First loves are like a first swim in the ocean...you never forget.

To my mother, the cool and salty Nancy Painter. Blessed beyond measure to call you mine.

SONGS APPEARING IN HOLIDAY ON THE ROCKS

HOLY SMOKES | Bailey Zimmerman
THREE SIX FIVE| Shinedown
STYLE (Taylor's Version) | Taylor Swift
THE SOUND OF SILENCE | Disturbed
I LOVE IT (feat. Chali XCX) | Icona Pop, Charli xcx
YOU BROKE ME FIRST | Tate McRae
DIAL DRUNK (With Post Malone) | Noah Kahan, Post Malone
FAR AWAY | Nickleback
BACK TO DECEMBER | Taylor Swift
BRASS MONKEY | Beastie Boys
I REMEMBER EVERYTHING | Zach Bryan, Kacey Musgraves
MILLION DOLLAR BABY | Tommy Richman
TEQUILA | Dan + Shay
MORE THAN A FEELING | Boston
BLISTER IN THE SUN | Violent Femmes
NO ONE NOTICED | The Marias
EYES CLOSED | Ed Sheeran

WATERMELON MOONSHINE | Lainey Wilson
CRASH INTO ME | Dave Matthews Band
MARRY ME | Bruno Mars
OCEAN EYES | Billie Eilish
PONY | Ginuwine
TENERIFE SEA | Ed Sheeran
CANON IN D | Brooklyn Duo

SEVEN YEARS AGO

I grabbed my birth certificate from the little metal box my mother kept on the top shelf of her closet, shoved it into my suitcase, and went to wait for him on the sidewalk. My parents left for work already, so it would be at least seven hours before they'd even notice I was gone.

The October sun was warm on my face as I sat on my suitcase. Rachel's car pulled to a stop at the curb before she and Lexi sprung out.

"This is the worst idea ever, Allie." Rachel, my girl since the third grade, stood in front of me. "You can't do this."

I laughed. "I'm eighteen today, I can do anything now."

"He—"

"He proposed last night on the Sugar Creek Bridge. The spot of our very first kiss." Sigh.

"He's bad news." Lexi rubbed her temples. "I think you've given me my first migraine."

"He's not bad news. We've dated a year, and my 4.0 GPA hasn't wavered a bit."

Rachel pulled me to my feet. "What the bibbity boppy f-ball is this? You're smart. Wait until next year. You already have scholarships for college, if he's the one this can wait."

"I'm still going to college." Why did the wrinkle between her brows crack me up? My laughter was *not* well received. "He'll come with me wherever I go."

Lexi let out a huff. "*Levi Dawson* in college? No freaking way."

I put my hands on her shoulders. "I'll go to college and he'll do what he wants. But we'll be together."

Rachel's eyes rolled. "Come on, you're the most intelligent person I know. He was just arrested last week!"

I did a little dance that had smoke coming from Lexi's ears. "For spray painting *my* name on the water tower in town." My hand covered my heart as giggles shot out of me. "Have you ever heard of anything more romantic?"

"Allie, please—"

"My parents are talking about sending me to live with my grandparents, but there's nothing to be afraid of. He's amazing if anyone would bother to give him a chance. I love him so much, and we can't *not* be together. We'll be married and then there's no stopping us."

Rachel let out a sigh. "This isn't the way. Stay with us, don't do this."

I quoted my favorite. *"Stay where it's safe, they said, but my heart only beats where the wild things grow."*

Her face grew red. "For fuck's sake Allie—"

I gave her a hug. "You both are my best friends. We grew boobs and read dirty books together. I need a sworn promise on *my* life that you won't tell anyone where we're going. I left a note for my parents so they won't worry, Levi and I will be back here on Thursday."

My heart hiccupped when I saw him rolling toward us in his uncle's "borrowed" car. I gave a wave as he pulled to a stop.

Levi grinned as he got out and the sight of him took my breath away. Tall, dark brown hair that was a little longer in back, and those green eyes framed by thick eyelashes that were unfair to women everywhere. Queue up Taylor's *Style*.

"Ladies."

Between the wink he gave me and the t-shirt that high-lighted his pecs and biceps, I was already melty. He opened his arms, and I stepped into the space that fit me perfectly as his arms wrapped around me.

"Levi, if you have a brain in your skull, you won't do this," Rachel said.

I looked up at his strong jaw. "All I want to do is protect and love her. She's my everything."

ONE
ALLIE

Present Day

"It's a blizzard, Allie. You're lucky your plane made it there today. It's just mother nature." Lexi let out an annoyed huff.

"Well, mother nature is clearly a psycho bitch with multiple personalities." I white knuckled the rental car steering wheel as I curved through the snowy Colorado mountains."

"Just get to the Vrbo and relax. The photos looked stunning."

"Yeah, but a woman alone in the middle of nowhere by herself? I think I've seen this movie and it does not end well." I groaned.

"Well, some of the crew might have made it before the storm. Maybe you won't be alone."

"Why in the hell is our friend the one person who thinks a winter wedding is a good idea?"

Lexi laughed. "You watch it. Emily is in a delicate mental place right now with the entire Midwest on a snow lock down a few days before her wedding."

That's when I heard her voice in the background. Yes, Emily's an emotional fruit loop on a good day, so the last thing I needed was a discussion with her. "Lexi, I'll let you go."

"Is that Allie?" Oh shit.

Before I knew it Lexi was replaced by Bridezilla.

"Allie, you made it to Colorado? I hadn't realized your plane left so early." Her voice had an eerie desperation to it I did not care for.

"Yes, I left at six this morning and landed before noon. But I really need to go, these mountain roads are slick—"

"You have *got* to go to the church first thing tomorrow. There are two fake Christmas trees I had shipped there. They set them in a storage room. You need to put them up, one on each side of the altar, exactly fifteen feet from one another. There're also boxes of ornaments and lights. You *have* to do this. The church must look like a magical Christmas vision. By the time I arrive I'll only have a day or two before the wedding, and I'm freaking out a little."

"Didn't I tell you last summer this was the worst idea ever?"

I think I heard an artery blow, and I giggled as she clearly spoke through gritted teeth. "I'm going to kill you if you don't shut your mouth."

"Be careful, I'm the only one here to set up your stupid magical Christmas trees. Maybe I'll just find a bar and *not* do any wedding stuff. You know tequila and I are close."

She let out a long breath. "I'm sorry for snapping. I would

owe you big if you just make sure the Church is decorated and beautiful. You know it's been my dream since college."

"I know, Emily. I promise you'll have the glorious holiday wedding of your dreams."

I took a curve and my stomach plunged as the tires slid.

"I've got to focus on driving. Text me when the blizzard blows over."

"Got it, love you, Allie."

"Right back at ya." I disconnected the call.

I slowed to fifteen miles an hour and had some control of my vehicle. It appeared I was the only dumbass zipping around the mountains. Maps said I was only seven miles away from the house. I could do this.

It was then I realized the Vrbo would have an empty kitchen. I had counted on anyone but me arriving first and filling the fridge with yummy food. Was there a Taco Bell anywhere close? Two hard shells and a Pepsi?

My stomach clenched as the tires slid left. I stood on the brake but the car didn't slow down. *At all*. I saw the edge of the road and the drop ahead of me. Oh mother trucker, it was happening.

I gripped the steering wheel as my stomach did a free fall when the hood of the car went over. Deep crunching sounds in combination with grinding while a scream escaped me at the same time cracking filled the air. Shards of glass slid across my face with instant stinging as cold air whooshed through the broken window.

My head hit the steering wheel as my seatbelt locked and dug into my hips. Airbags punched the side of my head and my face, and there was instant ringing in my ears from the force.

As the car rolled on and I saw an upside down tree and wondered what the fuck I ever did to Karma.

As the car rolled again, the red can of Coke I'd bought at the airport for later zipped past me, slammed into the front window, and then my forehead. Clearly the word of the day was fuck.

Abruptly the car stopped when it slammed into a tree and the seatbelt dug deeper into me. I took some breaths as I hung upside down attempting to get oxygen back into my lungs. My body shook uncontrollably, as warm blood ran down my face, well up my face since I was bottom up. I grimaced at the sting when my hand touched a cut on my forehead, and I pressed my glove against it attempting to stop the bleeding.

The past and present swirled together, and I couldn't control my tears. My heart pounded a violent beat as I reminded myself that this accident wasn't like the last; I was conscious. I could move my legs. I could get out of this.

But as hard as I tried I *couldn't* get out of this; my seatbelt was jammed. To top it off my cell phone was in my purse which wasn't visible anyway. I stretched my neck and couldn't even see the road I used to be on. Did anyone see me fly over the cliff? Was anyone coming for me?

Panic swirled up my back as my eyes bulged. Memories of weeks in the hospital that I'd blocked out ran through my mind like the one hundred meter dash. *This isn't the same.*

I was too young to die, I'd always figured by the time I kicked the bucket my winning column would outweigh my losing column, but that didn't appear to be the case. As I looked back at the success and failures, I couldn't help but to be proud that at least the potty training thing had stuck.

If I survived this I was going to join the cicadas this summer and just scream for six weeks straight.

"Hey!"

"Help!" Gratitude pumped into my bloodstream; someone was coming. Now I was happy and scared crying at the same time. I looked at my glove to find it saturated with blood, so I switched hands. I decided if I didn't die today I would have to kill Emily for planning a winter wedding in Colorado.

"Are you okay? I'm trying to get the door open." The man's voice filled my fucked up rental car. I looked through the passenger window that was now missing the glass to see a black coat outside. Crap, I probably should've opted for that extra insurance they babbled on about at the rental place. My bad.

"I think I'm okay." My voice was shaky and unfamiliar and as hard as I tried, the hot water wouldn't stop coming from my eyes. "Thank you for helping me."

"Fuck, the door is jammed." The man's voice was deep. "Sorry for the language." I could see him tugging on the door.

A nervous laugh popped out. "They say smart people swear more than stupid mother fuckers."

"That's funny."

"Yeah, I'm a hoot in life threating situations."

"I don't know if I can get this door open enough."

My teeth started chattering. "You can do it. Do crackheads say *I can't get high today because I'm broke*? No, they make it happen. Don't let a crackhead hustle harder than you."

A deep laugh filled the car. "Look at this. Chick hanging upside down is the new Tony Robbins over there."

After a minute more he pulled the door open and leaned inside. "Oh shit, you're bleeding pretty bad."

He crawled into the car and that was when I died.

"Allie?"

Even upside down with blood everywhere, his eyes cut me more than any glass ever could.

"Levi? Are you kidding me right now?" I could feel my heart beating in my neck. "Have I died and gone to fucking hell?"

"I—"

"You son of a bitch." I hissed. "Get away from me!"

"Allie, I need to get you out of here."

"I'd rather bleed out in this car than be *anywhere* near you!

"Langley, we need to get you down."

"So you ended up in Colorado? I knew I'd hate the 38th state in the Union!"

He crawled further into the car and every muscle in my body jumped when we were upside down face to face.

"Of course your brain would know that fact."

"Do *not* talk about my brain!" I slapped his hand away.

"Langley, calm your ass down."

"Don't tell me to calm down. You shut up and get the hell out of here!" He took something from his pocket and pressed it against my cut.

"Apply pressure, and I'll get you down."

"I'd rather freeze to death."

His hand against my stomach as he started working on the seatbelt caused fire to shoot through my body, and I closed my eyes. How could he be here? Every cell in me rolled into the fetal position.

"I think I've got it."

I looked up at him remembering so many times we'd been

in a car together. Hands everywhere, windows fogged, and an energy weaving between us that tested my sanity.

The seatbelt clicked open and he grabbed me before I dropped down on my head.

He set me down as the blood rushed away from my brain leaving me dizzy.

"Just sit for a minute."

I looked into the face that was so ruggedly handsome it was unfair to all other men in the world.

"I'll always hate you, Levi."

He nodded. "I know."

He got out of the car and extended his hand, and I pushed it away like an ornery child because I despise him to the depths of my soul. I crawled out of the car and stood up in the snow, but immediately fell down.

"Just let me help you."

I got to my feet and looked at the ground. I was messed up already, but being close to him made me wonky to the core. It was too much and a few tears escaped.

"Allie, please don't cry."

All I could do was shake my head. I suddenly didn't know if I was crying because of the car accident or seeing his face. Bringing it all back like a scab being ripped off of a wound.

"It's steep and snowy, please let me just get your out of here, okay?"

"I don't want your help."

"I know." He pulled off one of his gloves and used it to wipe some blood from my face. "But you're getting it anyway. I'm going to bend down and you're going to get on my back, and I'll get you up to the road." He flashed me a grin that had my stitched up heart shaking her fist at me. "Then you can hate me again, okay?"

I looked at the snowy hill before me. "I'll do it myself."

"No," his deep voice rumbled. "You hold my glove against your cut, there's a lot of blood." He reached in the car and grabbed my purse.

"Levi—"

"Langley." He turned around. "Get on my back now."

I grumbled as I held onto his shoulder with one hand and jumped. He caught my legs, and they went around his waist.

My body was on his body. The thought sent more spots in front of my eyes. While my head was throbbing, my mind went back. Our bodies intertwined in an empty train car tasting the tequila on his lips.

I shook my head and focused on right now.

Right now I had my arms wrapped around the tall and strong Levi who'd haunted me for years.

"You okay back there?"

I looked at his profile, my tummy twisted, and I couldn't say a word. Once on the road I immediately squirmed off his back and onto my feet. But I found out my feet weren't ready yet, and I fell to the snowy ground yet again.

I was lifted up and in his arms and my body was rested against his chest. I hated it.

I wished I hated it. I was unable to utter a syllable as he carried me to an SUV and opened the passenger door.

"There's probably a hospital in the next town."

"Just call me an Uber. I don't want to go anywhere with you."

He put me in the passenger seat and his eyes on me put fire

in my face. "We have to get you looked at and then I'll drive you home." He shifted his weight. "Do you live here?"

My eyes rolled. "No. I'm here for a stupid wedding of a friend."

He nodded. "Is that so?"

"Duh. Why would I say it if that wasn't so? You're stupid, Levi."

"Wow."

I leaned my head against the seat. "My head hurts."

He shut the door and got behind the wheel. "Close your eyes and rest."

"Don't tell me what to do." I pulled my hood up. "Let's play the silent game."

He started the car. "I'm visiting Colorado also."

"Clearly the universe hates me and you have no concept of the quiet game."

"Well, aren't you just a little ray of dark black. Do you want me to climb down and get your suitcase? Or are you planning to wear bloody sweats for a wedding?"

Even one look from those green eyes could still turn me to Jello. *I* was in the same place as him. I was in the same place as *him*.

"Should I take your silence as a *yes please, Levi*?"

I shrugged. "I guess."

"Do you have the rental company papers in the car? You'll need those."

"Of course I do, do you think I'm an idiot?"

"Would you like me to grab those as well, or are you going back down the cliff?" I hated the way he drummed his fingertips on the steering wheel.

"Fine."

"I'm sure you mean yes, please."

I looked over to see a smug grin. "What I mean to say is go to hell. Like tonight would be perfect."

He got out and slammed the door while I watched his fine self cross the highway as I attempted to regulate my racing heart. And spinning head. And the sudden realization that I was going to hurl at any second.

I pushed the door open as vomit spewed from my mouth and slapped on the concrete below.

The pain in my head came in a wave, and I sat with my head in my hands.

"Allie?"

I kept my eyes closed as Levi took my face in his hands. "Langley, look at me."

I opened my eyes but it was too much. "Go away."

He pushed me gently back into the vehicle. "We have to get you to the hospital. You might have a concussion."

TWO
LEVI

IN HER PRESENCE

She held the sides of her head with her hands. "Just don't talk to me."

We drove in silence and the amount of time my eyes were on her instead of the road might not have been the safest. I'd day dreamed of this moment so many times, being in the same place with her, but in every thought, I'd always had the perfect thing to say, you know, smartassy and clever, but now my ability to spit out the English language seemed to be on hiatus.

It was too quiet. I needed to say something. *Anything.*

I cleared my throat. "So." Yup, that was all I had.

She glared in my direction and panic shot through me. My eyes landed on the bag of candy sitting on the dash. "Skittle?"

She huffed as she adjusted the blood soaked glove against her head. "What?"

I grabbed the pack and meant to offer it to her, but I moved too quickly and several shot out and bounced off her face.

"Sorry."

I pulled up to the emergency room entrance, opened her

door, and extended my hand which she swatted away. "I don't want your help."

"Will you quit being stubborn, Langley?"

She stood and closed her eyes as she leaned against my vehicle. In an instant I scooped her up and walked through the double doors. While I half expected a punch to my jaw, instead she kind of settled in.

I never wanted to move again.

I held her and got her checked in and the nurse led us to an exam room where I set her on the exam table and she immediately lay down and closed her eyes.

I stood near her as the nurse examined and cleaned the gouge on her hairline.

"The doctor will be in shortly. You're going to need some stitches."

The door was closed and she rolled on her side. "Please just go."

"I don't want to."

"Well you narcissistic douche canoe. How can I help the world revolve around *you* today?"

"Allie, I know you hate me—"

"We've clearly gotten off on the wrong foot, Levi. It's throat punch Thursday. Step on over and we'll celebrate."

"Langley—"

She groaned and put her hands over her eyes. "The sound of your stupid voice makes me want to get tanked by noon."

"Come on—"

"Please leave now."

"I'm not leaving you here in the hospital."

She rolled over and her eyes cut me. "Why not? You're an expert on that front."

An ice pick to my chest. "It was a long time ago."

"Fuck you."

She faced the wall as I took a chair. The room was too quiet. The annoying tick of a clock above my head filled the space where the air was too heavy. My eyes stuck to Allie rolled on her side, and I couldn't help but notice she still had the perfect tush. What was she thinking?

"OMG Levi, do you have to breathe so freaking loud?"

Question answered.

The door opened and a female doctor entered. She was tall with dark hair piled on top of her head in a bun.

"Hello, I'm Dr. DeWater."

Allie sat up and flashed a little smile. "I'm Allie."

The doctor looked over at me and smiled. "And you are?"

Allie huffed. "Ignore him. He's nobody."

The doctor's brows popped up. "Okay. Well, I'm going to take a peek." She looked at Allie's head. "This is a good gouge you have here. We'll do some stitches and get you some pain reliever. On a positive note, since the laceration is on your hairline the scarring will be minimal. I'm going to take care of this first and then I'll do a little exam."

Allie nodded and looked down and the doctor touched her arm. "It's okay. I'm going to numb you up and get this fixed."

The nurse returned and they had everything ready. I stood and walked to Allie who was visibly shaking.

"Okay, we're going to get started now."

She nodded as a tear escaped. "I'm sorry. I just, I hate hospitals and doctors." She flashed a little grin as she wiped her eyes. "Except for you, you seem super cool."

The doctor patted her on the shoulder. "It's okay to be scared. Don't worry, I've got this."

I held my hand out and without looking she grabbed and squeezed tightly while they administered a local, then started stitching her up. I never wanted to move again.

I looked at her small hand on mine. The pale pink polish on her nails and the finger that had no ring on it. Thank God.

As soon as they finished she swatted my hand away. After an exam she was given some medication to take with her for her mild concussion.

We stood by the hospital ER door. "I'll take an Uber to where I'm staying."

"No, I'll drive you, come on. I just want to make sure you're safe."

She wrinkled her nose. "I'm sorry, I couldn't hear you over the little voice in my head screaming *what a load of crap*."

"You have a concussion, and I'm just trying to get you where you're going. I'm attempting to help."

She huffed. "I'm pretty sure you being in Colorado caused this whole thing."

"So I did this?"

"Probably, somehow. I don't know, just shut up."

"Your attitude sucks. I think certain people should use a glue stick instead of Chapstick right about now."

She spoke through gritted teeth. "You are so annoying."

I leaned down and she jumped. "I'm driving you where you're going. No option."

We got into my vehicle, and I could only stare at her profile as those auburn curls fell over her shoulder. God she was even more beautiful. The visions of the last time we were in a car together. Hands everywhere, her clothes on the floor, and the desperate kisses. *I can't wait to be yours, Levi.*

She looked over and our eyes locked for a moment. It was

clear the same memories were rolling through her mind by the way she swallowed hard.

She grabbed a cell phone from her purse and scrolled. "I have the address. Why are you in Colorado anyway? You make Colorado suck. You being in the same state makes me wonder what I did in a previous life to deserve this shit. Serial killer? Kicker of cats?"

Did I feel bad that I was about to lie to the most beautiful girl in the world in order to be close and breathe the same air as her? Nope. But were my words about to cause her to quickly become a gun toting maniac murderer? Hard yes.

Sure, she'd have to get a gun, but I had all the confidence in Colorado she could; and I already knew she was a good shot.

"My cousin Evan is here for a wedding and invited me. The last place I wanted to be was here for a Christmas wedding of people I don't know." That sounded all natural, huh?

"What?"

"Everybody's staying at some big house on Winding Ridge Road. Who's stupid enough to plan that shit in December?"

She looked forward and inhaled sharply, which I liked very much. "Emily."

"What?"

"My friend Emily is stupid enough to plan that shit." She looked over with fire shooting from her eye sockets. "Your cousin is *Evan*? The Evan dating Rachel?"

"Rachel? Wait, *your* Rachel? My cousin is dating Rachel from high school?"

"How in the bloody hell do you not know Rachel is Evan's girlfriend?"

She sat blinking at me.

"I've been out of the country since Evan's been with her. I

19

guess because there are millions of Rachels in the world, I would've *never* imagined it was Rachel from high school."

"No, no, no." She leaned her head back against the seat. "You can *not* be at the wedding or any of this. I need you the hell outta here."

THREE
ALLIE

THIS CAN'T BE HAPPENING

N o. Freaking. Way. No *way* could this be happening. My car flying over a stinking cliff, stitches, and a concussion in my first two hours in Colorado, and now Levi. WTF!

"You can't be here." Panic had me in a headlock at the thought as instant jitters roared through my veins. I could *not* be in the same place as him. Not happening. His presence made me unbalanced and gave me an instant headache. Well, that could be from rolling down a fucking mountain, but he was a factor in this shit show, and I needed him gone.

A smug smile slid across those lips. "But my cousin invited me."

My pulse ticked up. "You just said you didn't even want to be here." I held my finger up. "Wait, you can just go back to the airport, jump on a plane, and go back to wherever the hell you came from. A solid plan."

He let out a little chuckle that made me want to give him a high five in the head with a chair. "I would walk through fire for my cousin."

"Come on! This is one of my *best friends*, I can't leave. And

21

you can't stay. You'll ruin everything. How could you not know this?"

"I guess I haven't seen any pictures of her to put it all together. I've spent the last two years in Brazil and got off social media long ago because it sucks."

"Now I feel sorry for Brazil since it's had to put up with stupid you. The dumbass, jerk, asshole. Yup, ruining a country sounds like a Levi thing for sure. But the bottom line is *you're* not staying here."

He used an announcer's voice. "We apologize, but your request for victim status has been denied. You are being referred to the big girl panties department. Please stand by."

Heat went to my cheeks. "Rachel and Lexi will *literally* kill you."

He grimaced. "They were always a little frightening."

"A little? Yeah, they're still scary and have grown into bat shit crazy. You'd better reconsider this stay or you may go back to wherever the hell you came from in a body bag."

He buckled his seatbelt and looked back at me. Those eyes that had been missing for seven years were turning me into a mushy mess.

"I will always hate you." I hit continue on my Maps. "The very least you can do is disappear. You're *just* a cousin; you aren't needed at this wedding. I'm a bridesmaid. Totally needed."

He shook his head of Prince Charming hair before he looked out the window. As much as I fought it, my eyes soaked in his perfect profile and strong jawline. *Stop!*

"Sorry sweetheart, I'm staying." He glanced back with a cocky grin.

My stomach tripped over his words. "Well, you'll have to

stay in a hotel. No way in hell you're staying under the same roof as me." I hated the crack in my voice and quickly cleared my throat.

"I've heard the house is huge. This isn't a big deal."

The way his green eyes messed with my equilibrium *was* a big deal. He was still the most beautifully handsome man to ever walk the earth. It wasn't fair that I had to stare into the face of the man who left me shattered.

My heart was thumping against my ribs while I assessed the shitty situation I was in. I didn't know if I needed a hug, hammer, Xanax, five shots of vodka, or to beat the shit out of Emily, but I couldn't come up with an option that didn't end with me behind bars.

I took a controlled breath. I could do this. I had to do this. I was no longer the young woman he'd crushed. I would deal with this situation with the maturity I lived by each and every day of my life.

"I hate you. I hate your stupid face, and you suck ass."

Clearly maturity had run screaming through the forest, flung herself over a cliff, and died a bloody death.

We drove the remaining seven miles in silence. He flipped on the radio and after ten seconds of *Rudolph the Red Nosed Reindeer*, I flipped it off because I was in my *bitchy to Levi Era*.

I closed my eyes tightly trying to *not* remember what his fingertips felt like sliding up my thighs. *"It'll always be you and me, Allie."*

I jumped at a horrid screeching sound that filled the SUV. He grabbed his phone from the dash and before he answered I got a glimpse of a woman with dark hair that popped up on the screen.

"Hey."

I looked out the window and hated everything. A woman was calling Levi. He had a life and people in it.

"Yeah, go ahead, it's fine."

What was he talking about?

There was a pause and my chest cracked open when his laughter bounced around me. The great laugh was the same and it hurt.

"Got it. Talk soon, bye."

How was I going to survive a Christmas Eve wedding with *him*?

The car finally reached the house that looked large enough to be a hotel. The exterior was stunning with stone and wood crawling up the front and windows everywhere with views of the snowy mountains and trees as far as the eye could see.

Our group decided renting this ginormous house with seven bedrooms, indoor pool, land out back for bon fires just off of a ski resort, was the perfect fit. The wedding party was just our group so we would stay here together except for the bride, groom, and their families who were staying at a hotel in town.

It sounded like a good plan until now.

Levi leaned up in his seat. "Holy shitballs, look at this place."

FOUR
LEVI

HATING LEVI

Allie hopped out of the car so fast she was a blur, and in a second her bag was out of the trunk.

I got out and looked over at the same second Allie stopped and flew back in my direction. What was happening?

"There's a hissing raccoon! Hissing raccoon!"

I wish I could say she ran past me, but nope. Her suitcase hit my leg when she ran past at full speed resulting in both of us landing in the snow. Did I mention it was about three feet of snow? I sat up to find I not only had snow in my ear, but I was covered in it. As I looked around, Allie's head popped up out of the snow a few feet away. It was in that second all oxygen was sucked from my lungs as her laughter bounced off the trees around me.

The past and present mixed together as the laughter of the girl I loved years ago was the same as I remembered. I couldn't look at her smile without memories of her hands on my chest and my fingers digging into her hips, and it was torturing me from the inside out.

Her auburn hair and rosy cheeks made her look like a snow angel.

"A mother fucking raccoon!"

Okay, maybe her halo was held up by pitch forks, but seeing that face was a lightning strike.

I got up and extended my hand to her. She took it and as soon as we were vertical she remembered she was in *Levi hate mode*, and snatched it away.

We entered the house, and I was a little blown away. We stood in the enormous living room that was so festive I wondered if the actual Santa resided there. Rich wood floors ran the length of the room and a large deep burgundy rug lay under the leather sofas and chairs. A fireplace sat in the corner with stone crawling up to the ceiling. Christmas wreaths hung around the room along with holiday pillows on the chairs and an acoustic guitar leaned against the wall near the fireplace. I looked over to see her eyes on it as well, and when they shifted to me her cheeks grew pink. Me playing for her while she lay in my bed was as clear in my mind as the day it happened.

"Wow, this is so Christmasy and cool."

Her eyes rolled. "I'd almost forgotten you have a weird obsession with Christmas decorations. Kinda thought a grown ass man would've outgrown that. I'm following doctor's orders and going to rest, and probably never coming out again." She picked up her suitcase.

"Allie, I have to say something."

"No. Once upon a time I didn't care. Still don't. The end."

"I just—"

"Not a word, Levi. It's bad enough I'm stuck here with you."

"Come on—"

She spoke through gritted teeth. "No! Say nothing."

"I just really have to—what happened—"

Her cheeks were pink. "Shut up, Levi."

"Allie—"

She dropped her suitcase. "You didn't fight for me! You let it all go!" Her nose winkled. "You just left me there."

"I was trying—"

"Nobody would tell me where you were." Her whisper strangled me. "I couldn't find you."

"Let me—"

I took a step and her hand shot out. "No! Leave me alone. You're a pot hole in the fucking rearview mirror, and I don't want to ever see you or hear you again."

She turned on her heel and disappeared up the stairs.

I deserved her hatred. Earned it. Expected it. The only light at the end of this tunnel was the days I had to try to change things.

FIVE
ALLIE
DREAMING

I walked down the hall with my legs shaking like a blade of grass in a tornado. I hated his presence. I hated what he did and what an ass he was.

I hated that I didn't hate it quite as much as I wanted to hate it.

I selected a room at the end of the hall. It had a queen bed covered with a luxurious white comforter, white bedside tables holding charcoal grey lamps, and even a vase of red and white flowers. The view from the wide window was one that belonged on a holiday card. The afternoon sun shined down on the mountains and trees which were wrapped in a thick layer of snow. There was a bathroom containing a deep soaker tub (Yes, please), huge white walk in marbled shower, and a black and white swirly vanity.

I grabbed the first thing I could find out of my suitcase and threw it on because I didn't give a rip about the other person in this house. Nope. I was staying in my room until everybody arrived.

I popped another pain reliever tablet, pulled the curtains

shut, and crawled into bed. My head sunk into the softest pillow ever, and I felt the first peace I'd had in hours. While I was worried about my brain not allowing me to rest because of the *huge* problem downstairs, once the perfectly thick comforter that smelled like lavender was around me, I drifted off.

I don't know how long I was sleeping when I started dreaming. My arm was nudged, and I cracked open my eyes to see the most handsome man in the world. The room was dark, and I hated to admit my past still owned a chunk of my heart.

Levi's voice was low. "Hi."

"Hmmm." His smile alone sent a shiver up my spine, and I loved when he visited me in my dreams. "You're here." I closed my eyes and snuggled into my comforter. "Good."

"How are you sleeping?" His voice was deep and quiet as it rolled over to me.

"Mmmm." I wanted to sleep forever. "I'm so tired."

"I wanted to check on you."

I kept my eyes closed. "I like that." I reached out and took his warm hand in mine.

He whispered, "The doctor said you needed to check your pupils every hour if you sleep."

Alarms and bells went off in my head as I shot to a sitting position. "What?"

Oh crap, this wasn't a dream; he was there and I'd held his hand. And was *nice* to him. WTH?

"Levi! What are you doing in here?"

He was on his knees on the side of the bed nearly face to face with me. "The doctor said if you slept more than an hour this afternoon, you needed to check your pupils."

I scooted back. "I know that!" I ran my hands over my hair.

He was leaning on my bed. *Leaning on the bed for God's sake!* "I'm not stupid."

"I didn't say you were." He stood. "Calm down, Langley."

"Don't tell me to calm down. Whoever calms down when told to calm down? You're dumb."

"Can I take a peek real quick and then you go back to sleep and hopefully wake up in a better mood."

"No."

His head tilted and his hair fell over his brow. "You let me check or I throw you over my shoulder right now and take you kicking and screaming back to the hospital. Do you hear me?"

"I'm good."

His crooked smile was annoying as shit as he reached over and turned on the lamp and grabbed my magic eight ball. "What is this? Langley giving life choices over to magic?"

"Shut your face." I tried to grab it from him but he pulled it away.

"Let's let this little thing decide. Agreed?"

"Fine! If it'll get you out of here!"

His big hands gave it a shake before he read. "Definitely fucking so." He chuckled. "What kind of magic eight ball is this?"

My eyes rolled. "Shut up."

Every nerve in me jumped when he sat on the edge of my bed. His face was inches from mine and my stomach twisted into a knot, and I hated it.

Well, maybe not totally hated it.

"I'm going to lean in a little so I can see your eyes, okay?" I felt his breath on my face and panic flooded me.

I nodded as my heart beat so violently I swore he must've

heard it. I swallowed hard as he moved closer while the memory of our first kiss streaked through my mind.

My nerves were on full display while we sat with our feet dangling off of the Sugar Creek Bridge just outside of town surrounded by wheat fields. The sun had sunk over the horizon on a warm summer night in June with only the sound of crickets in the distance.

Now he was the man I'd hate forever.

When he leaned in the mattress dipped and everything in me went on a tilt when his emerald eyes stared into mine. I held my breath as heat swirled up my spine. I sat frozen for a long moment until he sat back. "They look great." He jumped up. "I mean they look normal. Yeah, your eyes there're, uh, totally normal."

He flipped off the lamp. "I guess I'll see you later."

He exited the room quickly and pulled the door closed behind him as I gasped for air, and attempted to regulate my pulse which I was certain was at least five hundred beats a freaking minute.

But after a half an hour of reliving the most exciting eye exam of my life, my tummy was growling. I dug in my purse and found three Jolly Ranchers, piece of gum, and a yellow Tic Tac which would *not* take the place of dinner very well. Twelve minutes later I knew I had to get to the kitchen and hope a previous guest had left some snacks or something. I was sure Levi was in a bedroom by now, so the coast was clear.

As much as I fought myself, before I headed downstairs I changed my clothes into black leggings and the blue Lululemon zippy jacket which I knew made my eyes look nice.

I'd like to say I brushed my hair, but my hair isn't the brushy kind. My curls ran wild most of the time and while I used to straighten and attempt to tame, I'd just accepted the fact that they'll never listen to me.

Did it stop there? Nope. Loser me put on mascara and a little blush topped off by lip gloss.

But it's just because I believe in looking my best for *myself*. Yes, self-love is important.

Shut up.

I tip-toed down the stairs realizing this humungo house was eerily quiet. I imagined there were a zillion places a murder could hide and then kill me while I slept. Danger was around every corner.

I made it to the kitchen and scoured the cabinets to find nothing but condiments. Did I squirt some caramel sauce into my mouth and top it off with a shot of whipped cream from a can in the refrigerator? Of course not, that would be ridiculous.

The most annoying ring tone in the entire world pierced my ears, again, as Levi's phone sat on the kitchen table across the room. I looked around and he appeared to be MIA.

My eyes were shooting in all directions when I took a few steps toward the table. I stretched my neck as far as I could and on his screen was the photo of a blond woman and my heart sputtered as the phone stopped ringing. I scolded myself; it had been too long to still feel the sting of Levi.

I shoved it out of my mind and walked through the kitchen and came upon a glass door leading to the indoor pool. This wasn't just an "indoor pool". This masterpiece belonged in an issue of Architectural Digest or on one of those million dollar pool shows on HGTV.

An oval pool was in the center surrounded by a complete wall of windows, floor to ceiling, with a breathtaking view of the snowy trees and mountains outside. Yes, one would be able to lie on a pool float while watching deer or whatever kind of animals were in the vicinity.

I walked inside with chlorine hitting my nostrils while humidity and heat wrapped around me. I could almost feel the curls on my head tightening up.

"Hey."

I jumped and spun around to see stupid Levi in the hot tub. I attempted to control my internal body temperature as my eyes skimmed over his well-developed chest and muscular arms. Holy fudgeballs he was built.

He had a tattoo scrolling around his bicep that was sexy as hell, and my heart fell flat on its face at the sight of his other tattoo. Our tattoo. Holding hands while he insisted my initials be in the design was a dull pain in my stomach now.

As a smirk snaked across his lips I quickly looked away. "I didn't know you were in here."

"Yes, I see your *never coming out* has ended."

"I'm going to get myself something to eat."

"I'll come."

"No, you won't."

"First of all, if I recall correctly, your car is a mangled mess down a cliff. So unless you're hoofing it, I'm coming."

I needed him gone.

"Fine. Then I'm going to my room and—"

"I know, I know. You're *never* coming out."

"I hate you."

"Yes, you've established that." He pointed to a table in the corner. "Would you throw me that towel?"

I crossed my arms over my chest. "Get it yourself. I'm leaving in five minutes."

His head shook. "Can you just toss me the towel, please?"

"No."

With that the man stood up wearing only black boxer briefs. The nearly naked man with the perfect pecs and biceps. Holy shit! I quickly turned my head as he walked past me, and I spun the other direction. "What in the hell are you doing?"

"I asked you nicely to hand me the towel. Twice."

"You're offending my eyes."

I heard a chuckle from behind me. "You're no more offended then you were back then."

The air swooshed out of me; I needed to be as far away from this guy as possible because his words were true. "You're arrogant, and I'm calling a cab."

I walked past him and he caught my hand. "I'm getting my clothes from the dryer and you're waiting for me because you're not getting into a car with a stranger. Not happening."

I looked up at him as visions of being wrapped up in those arms marched through my brain like the Macy's Thanksgiving Day Parade. I jerked my hand away and walked to the door. "I'll be outside."

I sat in his vehicle after digging in my purse and making the joyful call to the car rental company about my car and its location so they could tow it out. Wow, it didn't take long for the universe to blow up my first fucking day in Colorado. Yeah, not everything happens for a reason. Sometimes life just sucks. Screw you Zig Ziglar.

I watched Levi approach the vehicle and had a shot of pure joy entered my bloodstream when I laid on the horn and he jumped.

Once behind the wheel *Jingle All the Way* hit my ears, and I quickly flipped off the radio.

He grinned. "I thought some chipper Christmas tunes might be nice."

I folded my arms over my chest. "An actual wood chipper would be better."

"You'd kill me by wood chipper?"

"No, you're too damn tall to just shove through the chipper." I flashed him a toothy smile. "I'd have to cut you into pieces first. Then through the wood chipper you'd go ending in the perfectly deserved crime."

"Glad to see you haven't spent too much time contemplating my demise."

"It takes a hot minute to come up with a murder plot. I've killed you five times in my mind already."

His laughter was as annoying as a soggy donut. "I get it, you hate me—"

"I don't want to hate you. Wait, that's a lie. I want to hate you and touch your face with a shovel...really hard."

He pulled onto the road. "This does not feel good. When did you say people were arriving at the house?"

"It's all question marks with the blizzard." I looked over. "But I doubt I'll take you out at this time."

"That should be comforting?"

"I'm not the least bit concerned about your *comfort*."

SIX
LEVI
NOT DEAD...YET

So I was taking her *not* killing me as a positive step forward. That was the key, I needed to stay positive and on task.

Be like a postage stamp; stick to one thing until you get there.

The difference between try and triumph is just a little umph (come on, you like that one.)

When life gives you lemons make lemonade and find someone with vodka?

Onward buttercup, there's fuckery to spread.

Okay, I'm getting a little off track.

Anyway, I looked over and her eyes shot to me for a second before returning to the road. I examined her profile and there was the same pull. From the second I saw her, my body had overtaken my brain.

While she was the uber intelligent girl in high school who should've never looked my way, the second she did I pulled out all the stops. The effect she had on me was all consuming, and in seven years it hadn't changed.

After the times I'd dream of being in the same space as her, it was happening. Did I put the puzzle of Rachel being Evan's girlfriend together three weeks ago? Yes. A few months back it sounded fun to fly in and hang with Evan and his friends in Colorado. I'd been out of the country for a few years and hadn't met Rachel, his girlfriend, but in a text, he referred to Allison Langley, and I couldn't help but wonder if the universe or something bigger was at work.

Evan only knew her as the Allie from my past, and would've never imagined it was the same person. He and his family put me back together after her, when I went to live with them in Wisconsin when all hell broke loose. He would've never wanted me at this house if he was aware it was the same Allison. Yeah, if Lexi or Rachel knew I'd be here, they would've likely hired an assassin to take me out altogether. Since I'd flown under the radar and made it to the Christmasy Colorado mountains, I wondered what the odds were of me chipping away at the icy exterior beside me.

There was an unmistakable noise. "Langley, was that your tummy growling?"

"Don't you be listening to my stomach." She grumbled as she turned the radio on and *Frosty the Snowman* filled the front seat. "I haven't eaten since this morning."

We turned onto a road that screamed Christmas ski resort town. On both sides of the street were shops, boutiques, and restaurants. Above were holiday lights strung from one side of the street to the other casting a warm glow on the folks strolling down the congested sidewalk.

"Wow, this is cute." She pointed. "The Summit Sip coffee shop. Adorbs. I'm making a mental note of that one."

"Hey, there's an Earth and Fire BBQ."

"Yes, I remember you love bar-be-cue." She glared at me. "I don't want to eat there."

"There's just no winning with you."

A sarcastic laugh bounced off my window. "Nice to see you realize that."

At the end of the street was an enormous ski lodge. I pulled into the parking lot. "I'd like to check this out."

"Do you realize how annoying your voice is?" She zipped up her coat.

"Isn't hating me *every* second of today exhausting?"

Her head shook. "Nope. Actually, I hate you so much it almost feels good. Yeah, like I've climbed the Everest of hate. Accomplished what few others could."

She bolted from the car like I was toe fungus and walked a step ahead of me through the parking lot while light snowflakes dropped from above. There were a few in her auburn hair that made her look angelic.

"Levi, we're finding a restaurant in here and sitting at separate tables so I don't have to look at your face."

It felt good. "Quick question. Is this your mood just now or like always?"

She laughed. "Well, Levi, I'm in a *I'd like to set someone's face on fire and put it out with a fork* kinda mood."

I chuckled. "So that's just tonight?"

Her hand flew into the air. "Did you ever just see someone and think yes, this is the night I'll be arrested for assault?"

We stepped inside the lodge with soaring ceilings and people everywhere. There were several Christmas trees filled with an obscene amount of lights, green wreaths hanging on the walls, and several seating areas with burgundy sofas and stately brown leather chairs.

Mahogany floors ran under foot and marble pillars in the distance screamed we'd arrived where the whole town wanted to be. There was a large wall of windows ahead of us show-casing the mountains, snowy trees, and ski lifts. The vibe of the whole place was *Holiday Vacation*.

We checked our coats at the door, and I followed her into a dimly lit bar where a woman in her late twenties stood. "Wel-come, two?"

Allie shook her head. "Oh God no, I'm *not* with him. Just one."

The hostess's eyes darted between us. "Okay, please follow me."

She was seated at a small table to the right of the bar, while my sad seat was a few tables over. I glanced at the menu and did the only thing I could; order a thick steak, side of mashed, and a Miller Lite.

As I drank my beer and waited for my chow, my attention wouldn't leave her. With a flick of her wrist she brushed away a stray curl from her face while her pink pouty lips were stran-gling me. She was literally the most beautiful woman I'd ever seen; then and now.

Her sunny smile appeared and punched me in the gut as the waitress took her order. The one I'd spent countless hours dreaming about as I sat staring and obsessing like a crazed stalker. It was then she noticed my gaze and immediately hopped to the seat across from her, so my view was now of the back of her head.

Still good.

The waitress set a margarita in front of her. Oh how I wanted to lick the salt from her lips. Yes, I'm the definition of what gives men a bad name. Sue me.

I finished dinner and my beer when my pulse spiked as a guy who was at the bar a second ago, was now seated at her table. But this was okay, I couldn't blame him, and I knew it was cool. But when she slurped down her margarita in record time and threw her head back and laughed, I realized this was not okay.

The guy said something to her and exited. As bad of an idea it was, I walked to her table. "Are you ready to go?"

She looked over and her flushed cheeks confirmed she still wasn't a big drinker. "No, I'm not ready. You just go over there, or I'll take an Uber back."

"You're in a bar with a stranger. We both know what happens when you drink."

Giggles. "You don't know me anymore. I'm a grown up now. Please go away."

"I know me being here is a problem—"

"Well, the answer to this problem may *not* be at the bottom of this margarita glass, but I'm going to be checking it hard."

"You have a concussion."

Her eyes rolled. "A *minor* concussion. My headache is gone and it's none of your business anyway."

"It's not good for you—"

Instantly she reached into her purse, pulled out her magic eight ball, and shook it. "Do I give a shit what stupid Levi thinks about anything?" Her eyes looked into the little triangle window. "It says fuck no."

"It does not."

"Does too." She set it on the table.

"No it doesn't."

She dramatically held it out and sure as shit she was right. "Huh, I—"

"Don't know anything?" She crossed her arms over her perfect chest. "Bye bye now."

"Alcohol isn't good for you—"

"There are a *lot* of things that haven't been good for me, and I pulled through just fine." Her eyes narrowed. "You can go now."

"I'll wait at my table."

"Words cannot express how much I don't care."

It felt as good as a swift kick to the balls. By the time I reached my table dumbass had returned with a second margarita in hand for Allie who was now clapping her hands. He was loud and clearly a little trashed. He plopped down and stared at her while he downed a drink, and I suddenly didn't know how this evening wouldn't end without him going through a wall.

SEVEN
ALLIE

LOSER LEVI

I peeked over my shoulder and pure joy shot through my veins to see Levi sitting with his arms crossed over his chest glaring at me. Serves him right. *Yeah buddy, you crushed me back in the day, but look at what you lost.*

After a few more chugs I realized he'd lost a lush.

The guy at my table was Toby who was on a ski vacation with friends.

"How about you and me head to the lounge down the hall?"

"Well, I think I need to get going."

He leaned in close and smelled as if he'd bathed in some bourbon out back.

"I think you're pretty." His hand rested on mine. "Come on, just for a little bit."

I scooted my chair out. "Thanks, but I need to be heading out."

We both stood. "It was nice meeting you."

"You too."

I walked past the bar and into the bathroom. When I

finished washing my hands, I jumped when I saw Toby's refection in the mirror.

"Uh, you can't be in here."

He took a step toward me. "I just wanted to say good night."

I eyed the door and took a quick step left when his hands had my upper arms and he pushed my back against the wall.

"Stop!"

I shoved his chest but he didn't budge. His fingers dug into my arms before his mouth came down hard on mine. I got an arm free and punched him in the side of the face.

A millisecond later Toby was no longer holding me at all, instead he had flown into the other wall, and Levi was in front of me.

I shuddered at the look in his eyes as he punched Toby who took a swing and got Levi in the jaw. He stumbled back before he went at it.

One after another, not a second's pause, until Toby was on the ground. A flashback of Levi beating the shit out of a guy who grabbed my rear when we were at the beach. He had grown up on the rough side of town and had that "I will fuck you up if you mess with me" woven into his DNA.

A man shot through the door.

"Stop!"

He grabbed Levi's arm and pulled him. Levi backed off and stood up.

"What are you—"

Levi was winded. "He followed her in here."

The man's eyes traveled to me and I nodded. He looked back down at Toby who slowly sat up before using the back of his hand to wipe the blood coming from his nose.

Levi leaned down and spoke through gritted teeth. "I should—"

"I'm sorry." Toby put a hand up. "I am, I'm sorry, I know I was out of line."

I felt the weight of everything dog piling on me. The stupid car accident, being stuck with Levi, which was rattling me to my bones, and the helplessness of being held against the wall by a stranger. I felt weak, stupid, and utterly disappointed in myself.

Levi took my hand and led me into the hall and stopped. He leaned down. "Are you okay?"

As I looked into those eyes I realized I was *not okay* on all fronts. Nothing in my life had prepared me for how quickly things could catch on fire. Again. I wanted to hop in a time machine and go back to my childhood to learn some shit because clearly someone failed me somewhere.

Fuck you Elmo.

He leaned down more. "Allie?"

"I'm okay. I just want to leave."

EIGHT
LEVI
DISTRACTION

We walked to my SUV in silence until her purse dropped on the ground and crap was everywhere.

"Let me get it." I opened the passenger door.

She used her coat to dab her eyes. "Are you being bossy right now?"

"Yes I am. After all that's happened today, can we call an hour's truce? Just *not* hate me for sixty minutes so we can make sure you're okay? You know, Langley, *not* fantasizing about me being attacked by honey badgers, barefoot in a desert of Lego bricks near a Bieber concert."

She looked down.

"I know what the car accident today was for you. It hits in a different way for you than it would for anyone else. I also know the ER only sent you with a few Tylenol, so let's pick some up to keep you comfortable. So just take a quick hate break, okay?"

She chewed on her lip for second. "But I thrive on the hate thing and you expect me to just let it go?"

"Of course not. Come on, all that time and energy put into

the hatred of Levi Dawson? I would *never* want you to give that up. But you've had some shit go down today. We can be civil for an hour, right?"

She shifted her weight and looked away. I grabbed the magic eight ball that was just behind the tire and handed it to her. "What do you think?"

She took it, shook it, and looked into the little window. A tiny grin slithered across those pale pink lips as she held it out for me to see.

"Why the fuck not?" I shook my head. "Best decision maker in the history of time."

She gave the smallest nod before climbing into the passenger seat. I shut the door before grabbing the last items from her purse and got into the driver's seat.

"Langley, why do you have taco seasoning and socks in your purse?" I grabbed my phone.

"I get hungry and cold sometimes."

"Of course you do." Her blue eyes zapped me. "My phone said there's a twenty-four hour grocery story a mile from here. Would it be okay if I run in to grab Tylenol for your head and a few items for tomorrow?"

"Okay."

Her tension filled the vehicle as she stared straight out the window. I knew between the car thing and the guy holding her against the wall she was shaken up, and I didn't know how to make it better. I did the only thing I could; turn up the tunes and belted out some Benson Boone. While she was silent, I chose to believe that my top shelf vocal abilities had just stunned her into silence. Yes, I was going with that.

Once parked, I turned to her. "You can wait here, I'll be—"

She laced her fingers together nervously. "No." She took a breath. "I don't want to stay here."

We walked into the empty store and the stress rolling off her was eating at me. Before I entirely knew what I was going to do, I scooped her up in my arms and put her in the back of the grocery cart as her laughter bounced off the wall behind us.

"What are you doing? I have to sit criss-cross-applesauce in a cart?" Her eyes lit up when she looked back at me.

"Today's been a lot, what you need is a distraction." I started pushing the cart down the cereal aisle and tossed a box into the cart. "You look like a Fruit Loop kinda gal."

"You'd better grab the Lucky Charms. With my luck I'll probably die the day after I finally get my shit together."

"Is Langley having a little pitty party?"

"No. It's just one of those days I'm glad we only live once because I can't do this crap again."

"It was just a bad day."

"Nope, the "L" in my luck has been replaced with an "F"."

"That's it. It is now my goal to get your mood out of this clusterfuck it's in."

"Goal?"

"Yup, I'm about to lock in like no one has ever locked in before. Just saying."

"I don't believe you're motivational speaking skills are necessary. Maybe I just need to simmer in the suckiness for a bit, and I'll bounce right back."

I whipped the cart in a circle. "You think the itsy bitsy spider gave a shit about the rain? No, it climbed the spout *again*. Lock in, Langley."

Her head shook. "Fine, cheer me up."

"Alrighty. When a door closes, open it again. It's a fucking door."

She shrugged.

"Sugar and spice and everything nice is *so* yesterday. From now on it's be defiant, salty, and extremely noncompliant."

"Hmmm, I do kinda like that."

"From this moment on we give everyone we meet the middle name of motherfuckin. Life is about to get interesting."

Her giggle circled me. "Can we start that now?"

"Absolutely, Allison motherfuckin Langley. I see my wise nuggets of wisdom are improving your mood."

"Maybe a little, Levi motherfuckin Dawson."

I leaned down. "To conclude my Ted Talk, a little tid bit that will make you smile the rest of the night." Her brow popped up as I whispered, "Boobytrap spelled backwards is partyboob. Carry on."

"Wow."

"You ready, girlie?"

"For what?"

I ran through the aisles pushing her in the cart while she screamed with laughter. *Jingle All The Way* blew through the store speakers while we sang along.

Memories of our Christmas past shot through my brain like a poisonous arrow. Allie knowing Christmas was something I was weirdly fond of, and her showing up at my dad's crap apartment dragging a Christmas tree behind her and a bag of decorations she'd picked up at the Dollar Tree. How she turned that shit hole into a beautiful place is still beyond me. While my father wouldn't admit it at the time, he spent the whole month of December in his recliner next the tree. At home almost every night. Most of his evenings involved bars and ladies and for him to be around, if even for a few weeks, was kind of like the sprinkles on a fucking donut.

She had so much fun with it she made it her New Year's resolution to make it permanent. She'd go to Goodwill and Thrift World and we'd load up treasures from a couch to cool shit for the walls and for the first time, I didn't hate being there. Everywhere she went she made things better without even trying.

"I need two pounds of butter."

I twirled the cart in a circle. "Is this a weird addiction?"

"No. I want to bake cookies for everyone when they arrive."

I tossed some butter and it bounced off her shoulder. "Sorry."

"Ya Ding Dong."

"I believe Ding Dongs, Ho Ho's, and all Little Debbie snacks would be found in aisle seven. Hold on."

NINE
ALLIE
TRUCE?

Did I imagine hauling ass down the aisles at the store in the back of a grocery cart would raise my spirits after flying off a cliff and the awful Ski resort experience? No. Was Levi being about the best person I could hope for right now? Appears so. Was laughing with him the thing I'd missed most? A concerned yes.

He stacked Christmas sprinkles, Hershey kisses, and frosting into the cart. Lastly we grabbed candy canes. No particular reason except it felt Christmasy.

I quickly scrolled through my phone which I hadn't looked at in hours. Messages from Emily about wedding details I never wanted to know, and one from Lexi assuming I'd gone to bed early and wasn't responding.

"Rachel sent money for me to get a little Christmas tree for the deck. She wants pictures with everyone by the outdoor fireplace. If we bought rope from the hardware aisle, do you think we could tie one from the holiday aisle to your SUV?"

"Oh, hell yes." He pointed. "We can get decorations here too."

I bit my lip at his smile which sent a little shock to my heart at 10:17 p.m. at cash register number thirteen.

Now that it was dark, the house looked even more beautiful as we pulled up on the circular drive. The bright moon above highlighted the thick Evergreen trees wrapped in snow and bright white twinkly lights that surrounded the house.

I put the groceries away while Levi got the tree into the tree stand before he put it on the deck.

"It's late, but I think I'm going to decorate it. You can go to bed."

The corner of his mouth turned up. "Are you kidding? Christmas is my favorite holiday. I'm staying. Besides, you're too short to get lights or anything even close to the top." He nodded. "Without me this thing will be all lopsided."

"I'm not short. I'm just cuteness in a concentrated, easy-to-carry-around container."

He let out a chuckle. "You know, they say short girls are mean because they're closer to hell."

"If you think I'm short, you should see my patience."

He shrugged. "Okay, I'm picking up what you're laying down, girl. Now brace yourself, Christmas music is coming." He hit a button on his phone and *Holly Jolly Christmas* filled the space. "Can't decorate without tunes, right?" He grabbed some lights.

"But Christmas songs can be a little crazy." I bit the sides of my cheeks to try to not smile as he did a weird thrusty dance, but failed.

"Crazy? What the hell are you talking about, Langley?"

"It's like the endless carousel of Christmas tunes is enough to make me want to set my hair on fire."

"Well, you sound like a Holiday card written by Gordon Ramsay over there."

An hour later the tree was twinkling at us like one million diamonds. It was filled with silver, red, and green ornaments and a big light up star sat at the very top.

We reached the stairs. "Well, good night. I guess I'll be heading to my wing now. If you need me I'm the third room to the right."

I popped my hands on my hips. "I will *not* be needing you."

His chuckle was like a warm blanket. "I mean as a friend, you perv."

"Whatever."

"You have to admit I've been a pretty good friend today."

My eyes locked with his emerald jewels. "Thank you."

It came out a husky whisper. "Anything for you, Allie."

His words socked me in the stomach as we both knew he'd spoken them to me the day we met at an outdoor concert. I'd told him I didn't want him to walk so far to get me pizza. *Anything for you, Allie.*

He gave me a wave before walking off.

I pulled on my grey sweats and sat in the corner of the room digesting the day. I took a few more pain meds as my head still had a little throb to it. There was quiet music, I thought. I checked my phone but not that. I opened the door and walked to the top of the stairs as the soft music was clearer and the organ in the center of my chest jumped. Down the stairs and on the leather sofa was the hot man strumming the guitar while one foot rested on the coffee table and the other on the floor.

I stood out of sight as he looked down at the strings. He'd gotten his guitar as a kid from his aunt for Christmas one year. By the time I met him it was a well-worn instrument that displayed what a natural musician he was. He'd taught himself and only played for me. I'd lie on his bed while he sat next to me and strummed beautiful songs as he looked down wearing that sexy ass grin.

He'd only played in public once. My mother ran the Christmas Pageant at our church and the day of the program the acoustic guitar player came down with the flu. I told her how amazing Levi played and after I begged him he caved. *Anything for you, Allie.* The entire congregation gasped when Levi appeared and slayed it as I sat in the first row falling even more in love with him.

This might've been a turned corner when it came to Levi and my parents, but they happen to catch him in my room at midnight the following evening and the full-blown *Kill Levi Era* continued on.

His fingers danced on the strings while I attempted to beat the desire that swam through me into submission.

I despised the fact that I wanted to stand there forever looking down at him.

I forced my feet to return to my room and plopped into bed. The music stopped and it was late, but I was not sleeping. Thoughts of Toby holding me against the bathroom wall along with Levi who was doing hurdles in my mind was the equivalent of a child high on Jelly Bellies and Lemon Heads; sleep was not happening.

I disliked that my hate was wavering a bit. Yeah, him saving me twice in one day was messing with me. I'd just steer clear of him tomorrow. Yes, that was the ticket. I gave team Allie a quick pep talk.

So he helped me out of a sticky situation today, death, but by tomorrow the hatred I'd had for Mr. Satan would return. He was still the scum of the earth, and if it wasn't for the life threatening thing today, the loathing hate I had for him would be as strong as it'd always been. Yup, a raging river of hate. So tomorrow I'd slip right back into my normal state of mind. The one that gives zero fucks for a dumbass.

A positive thought? I was positive Levi sucked.

I tossed and turned for what felt like an hour, and I was trying everything to get to sleep. Basically one sheep, two sheep, raccoon, cow, turtle, Old McDonald had a farm, heeey Macarena! Had I developed adult ADHD?

Me: I can do this. I can sleep.

Brain: Pssst.

Me: Yeah?

Brain: What disease do you think you have?

Deep breathing and thinking of Emily's wedding details that normally put me to sleep in a second, did nothing. I sang *Silent Night* and *Little Drummer Boy*, but still not sleepy.

Then there was a creak. What could be in a strange house in the Colorado mountains? My eyes darted around the dark room wondering if it was a bear outside my window or a serial killer in the hall. I thought I'd prefer a serial killer if I had to choose between the two, I guess. But I would fight a bear, not well, but I'd sure as shit give it a go. But not a grizzly bear, or a black bear. I'll take a Care Bear, please?

Yes, I definitely have adult ADHD.

I slowly climbed out of bed and went to the door. I pressed my ear to it but heard nothing. I nearly jumped out of my skin when the noise happened again. It was from outside but I couldn't make myself look.

What if I pulled open the curtain and a man was there staring at me? The thought sent a shiver up my arms.

Calm your ass down!

I went over and peeked out the window to see nothing but trees and snow. Whew. I got back into bed and after more tossing and turning, I finally grew tired.

My eyes opened and terror wrapped around me. I was back in the car again. I hung upside down with more blood appearing by the second. My gloves were soaked in it as hot tears streamed down my face.

The biting wind cut my skin like shards of glass as the cold seeped into my bones while I shivered uncontrollably. My fingers were numb and stiff, unable to feel the cold anymore. I knew it wouldn't be long before it was over. Before I was gone. The slow ache in my chest grew as my heart was turning to ice. I had no way out. I was alone and there was no hope. Nobody was coming for me. I was gone.

I sat up in bed unable to breathe with tears blurring my vision. *It was dream.* I attempted calming breaths which didn't do shit, as my mind swirled around my car going over a cliff. The crippling fear, blood on my face, and thinking of what could've happened. I was alone.

Before I could talk myself down, my feet were on the floor and out in the hall. The house was dark and quiet and scary. My lungs were tight and refused to let me draw in a breath while my skin was hot and cold at the same time. Could someone my age have a heart attack?

By the time I reached Levi's hallway I was jogging, and after three empty rooms, I stumbled into his, ran into a table by the door, and something crashed to the floor. The moonlight shined in the window, and before I could do anything he'd flown out of bed and was standing in front of me.

"What happened? Are you okay?"

"I, uh, I had a dream." My body was shaking as I took in shallow breaths. "I—"

He hit the switch on the wall and soft light from a lamp in the corner filled the room. I'd almost forgotten how tall he was as he stood wearing sweats and a red T-shirt with messy hair. I used my sleeve to wipe my eyes. "Oh, I'm sorry. I was just a little freaked out and, well, I don't know." My breathing was ragged and my pulse racing.

My heart squished when he pulled me to his chest and held me. It was so strange yet familiar; still a spot I seemed to feel utterly protected in. His arms around me made me soft as I melted into him. The right side of my brain was screaming to leave, while the left side was floating on a cloud in his presence. After a moment I pulled back and tried to get some air in. "I'm sorry, I can't catch my breath."

"You're shaking. Breathe through your nose, okay? This is anxiety messing with you."

He pushed a piece of hair from my face and it was intimate. Too intimate. I took another step back and crossed my arms over my braless chest feeling utterly exposed. My fear was shining through.

"You went through something traumatic today. Your mind isn't shutting off, I get it." He leaned in closer. "I know today rattled everything in you."

I nodded while still unable to get a good gulp of air.

His hands went around my biceps. "Langley, breathe through your nose and out your mouth, okay?"

Why was this so hard? "I can't."

His deep voice rumbled through my bones. "Let's breathe together."

I looked into his eyes while he took a deep breath, and I followed. Again and again and after a several minutes everything regulated.

"Better?"

I nodded. "Uh, I guess I should go back to my room. Sorry to have woken you."

I wanted my feet to move but they were stuck. After a few seconds his head tilted. "Why don't you just chill in here for a while? Maybe if you're not alone you can rest."

I stared into his twinkling eyes not certain of what I was asking, but his warm grin answered. "So you can sleep. I don't want you to be across this house if you have another bad dream. After all that's happened this is normal."

I didn't know what was happening, but I knew I wasn't going anywhere.

"Come on." I followed him and he pointed. "You take the bed, and I'll take the floor."

"That sounds kinda sucky for you."

"Langley, I spent half of my childhood in a sleeping bag when I didn't have a bed." He flashed me a smile. "It'll be fine."

"I don't know."

He walked to the closet and grabbed a blanket, pillow, and tossed it on the floor next to the bed. "I insist."

I nodded, climbed in, and no sooner did my head hit the

pillow, he reached down and pulled the comforter up to my chin. He walked over, turned the lamp off, and hit the floor.

My skin was prickly as the place I lay was still a little warm from his body that was there just moments ago. I sunk deeper into the mattress trying to feel it more. Did I inhale the pillow deeply searching for him? Of course not, I'm not a weird psyco. Come on.

Painful yet exhilarating memories of our last night together played on a loop that I wanted to stop.

Sort of.

Levi showing me what it was to belong to him. Hands everywhere while the things he made me feel, and the memory of it, caused an ache that filled me to the depths of my soul.

After a few minutes of silence his deep voice whispered, "You good up there?"

"Yes." I let out a breath.

"Things in life happen and they twist us up. But once you get some rest you'll feel like your old self." He let out a little gasp. "Did you hear that? I sound like I really know my shit, huh?"

I giggled. "Mr. Wisdom over there."

I stared at the ceiling almost afraid to close my eyes. Between Levi being next to me on the floor and the car debacle, my life was flying by at 15 WTF's a minute.

"I believe I hear your eyeballs blinking one hundred miles an hour up there. You're not going to have that dream again."

"How are you so sure?"

His chuckle hit my ears. "Well, with all this testosterone next to you, your subconscious knows your safe as a kitten here in this bed."

"OMG, did you really just say that?"

He nudged my arm and when I looked down he flexed. "Big guns don't lie."

"Barf." Sigh.

Heavy silence hung in the air. The past, the fact that we were sleeping in the same room, and the invisible string I wanted to deny, was still there.

Silence.

TEN
LEVI

IT SHOULD'VE BEEN

Being in the dark room with her, I knew this was how we should've been all along. The air was electric and all I wanted to do was fucking crawl in that bed. The place I belonged.

I wanted to kiss her and feel her soft skin against mine, but maybe a friend thing was a step closer to where I wanted to be.

"Do you think your group will be here tomorrow?" I wanted another day alone with her. One where we could be like this. Where her hate toward me was on a hiatus. One where I could give the lusty obsession I had with her a chance to grow legs. For her to realize it should be us.

"Not sure. The Midwest storm was still going a few hours ago."

She sighed, and I wanted to feel her breath against my skin.

"Lexi and Rach still the same?"

"Still wild women with no filter or patience." She yawned.

"We should sleep."

"Yeah."

I was fighting myself not to reach out and pull her down on me. "Who says friends can't sleep together?"

A whispery giggle wrapped around me. "Good night perv."

"Good night Langley."

ELEVEN
ALLIE
GOBBLE, GOBBLE

I rolled over as the morning sun shined on my pillow nearly blinding me. I peeked over at Levi who was facing me on the floor. I stared at his sleeping face and listened to his soft breathing. I curled up and just let my eyes soak him in. I wanted to memorize every bit of him. He was adorable and hotter than a jalapeno's armpit at the same time.

Memories of waking up with his arms around me, his body next to mine as I curled into him, warmed me from the inside out.

I slipped out of bed and back to my room to find a bazillion text messages from the girls.

Allie, how are you? I worry about you all alone in that big old house.

Why are you not answering me?

Allison Marie I am worried sick about you!

The snow is still coming down. Damn mother nature! What a freaking bitch!

Don't make me call the police, respond!

I grabbed clothes from my suitcase and dialed Lexi.

"Galloping gremlin, I've been so worried. I have been going crazy with zero responses to my texts! What in the frack are you doing to me?"

"First of all, it's been night time and I've been sleeping like a normal human. Secondly, why are you saying stupid words?" She was a head scratcher alright.

"I'm trying to clean up my language. I need to stop my swearing and pull my ship together."

"I'm rolling my eyes."

"No, I swear I'm doing it this time. No cursing while I'm in Colorado. Royce, get me a margarita."

"It's morning for God's sake. Do *not* have a margarita. Please no drinking at the airport. The last thing you need is to be hauled off another plane."

Her gasp nearly sucked my earring through the phone. "Mother trucker that was not my fault. I was just nervous about flying and my meds and the wine did not mix well. It happens, Allie."

"No, it doesn't. You were laughing and started screaming *we're going down*. Just when I thought it couldn't get any worse, you head butted the steward who was just doing his job."

"Hey! I didn't mean to do that, his big old head got in the way. We agreed to *never* discuss this topic again."

"You also agreed not to drink within five hundred feet of an airplane or any aviation facility. I think you even signed something."

"Whatever. Are you the fucking margarita police now? Great, now you ruined my no cursing thing."

"You can still not curse you know."

She huffed. "Why bother now? Let's face it, I love to curse and hate people. That's just me I guess."

"Yes, you suck."

"Not for free." She giggled. "People just need to be happy this blizzard hasn't turned me into a gun toting maniac."

"Wow, your life skills are top shelf."

"My life skills are fine but it's my tolerance for idiots that's low today. I used to have an immunity built up, but there must be a new strain of stupid out there."

"Damn stupid strains."

"Are you keeping the doors locked?"

"Of course I locked the doors. You're going to lose it when you see this place."

"I'm just worried about you being all alone."

"Evan has a cousin who got here the same day I did." I smiled at the memory of sleeping Levi with his messy hair and those pillow lips that did a little cha-cha through my frontal lobe. Yes, as much as I'd fought it, those lips were burned into my brain like a tattoo.

"And he's been nice? What's his name?"

A little horn blew in my mind.

"Shoot, my phone's going to die. When do you think you'll get here?"

"I'm hopeful in the next day or so."

"Love you. And Emily says to get your butt to the church to decorate this morning."

"I will."

"Bye-bye, babe."

I applied the ointment I was given at the ER to my stitches and popped two more pain reliever tablets before hopping in the shower with Levi on my mind.

I pulled on my favorite jeans that make my bum look nice, white tee, and topped it off with the Nike black zippy jacket I found thrifting. Score for me.

I put some gel in my hair to tame my curls and then spent thirty minutes getting the *natural look* with my make-up.

I bopped down the stairs and let my eyes take in the beautiful Christmas tree in front of the window while *I'm dreaming of a White Christmas* softly filled the room from some invisible speaker somewhere.

As I entered the kitchen the aroma of bacon gave me a hug, and the sight of Levi made me want to hurdle the center island and give him a hug. *Stop!*

"Hey." His hair was damp from a shower. A shower where his muscular chest that was holding up his shirt would have had hot, steamy water running over it.

He wore black joggers and an Adidas Blue sweatshirt that made his eyes pop. "You still only like boring scrambled eggs with zero cheese or veggies?"

He remembered. "Yup."

"You picky eaters."

"I don't want to be picky; it's just the way I'm wired." I gave a nod. "Proud to say I still eat from the kids menu."

"Really? The kids menu?" He slid a plate to me.

"First of all, it's an economically sound choice and most people don't think I'm too weird. Nothing makes me happier than a simple grilled cheese and fries."

"Kind of comforting to know some things never change."

The words hung in the air, and I forced out a weird fake cough.

"Uh, I have to go do church decorating for Emily. It figures all the work will fall on me today. Do you think I could borrow your SUV?" My entire being felt all twirly. I didn't know how to not hate Levi. It'd been a solid seven years, and now we were kind of people who talked to one another?

"I can help." He used the spatula to push some eggs onto my plate.

"It's okay, you just stay here." I needed to *not* have him close to me, bad idea. Why are the bad ideas always the fun ones to think about?

"I've got nothing but time, and we both know I have killer holiday decorating skills."

"Really, I'm fine doing this myself." My eyes dropped to my plate. "Yes, I'll do it."

I took a bite of the fluffy scrambled eggs and OMG; flipping fantastic. They didn't even need salt, they were perfectly perfect. I took another bite as a few pieces of bacon were dropped on my plate. I took a taste and wondered how in hell he had perfected bacon; crispy but not too crispy. Was it just this slice? I ate another and another to find out all the slices were perfect; yummy to the core. Had he taken a class? Become a chef? I had no flippin' clue, but wow.

I looked up mid-chew to find Levi leaning on the counter thoroughly amused as I had shoved his delectable breakfast into my mouth at record speed. My cheeks were hot as I swallowed and flashed a weak smile.

"Everything taste okay?"

I nodded. "Yeah, it's okay." For some reason I couldn't stop nodding.

"Good."

Still nodding. "Yeah, good."

"So what's up with the church stuff?"

I pulled out my phone and scrolled through messages.

"Well, Emily's had two Christmas trees shipped to the church so that's good." I looked up. "But I'll get it, really."

"You're going to haul two Christmas trees in, assemble them, put all the lights on, and decorate?"

"Yeah." Huh, that did *not* sound fun.

"That seems like a lot for one person."

"It kinda does."

"How about I come along and just help you get the trees up, and then I can take off?"

I didn't want to be near him. I didn't think I liked *not* hating him. I needed the hate.

"Levi—"

"I know we're not friends."

My eyes shot to him.

He cleared his throat. "I mean, I know how things are. But I want to help you get those big trees into the church. I just can't sit around here knowing I could lighten the load for you."

I popped a brow and he flexed.

"Come on."

Eyeroll. "Fine."

I looked back at my phone despising the fact that I might've been a tiny bit glad he was coming.

"So how do you know Emily?"

"We went to college together. She's great but is particular about things." I scrolled on. "Crap, she also wants me to go and cut twenty-five Evergreen branches, approximately fifteen inches in length, and use the ribbon she sent with the Christmas trees and attach a four inch bow to each of them and put at the end of each aisle. Clearly she's not a control freak, right?"

He tossed a piece of bacon into his mouth. OMG how could he make eating bacon sexy?

He pointed out the large kitchen window. "Easy peasey. We're surrounded by Evergreen trees." He rummaged through a drawer and held up a pair of pliers with a pointy tip. "You use these, and I'll find something in the garage to cut it with. Do you have boots?"

I let out a huff. "Do I have boots? Of course I came to Colorado with boots."

His hands clapped together. "Meet you outside in five minutes."

I pulled on my boots realizing this was maybe okay. Yeah, Levi helping with church stuff would be fine. He knows we'd never be friends so I'll use him for his muscles. Yes, that's almost hating him again.

I stomped through the snow while digesting my beautiful surroundings. The crisp air filled my lungs as my eyes dance around from the mountains in the distance to the snow covered trees in front of me, and I could think of no prettier place in the world to be.

I soaked in the sound. Or lack of. So different from my apartment in D.C. I'd only lived there for six months after I got an unbelievable job opportunity. I was strong and on my own and achieving my career goals. While I love living in the city with the hustle and bustle, this was a pallet cleanse for my senses. I couldn't hear a single car or noise at all. It was the sound of silence. (Cue up Disturbed)

But I did miss Chicago where I'd lived since after college and absolutely loved. You might be wondering why I'd moved away from a place that was amazing. Well, it turns out when I date people and start having a serious connection, I sort of cut and run sometimes. Edit: every time.

My only serious relationship was with Clint Jacobsen. He worked in finance for Northern Trust Corporation and we met when he was walking across the street. I had looked down when I dropped my Reese's Peanut Butter Cup in my lap, and when I looked back up he was right in front of me crossing the street. I screeched to a stop and didn't run him over by sheer inches.

After much apologizing he said he'd forgive me if I met him for dinner. Pretty cool pick up line I had to admit. He was handsome, sweet, and funny. As things grew a little more serious, the fear of being happy and things imploding almost consumed me. I secretly saw a therapist to try to get a grip, but after two sessions she wanted to focus on "resolving my Levi issues" and that was a fuck no. I'd done my best to bury that shit and no matter what a professional said, opening that box was not a thing I could do.

I knew with all my being that Clint was a good man, but what if he grew tired of me? What if one day he didn't want *us* anymore? What if I woke up and he was gone? This happens to people all over the globe, and it'd happened to me with the only man I'd loved, and it broke me.

The pain and thoughts of Levi 24/7 made me wish I hadn't survived the accident. He didn't just disappear; he took a part of me with him that would likely never return. The trust part, the part that jumped without a net knowing his arms would catch me. If he could do that after what I thought was the strongest love in existence, it would likely happen again. I mean maybe someday? Or not. I went to a dark place that took so long to climb out of, I didn't know if I could do it again.

While I'm no shrink, I knew the desperate job search I did in all states but my own confirmed I was just not ready for a serious relationship. Yes, I didn't have the balls to end it like a grown up so a perfect job offer across the country was an easy solution for those of us who don't like conflict. Sure we said we'd try the long distance thing but over time the calls became less frequent, and I brushed off him visiting or me going back to Chicago because of my crazy work schedule. But it was probably for the best.

I figure I'd get my first cat in the summer. I never dreamed I'd grow up to be a super cool crazy cat lady, but I'm pretty sure I'd kill it. Not the cat, just the living my life solo part.

Someone once said it's beautiful to be alone. To be alone does not mean to be lonely. It means the mind is not influenced or contaminated by society. Yeah, I'm clinging to that shit like the Kardashians' cling to filler.

I walked through the trees and before me stood a handsome Evergreen, and I got to it. I used my pliers but after cutting only three branches, there was rustling of leaves and loud cackles. WTH? I spun around to see three wild turkeys running in my direction. I let out a scream in an octave I wasn't even aware I could hit, threw my pliers at the leader of the killer turkey gang, and hauled ass. They were blocking my path back to the house so I bolted in the other direction.

In front of me stood a tree that had some low branches. Without a thought I jumped on a branch and climbed up. It was a little concerning that the lower branches seemed to be breaking right off the damn tree while I made my way up as I hoped to eventually climb down. After a few stumbles, I arrived at a high perch. Did I ever expect to have to climb a tree in a forest in Colorado to escape possible rabid turkeys? Short answer, no. Long answer, heeellll nnnooo.

As my attempted killers scampered around at the base of my tree, I immediately took the pine cones close by and threw them at my attackers. Why didn't I bring my cell freaking phone? I knew I'd run a little ways from the house, but certainly Levi would find me. Good news it appeared turkeys don't climb trees.

I sat quietly counting thirteen pine cones above me.

"Langley, Where are you?"

Relief washed through me as the deep voice echoed throughout the forest. "Allie!"

"I'm here! I climbed a tree!'"

"Why in the hell did you go tree climbing?" His voice moved closer.

"I was attacked by turkeys! They're at the bottom of my tree!"

His chuckle echoed everywhere. "Are you kidding me right now? You can't be left unsupervised for ten minutes?"

"It's not me!"

He spoke like a robot. "Warning, unsupervised adult may exhibit erratic behavior and will be highly unpredictable."

A few second later Levi was running, yelling, and waving his arms in the air and the turkeys took off. He looked up and shook his head. "I guess they like short people."

I chucked a pine cone and it bounced off his head. "You watch it. Short girls are like cute tiny ninjas of death who are the perfect height to do serious damage."

As my eyes looked down, I realized how far up in the tree I actually was. My heart hiccupped as I found I was a little more scared of heights than I'd realized.

"Come on down."

"Uh, okay." I held on to the branch my bum sat on and lowered my foot. "I'm not sure how to do this."

"You had a brother. Didn't you tree climb as a kid?"

"Will climbed trees. I played Barbies *under* the trees."

"Okay, I'll guide you down. Just follow my instructions."

"The ground looks so far away. And, as hard as it is to believe, I'm kinda a klutz."

"You don't think I remember that? The girl who was leaning too far over the ledge and literally landed on me?" He chuckled. "I still think you did that on purpose."

It was the perfect meet cute if we were a romcom movie. Me with Lexi and Rachel, I wasn't supposed to go but snuck out to go to a concert a few towns over. I was sitting on a railing I shouldn't have been on because it was stupid, and as I threw my arms in the air when Coldplay took the stage, I tumbled over and landed on Levi who was with his friends below me. We were connected at the hip for the next twelve hours. And the next year. There was an instant chemistry that wove between us. "Why in the hell would I *throw* myself over a ten foot ledge?"

He did a spin. "Clearly you found me irresistible."

"I did not." I was glad he couldn't see the crimson that came to my cheeks.

"Those kisses said different."

My words hopped on a train and bolted after the turkeys. I wanted to say he was wrong, but he wasn't.

"Here's how this is going to go. You are going to do what I say, and I'm going to guide you down. You ready?"

I nodded.

"Under your right foot is a sturdy branch. I want you to

reach your foot down until you feel it. It's about a ten inches below you."

I slid down and got my foot on the branch.

"Good girl. Now turn around and hold the branch you were just sitting on."

I followed directions while his deep toned *good girl* gave me a tummy flip.

"Nice. Now lower your left foot about ten inches and you'll feel another branch."

I held on for dear life and found the branch, but when I stepped on it there was a crack, and I pulled my foot back.

"Okay, we're going to go for the one just below that one."

I yelled. "Raise your hand if you're sick of this shit."

"Just do it."

"Don't be getting all bossy."

"You like a little bossy."

"Shut up. Don't flip my bitch switch, I warning you now."

I followed his directions and a few moments later I could see I was getting close.

"Alright, you're out of branches and probably don't want to fall six feet, so slowly turn yourself around, and I'll do the rest."

Memories of him *doing the rest* ran rampant and brought more heat to my face. I turned and saw his arms up as my feet slid down. His hands had my upper thighs then my waist, and a second later my body slid over his chest and my wobbly feet were on solid ground.

As I stared at his chest I realized his hands were still holding my waist. My breath hitched in my throat, and I knew if I looked up he'd read me like a book and know the effect he still had on me. I didn't want him to see that one look could wreck me. That the sound of his voice still awoke butterflies.

"Well, thank you." I spoke to his chest as we stood frozen. I took a small step backwards, but he didn't release me, and I didn't know how I felt about that.

My eyes climbed up his muscular chest, past his perfect jaw line to those eyes that were intense, and I was suddenly shaking a little. I gulped air as his eyes bore into me, and I didn't know if I wanted to whip off my shirt and rub against him like a cat, or haul ass into the forest to disappear to never been seen again.

"Hi."

My stomach fell to my feet when his eyes dropped to my lips. Was he going to kiss me? His eyelids drooped as his pupils flared. I knew I should step away, but also knew a stick of dynamite wouldn't have moved me from the place I stood. His eyes were asking permission, and I had no freaking clue what my eyes were saying back, but his hand went to the back of my neck as he closed the distance between us. We were just an inch apart and leaning in and the sides of our noses touched, and I felt his breath on my mouth.

This is so bad, step away!

My pulse spiked as he leaned closer and brushed his lips against mine. Once, twice, as my eyes closed, and I wanted his mouth on mine more than anything I'd ever wanted. Even chilled Dove chocolate. It was the wrongest of all wrongs, but he was my kryptonite. My brain had always been strong, but feeling his breath on my face was still a high; a euphoric state that sent a low hum throughout my body.

His smell, those eyes, and his hands on me were what I'd missed for seven years. But there I was, in a quiet snow-covered forest next to the house that would only contain us until the others arrived. Visions of his fingers sliding across my skin, the way his touch left me willing to give up anything for it to continue. I suddenly realized I had a hold of his jacket. A firm hold as if I was afraid, he'd step away from me.

My brain came to life as it hit me that things could happen here. *Things could happen!*

Oh, mother of pearl, WTH was I doing?

I pulled away with my mind feeling like a pile of useless mush. "This can't, we can't."

He whispered, "I know you feel whatever is going on between us. It's fire."

"We're the past. The past has to stay there." It was a strong sentence but came out a weak airy whisper.

He leaned down and kissed my cheek and my eyes closed as his mouth slipped down to my jaw while my tummy twisted.

My voice cracked. "We're just friends for a few days, then nothing. It's the way it is."

A tingle slithered up my spine when his whiskers slid down my neck. It felt so good I was melting. Even with the slightest of friction between us every nerve ending in my body stood at attention. I was certain I'd end up a puddle on the ground at any second. His presence was a magnet that drew me in. My body betrayed me with even one glance.

He muttered against my neck. "Friends?"

I stepped back and straightened my coat. "That's what we are. Sort of. Maybe not." Could I sound more like an idiot?

The corner of his mouth turned up as if the ring master was patronizing me. "I got it."

I needed to be strong. I knew what it was like after he was gone. I'd lived it and there unbearable pain, and while I stitched up my heart, it took far too long to get over him.

"Well, that's good. I'm glad we're on the same page." I cleared my throat. "Let me cut these branches so I can go to the church." I side eyed him. "And you can totally stay here. I can do it myself."

"I'll help now and at the church." His arm nudged mine as he passed. "You better stick close to me. You never know when the turkeys will return for shorty and superhero Levi will have to come to the rescue."

While I gave an annoyed huff as he walked away, I made sure he was in sight as I shoved the image of a bare-chested Levi in a superhero cape out my ear.

TWELVE
LEVI

UH-OH

The ride to the church was quiet, and I knew by how she chewed on her lip what was on her mind. Her lips and taste, even for a second, were now branded into me and the only thing my mind was willing to entertain.

We entered the front office of the church where a woman in her sixties wearing a turtleneck with her dark hair piled on top of her head in a bun sat behind a desk.

"Good morning."

Allie smiled. And what a smile. "I'm Allie Langley, and my friend is getting married here on Saturday."

The woman nodded. "Yes, Emily."

"She had some items sent to decorate the sanctuary."

The woman stood up and laughed. "She surely did. Enough to nearly fill up our storage room. Come with me."

We followed her down a hallway and my eyes were glued to Allie's tush. *Down boy!*

The lady stopped. "It's all in here." She unlocked it and handed Allie the key. "I'm leaving to attend a meeting shortly, so here's the closet key if you need to lock up before I return."

"Thank you so much."

The woman gave a wave and disappeared.

Allie set her purse in the hall, and we entered to find two large boxes containing Christmas trees and another holding ornaments and lights.

She kicked a box. "This sucks. The chains on my mood swing just snapped. Would a handful of Xanax count as Emily's *something blue*? She's crazy."

I pulled off my jacket and tossed it on a table in the corner. "Crazy or eccentric?"

"Crazy. I think." Allie set her coat next to mine.

"There's a fine line between eccentric and crazy, and I ride that shit like a circus bear on a unicycle. She might too."

She pulled open of the boxes and groaned. "Stop."

"When you say stop, I don't know if you mean it's hammer time, or if I should collaborate and listen."

She huffed. "You make me need something that's more than coffee but less than cocaine."

"Wow." I laughed and opened the Christmas tree box. "Have you lost some of your sweetness with age?"

"I think so. The older I get the meaner I seem to become. It won't be long before I'm biting people."

"And that's bad?"

Even in the dimly lit closet I could see her cheeks get rosy as she cleared her throat.

Her grin socked me in the gut. "Thanks for helping me. I don't think it'll take too long, right?"

"Teamwork makes the dream work. Wait, is that right?" I scratched my head. "That doesn't sound right. What's that saying?"

"Hmmm. Not sure. But if you take out the team in team-work, it's just work. Who wants that?"

"Teamwork means never having to take all the blame yourself."

She pointed at me. "I like that one. Yes, Bridezilla will kill both of us."

"I'll get the Christmas tree box if you'll get the door."

I lifted it and watched her fine backside walk away.

"Wait, it's locked." She looked around. "Where's my purse?"

"You left it in the hall."

Her mouth made an "O". "Oops."

"Oops?"

"Oh mother hubbard, we're in a pickle."

"Huh?"

"I put the keys in my purse so I wouldn't lose them. Clearly my brain isn't braining today." Her eyes closed. "The door must lock automatically or something."

A jolt of pure joy entered my bloodstream. I was locked in a closet with the most beautiful girl in the world? I swear to God I felt the universe give me a high-effing-five.

She gritted her teeth and kicked the door, and I couldn't control my laughter.

"Stop laughing at me."

"It's just, well, is it wrong that you look a little hot when you're angry?"

A grin snaked across those lips as she ran her hand through her hair. "Well, when I woke up today, I had no plans of being *this* sexy. But hey, shit happens."

I set down the box and leaned against the wall. "It does."

Clearly I needed to tell my facial expressions to use their

indoor voice, because with one look her eyes went wide as our situation registered in her brain.

Her nerves entered from stage right. "But there's got to be a way out of here, right?"

She shuffled over to a metal cabinet in the corner and pulled open a door before rummaging through stuff. "Yeah, I'm sure there's a hammer here or something."

"You're going to hammer us outta here?" Why was her panic spurring me on?

She glanced over her shoulder. "Maybe?"

She bent down and pulled some tools from the bottom shelf. "Wait, I might have the answer."

Could the answer be to hold her against the wall and kiss all of the lip gloss from her mouth?

She sprung to her feet and held out a wrench. "This might do the trick." She nodded like a bobble head as she went to the door and dropped to her knees. I liked it very much. "Yeah, I could use this tool to kinda grab the screws and pull out the knob?"

"It's a wrench."

More nodding. "That's what I thought. A wrench."

"Wrenches are used to tighten or loosen nuts and bolts."

"Perfect. Yes, I need to loosen these so I'm good."

"Those aren't nuts or bolts."

She let out a sigh. "I'm sure this will work, maybe."

"I'm sure it will *not* work." I walked over to the metal cabinet, turned on the flashlight in my phone, and took a look. "I don't think the right tools are here for that."

I turned around to see her stand while she shifted on her feet nervously. "We have to get out of here. There has to be some tool that will work."

"Don't think so, sweetie."

She inhaled sharply, which lit something it shouldn't, before she walked over and grabbed my phone. She shined the flashlight, bent down, and looked through the contents in a drawer before standing, handing me my phone, and looking down. "I *need* you to find a way to get that door open." Her fingers laced together.

"Are you claustrophobic?"

"Huh?"

"Afraid of being trapped in small spaces?"

She took a little step back and spoke in a whisper. "I'm afraid of being trapped in small spaces with you."

Her words hung in the air. "You're not afraid of me." I took a step toward her while she took another back. "Are you afraid of *you*?"

Her head shook as I took another step when her eyes drop to my lips before she quickly looked away.

"I don't know what it is between you and me." I took another small step while she took one back.

"There's nothing between us." She gulped. "We're friends for a few days. Or not."

I chuckled. "Sure."

Our dance continued but as she took one more step her back was against the wall. I closed the distance between us as she let out a breath. We stood silently, and I swear I could feel her heart beating.

"You feel it. Like back then."

She shook her head. "It's just physical."

"*Just* physical? You've never thought of me?"

"I don't ever want to think of you."

We stood silently, but she didn't move. She didn't step away.

"Do you want me to kiss you?"

Her head shook. "No."

I held her eyes for a long minute. "All you have to do is step away. Why are you still here in this corner?"

She spoke in a broken whisper. "I don't know."

I leaned in closer. Her being so close made the air thick with an intoxicating scent of desire. "Do you want *me* to move?"

"No. Yes." Her breath was on my face.

I whispered, "I think we're in a fucktangular."

The corner of her mouth turned up. "What?"

"A fucktangular is a situation which is complicated and messy in multiple *pleasant* ways."

She swallowed hard.

"Do you want me to kiss you, Allie?"

"No."

I was about to step away when she threw her arms around my neck and pulled me to her, our lips a breath apart. Every muscle in me was pulsing. Gently, slowly as our mouths still fit together perfectly. Her lips led mine while my hand traveled to her neck and into her hair as hers travelled to my chest.

The kiss was torturously slow and hot. She felt so fucking good, and I had to catch my breath when she pressed her chest into mine. My hand traveled to the small of her back, and I pulled her closer while a quiet gasp escaped her. I wanted to possess her, body and soul.

But she had control, and I'd have it no other way. She clung to my shoulders while she was restless in my arms. Her hands raked through my hair as the kisses grew deeper and faster like we'd been starving forever.

We'd been starving forever.

THIRTEEN
ALLIE
TIME WARP

I was in a time warp, and I couldn't get close enough. My mind was thrashing like a boat on out-of-control waves; I didn't want what I wanted. It was a dark, primal desire that I knew could never truly be quenched.

I was jittery with a spinning head as I realized he was tasting me like someone who'd been living on Ramen and was suddenly served filet mignon. His fingers slid through my hair as we pressed together. His body heat wrapped around me like a blanket leaving my brain oozy, and I wanted more and more and more.

For years I'd fought the memories of Levi. But under the surface I'd craved the man who could be both a gentleman and the beast that would hold me by my wrists and take what he wanted.

His hand traveled to my neck and his thumb glided over my collar bone. A low groan went from his mouth to mine and was fuel being poured on the fire that was me as I pulled him closer. My thighs were trembling as his lips trailed down my neck to the sensitive area below my ear.

Ohmygoshohmygoshohmygosh...

My common sense was being drowned by the sensations firing through every cell in my body. My legs were the consistency of water as I held onto his shoulders as falling down was something I did often.

I don't know what force overtook my body and beat my brain into submission, but the next thing I knew my fingers had slid under his shirt and the heat of his skin burned my fingertips in the best possible way. A low rumble went from his mouth to mine before his hands slid down and held my bottom.

His taste and touch brought it back like the recovering heroin addict being served up a platter of the one thing that could destroy her after providing the high that only it could. As he caged me against the wall in the storage closet, I knew we were on a speeding train that would be impossible to stop. Could anything stop this?

"Hello?"

It turns out the church receptionist could derail it in an instant.

There was a knock, and I ran my hands over my hair after pushing Levi away. "Shit, what should I do?"

He stepped back, pulled his shirt down, and flashed a grin. "I say never make eye contact while eating a banana."

"What?"

"I thought you were seeking general advice." His dirty grin slugged me. "Maybe say hello?"

"Hi!" It came out as a screechy little scream. "The door locked, and the keys are in my purse out there."

"I see them."

As the door opened, I jumped away from Levi. A second

later the lady's head tilted as her eyes bounced between the tall handsome man and me. My cheeks caught on fire.

"Thank you so much." I quickly grabbed a box containing ornaments. "Now we can start decorating for the Christmas wedding. There's nothing like a Christmas wedding, am I right or am I right?" I threw my shoulders back and walked out of the storage closet as if my entire world hadn't just been rocked to the core.

We silently got two Christmas trees assembled and set one on each side of the altar before I pulled out boxes of white lights.

Levi reached down and grabbed a box. "You okay?"

"Quit, Levi."

"I am unable to quit as I am currently too legit."

Eye roll. "That can't happen again." I looked at that handsome face knowing I was going to pay a price for being close to him again.

"But you—"

"I know I kissed you. But it can't happen twice."

"Okay, not twice." He raised a questioning eyebrow. "Maybe five times?"

"Shut up, please."

"Let's calm down. This isn't a big deal. We can forget it and move on." He gave a dip of his chin. "See? I can be the voice of reason."

My blood pressure ticked up. "If I'm ever in a situation where *you're* the voice of reason, then we are in a very bad place."

"Ouch."

I took a cleansing breath trying to lasso my brain which

seemed to still be in the storage room. "It just can't happen again. Everything about you is in the past and that's where I want it." There we go. I'm a grown ass woman taking control and making brave decisions; silence, saying no, and walking away.

"But—"

I flashed my strongest smile. "No buts."

He opened the box and nodded slowly before giving me a wink. "Got it."

He hit a button on his phone and *We Wish You a Merry Christmas* filled the room. We remained silent, and I was proud of achieving my first wise decision in recent times. As I focused on the decorating task at hand, I looked over to see him with a big red ornament hanging from each ear, green little ribbons tied into his hair, and a red velvet rope with bells on it wrapped around his waist.

A laugh popped out at the same time he held up a finger and started galloping around the tree with his dinging bells ringing out.

Why did he have to be so handsome, charming, funny, adorable, tall, and handsome? Did I say that twice?

And dangerous to every part of me. I tried to grasp at the wise decisions again, but they seemed to have vaporized into thin air.

For my next trick I will dazzle you with the illusion that I have my shit together.

As we got closer to the house, my mind put on its mental

armor to fight Levi as I was suddenly a ball of stress. If stress brings on weight loss, I should be invisible by morning.

I jumped when his phone started screaming *Warning; an idiot is calling you.*

"Sorry." He grabbed the phone. "I changed my ringtone, you like?"

"Sure, if you're a thirteen-year-old dude."

He chuckled and put it to his ear. "Yo."

I looked out the window as my super-sonic ears thought they heard a female voice.

"That's fine." Pause. "Nothing, just out of town for a bit."

Nothing? Was he asked what he was doing and wrote off the entire storage closet situation as nothing?

He pulled onto the long driveway. "That works. Ciao."

Wow. A reminder that he had a life. He'd lived years in another country where he did stuff every day with what appeared to be *many* people, Things that had nothing to do with me.

A weird irritation entered my body like a shot because Levi was messing everything up. He was messing *me* up. Sure, I kissed him first, but I didn't want his presence, and I needed him to go. This was too hard. It took years for me to get my life back together, and I wouldn't let that all go for a kiss. Nope, I was done.

As a matter of fact, he was kind of a jerk. *He* was the one who crushed me. And now Levi Dawson had the audacity to use his hotness to try to get some action while in Colorado? How dare he? He crushed me, left me, and never *ever* reached out again. Not once. Who does that? Only a cold-hearted bastard, that's who. He just wants to get his kicks. Well, not happening!

Suddenly another car pulled up beside us, and I hopped out to see a man in jeans and a black jacket. "I have your grocery order."

"Who ordered them?" I tried to ignore Levi and his orgasmic cologne as he stepped beside me.

"Lexi Golden."

"Whoa." Levi scrunched his nose. "Her name still gives me instant heart burn. Maybe I should go into the forest and search for portals to other dimensions in case needed upon her arrival."

"Solid plan, Levi." I looked back to the man. "I can help you with the groceries."

Levi stepped away from me. "I'll get them. You go inside."

"Don't tell me what to do." Who did he think he was? "Don't tell me to go inside."

The delivery driver's brow lifted as Levi flashed me a smile. "Yes, dear."

Fire shot through me. "Don't call me that."

Levi picked up a bag and nodded with a hint of amusement. "I'm joking, Langley." He whispered to the man, "Old ball n chain's getting cranky."

"You shut up." The delivery driver narrowed his eyes at me. "We are *not* together."

Levi huffed out a single laugh. "Well, we just made out in a storage closet for twenty minutes, so whatever."

I stomped my foot. "And now I hate you again." How was I going to survive this effing week?

Levi picked up another bag and gave me a cocky chin nod. "Sure, you do."

He could see through me.

As I watched him enter the house, I knew I could not. Not

now. I would either kill him or rip off my shirt and do a dance for him in the kitchen. I couldn't trust him or his dark motives, and I sure as shit couldn't trust my dumbass self. *Uuuggghhh.* Instead of entering the house, I just reached inside the front door, tossed off my shoes, pulled on my boots, and walked around to the back of the house.

I avoided the turkey infested forest to my right and headed down toward the frozen lake behind the house. For December in Colorado, it felt pretty warm, so I tromped through the snow that glistened like one thousand rhinestones under the sun.

The silence of the land was a vacation for my ears, and I knew it would help me wrap my head around how to ensure I steer clear of the green eyed monster.

I had to be strong and would ignore Levi. He remembered the effect he had on me, but it would go no further. Inhale. Exhale.

While I tried to forget the eyes that paralyzed me, I realized this was a ten out of ten Vrbo. There was a bench next to the frozen water, and I took a seat and absorbed the view in front of me which belonged in a Christmas movie. Fire pit with logs beside me, trees sprinkled with snow, and the mountains in the distance were breathtaking.

If it wasn't for Levi this would be the perfect Christmas in Colorado.

Beside me was a large wooden box with a lid. I peeked inside to see kerosene, long matches, and more wood. Nice.

While I couldn't recall ever lighting a bonfire before, it felt right. I poured on some of the magical fluid, tossed a match, and boom, this gal made fire.

I lifted a lid of another box right next to the lake to see many pairs of ice skates in various sizes. Well, slap my ass and call me Larry, I did *not* know I'd be learning to ice skate today.

These activities would keep my mind away from the hottie in the house.

FOURTEEN
LEVI
BACK AT IT

Her shoes were inside the door, but no sign of Allie. It appeared she was slipping back into hate mode, so maybe she was relaxing in her room. Or taking a bubble bath. A bubble bath where her hot slippery body soaks in the steamy water. That would be super cool.

I walked past her room, and the door was open, but no Langley wrapped in a towel or anything. Bummer.

I checked the pool area, out front, and the game room in the basement, but she was MIA. I grabbed a Rockstar and sat on the deck for a minute and that's when I saw it.

Down the hill in the distance was a fire and a tiny person. I narrowed my eyes and the auburn hair with the backdrop of winter white snow answered the question of who it was.

Did I immediately run down the hill so I could be by her and the fire? Nope. Instead, I grabbed a toboggan from the shelf in the garage and slid my ass all the way down the hill in style. While I'd like to say I hadn't gained speed quickly and ran into some huge wooden box, I can't. I hopped up realizing any chance of playing it cool had stayed back at the house. Allie skated toward me.

"I'm fine."

Her eyes rolled. "I didn't ask."

I stood by the fire and dusted myself off. "I'm sorry for what I said by the car. I was joking, but it was in bad taste."

"Let's play the quiet game, okay?" She skated in a circle.

"I think—"

"Clearly you *still* have no concept of the quiet game."

She propelled in the other direction and stayed about as far from me as possible. Every minute around her was stoking a fire I knew would eventually grow out of control; she was still the only thing I wanted. There had been many women in my life, hookups and purposeful dead ends, because nobody could be what she was, so why try? I'd regretted shutting it down from the day I had.

There were chairs on the ice in the distance, several areas where people had been ice fishing recently. I walked across the ice toward her.

"Hey! Watch for ice holes! It'll be weaker there." My voice rolled across the frozen lake.

"I don't want to hear from you. I'm going back to the house."

"Come on, Allie. Let's talk about this."

"No. I don't want to talk about anything. I just want to forget it and never speak to you again."

"Accept it; you can't steer clear of me. Not then or now."

"I'm sorry. I couldn't hear you over the little voice in my head screaming you're an idiot. No talking anymore. Stay away."

"Langley—"

"Everything is done."

"I hear ya honey, and I guess it's your lie to believe then. I just—"

She let a sarcastic laugh fly. "Please hold while I connect you with someone who gives a shit."

She skated to the bench, pulled off her skates, put on her boots, and tossed her skates in the box before heading up the hill toward the house.

She needed space. I'd just stay out here for a bit. It was warm for December so I'd just chill and try to *not* think about her. I walked across the ice realizing a little time was needed. That plan was shot to hell when the ice beneath my feet cracked.

FIFTEEN
ALLIE

THIS IS DONE

As I walked up the hill I decided if I stayed in my bedroom until everyone else arrived, I'd be able to control myself as the storage closet incident was playing on a loop in my noggin. Because I didn't like that I liked thinking of the low groan that rumbled through him when my fingers touched his skin.

And the phone calls. Clearly, he's meeting up with some chick at 7:00 to do something when he goes home.

Yes, I'd focus on the staying-in-my-room plan. The staying-away-from-the-hot-one plan. Then my mind grew exceptionally quiet. I was suddenly suspicious that I was up to something I didn't want me to know about. Whoever is in charge of making sure I don't do stupid shit is fired.

After hiking up the hill that was steeper than I remembered when going down, I reached the deck and looked over my shoulder to see Levi was gone. I glanced to the forest, but he wasn't in sight. Maybe he went for a walk and would just keep on walking. I needed to learn to love the sound of my feet walking away from things that aren't good for me because those kisses could take me out altogether.

Suddenly the world around me faded away as I saw Levi's shoulders and head come up from the ice and then disappear again; the ice had broken. A cold wave washed over me as I kicked into gear and ran back toward the lake.

"I'm coming!"

I ran down the hill and grabbed the toboggan Levi had sled down on before my legs sprinted across the ice and toward him as his head and shoulders appeared again.

"Levi!"

As I approached, he grabbed onto the ice around him trying to pull his body out. "Stop right there!" His teeth were chattering and the fear in his eyes squeezed my heart so hard I was dizzy. "Everything I'm grabbing is breaking. Stay back!"

"I'm going to slide the sled to you. I'll hold the rope, you climb on in the water, and I'll pull you out."

His body went back into the water except for his head. "Lookey here, does Langley have a side-hustle as a superhero?"

"Bet your ass I do. I'll be damned if you're going die here on the ice." I dropped to my knees and pushed the sled across toward him. "I have plans for that later."

He chuckled. "Going out in a blaze of glory, am I?"

I lay on my stomach realizing that was the only way I could keep hold of the rope tied to the toboggan. Fear was crushing me as I looked at the face that tore at every one of my senses. "I felt a spree coming on this morning. I wasn't sure if it was shopping or killing at the time, so I came up with a few options for both."

He grabbed the sled. "I think the ice will break, I don't want you to—"

I forced a smile as a tear rolled down my cheek. "We've got this."

He set the sled on the edge of the ice as his teeth were chattering harder. "Allie, please don't cry."

I wiped my face with the back of my hand. "Big girls don't cry. They pop a couple of Xanax, wash it down with vodka, and set your car on fire. Now let's get this show on the road so I can partake in all of those."

His hands rested on the sled.

"Hold on!"

I got to my feet and slowly pulled the heavy sled, but with every inch I pulled, the ice around the sled broke and Levi remained in the water.

"Okay, let's try this. You push the sled up and jump on so we can get it on top of the ice, and I'll run like hell."

"I've seen you run, and *like hell* would not be a synonym for that action."

"Okay, smartass. Is this really the time to be insulting my athletic abilities? *Never* pick a fight with a woman, we're full of rage and sick of everyone's shit. Now, you ready?"

"Yes."

I held the rope and started to run at the same time the sled popped out of the water with Levi on it. I ran as fast as my legs would take me, and after a moment I looked back to see him sliding on top of the ice away from the water.

With a new fear of frozen lakes, I kept running until we reached the bench.

I helped him stand as his body was shaking out of control. I ripped off my coat and put it over him.

I put his arm over my shoulder and led him up the hill.

"Well, this blows ass." His soaking wet clothing was

quickly saturating my shirt. "I think we just had a fuck-tastrophy."

"Yes. Clearly ice was a bad idea."

His teeth chattered as he laughed. "Just because it's a bad idea doesn't mean it can't be fun."

Boy, could that be my new life mantra or what?

We got to the back door, and I pushed it open and led him upstairs. "I'll turn on the tub for you."

We reached his room and went into the bathroom where a deep soaker tub awaited. I turned it on and when I spun around, he stood pale and shaking out of control looking dazed.

"Why don't you get out of those clothes?" I grabbed a towel from the hook on the wall.

His teeth chattered. "Now you're talking."

"Watch it. I've had enough to deal with today without having to make your death look like an accident. Don't make me sorry I saved you."

"Thanks for that, by the way."

"I'll go grab you some new clothes from your suitcase, okay?"

He was staring at the filling tub in silence. "Do you want me to help you?"

He stood as if I hadn't said a word. Could he hear me?

"Levi?"

"What? I'm having trouble, uh, I don't know."

"Let me help you." I pulled off his coat and set it in the sink. I pushed it up exposing his bare chest while he stood silently shaking. My eyes skimmed over his tattoo. My heart was thumping in my ears. Memories swarmed me like bees around a hive as I helped get his arm out of his shirt as water dripped on the floor.

Me sitting on his lap in the tattoo parlor as he held my hand. The tattoo he designed on the back of the room service menu in our hotel room. The tattoo he got on our wedding day.

I looked up to see his mind was back in lake. In the icy water reliving what could've happened. My stomach cinched at the thought and the back of my eyes burned before I cleared my throat.

"Levi, let's get you into the warm water."

He looked at me like I was speaking Bulgarian, but with a dip of his chin he acknowledged; he was in shock.

"I'll be right back." I took a step toward the door when he caught my wrist, and I turned back to see his glassy eyes looking down at me.

"Thank you, Allison."

The wind was knocked out of me at the somber look in his eyes. "Now don't you go full naming me, Levi Andrew Dawson. I'm going to turn around, you get the rest of your clothes off, and I'll toss them into the washer."

I heard the soaking pants drop to the floor and the sound of water as he entered. I was in the same room as naked Levi. My twenty-four-hour ago self would've never believed this shit.

I scooped up the clothes and ran to the laundry room before I made some hot chocolate and returned to the bathroom with a knock.

"Here, drink this."

I set the mug on the corner of the tub as I covered my eyes to ensure I didn't see *anything*. I'd like to say his glorious smile had reappeared, but he lay back in the tub staring in the distance and it squished something in my middle. I pulled out my phone.

"I figure some of your magical Christmas music might get you out of this annoying funk." What was the most upbeat tune? I opted for *Rocking Around the Christmas Tree*. I set the phone on the vanity and turned back and realized how much it tore at me to see him this way.

"I'm going get you something to wear."

I went back into his room and stopped outside the door. This was his space. Where he slept, even if for only a few days. The place where he took off his clothes and maybe did push-ups naked. It was beyond bizarre when I approached his closet. I slowly slid the door open to find some clothing on hangers and some still inside his suitcase. I touched each shirt, and would it be weird if I smelled them? If so, I didn't do that.

These were his things. The stuff he bought at stores while not thinking of me. He'd built himself a new life after he'd left. Had he ever contemplated finding me? I left home the second I could to escape the memories of him, but how was he able to just move on and never look back? Did he think of me?

I grabbed a red hoodie from the hanger and rummaged through the suitcase to retrieve a pair of charcoal grey sweats. I inhaled his socks like a sick lunatic as the fresh sent of fabric softener slid across my nose as visions of Levi sliding down my body zipped through my noggin. *Stop!*

I closed the closet and couldn't help but notice his wallet on the dresser. It was totally out of line, but I opened it. He had a smoking hot driver's license photo which seemed unfair to the rest of the world, debit card, and credit card. As I flipped it over there was a little pocket. My heart stopped when I pulled out a photo. It was worn with bent corners, but there was no mistaking the faces. It was a laughing Levi sitting on the tailgate of his blue Ford truck, a fire below him, and me on his lap. My arms were wrapped around his neck while I kissed his cheek. Of course a bottle of tequila sat beside him because we walked the line of crazy and fucking crazy back then.

The brink of sanity at times, but the emotions and all-consuming love were my addiction. We couldn't get enough of each other, and it drove my parents crazy. My dad would ground me time after time, but there was no keeping me away from him. The straight A student with the hellion was a concern to an entire community. But being in his arms was all I wanted. Our connection was inexplicable. We brought the passion and craziness out of one another. While I'd like to say it was all a mistake, I think I'd been seeking anything like it since the day he left.

I put the photo back but quickly grabbed it once again and stared a little longer.

If I could go back in time, what would I do differently? Anything at all? I wished I could say yes. I wished there was a single day in the past seven years I hadn't thought of him. Craved him.

There was another little pocket and when I peeked inside, I heard the shattering of the deep emotions that stay hidden. The ones I threw into a hole and poured a thick layer of concrete over to never feel again burst through like a barrage.

His gold wedding band.

I held it between my fingers as the visions shot rapid fire. Road trip, wedding bands bought at a pawn shop outside of Las Vegas, and holding the hand of the man who was my everything.

I quickly put it back in the proper place and rested my back against the wall. A surge of caged up jitters hit me, and my legs were wobbly and heavy.

He still had the wedding ring. He carried it with him every day. He kept it but never came back for me? Never reached out once? Why would he have it if he didn't think of me?

After several cleansing breaths that didn't do shit, I knocked on the open bathroom door before setting the clothes on the vanity. "Here you go."

I looked over to see his head resting back on the tub with his eyes closed.

"I think I'm going to make those cookies I was talking about." No reaction. "So you're good in here?"

He didn't move an inch, just gave a small nod. I knew the expression he wore. The one when he was battling with himself to find strength. The one I saw when his father went on a bender and wasn't found for three days. When their power was shut off and an eviction notice delivered. Levi had the ability to dig deep, push through, and find solutions where there were none.

His mother left them when he was young and it was a scar that would never heal. The woman who just let him go. Packed up and left her beautiful little boy with an alcoholic father.

"Let me know if you need anything."

I exited as worry took a seat on my chest as the legs of the chair sunk into my ribs. I sat on the top step close to his room not certain why, but I couldn't move. Twenty minutes later I approached the bathroom again to see Levi dressed and standing at the vanity, hands resting on the counter, and his head down.

The air cracked with tension and unease, and I didn't

know if I should stay or go while *I'm Dreaming of a White Christmas* sang quietly from my phone on the counter.

"How're you doing?"

He inhaled through his nose but was still. I decided I should definitely leave. He just needed a moment to gather his thoughts after the water disaster. I turned but he caught my hand and before it could register in my mind, his embrace enveloped me.

I started to push away, like the brain-using-woman I was, but an instant later I melted into him. It was familiar but different. His smell, the way he held me, the instant reaction my body had to him. The organ in the center of my chest scolded me, and demanded I step away immediately, but my legs weighed one thousand pounds.

"Thank you, Allie," rumbled into my ear as it rested against his chest. "Today, uh, it's been a lot."

After a long moment he pulled back slightly, and I found myself staring at the center of his chest for the third time today. I wanted to look up, but fear was swimming through me. The seconds ticked by as quickly as water through a hair clogged drain.

Slowly my eyes walked up to see the warning behind his green irises as to what was about to happen. Almost as if he was giving me an out, but I didn't move.

His lips touched mine loaded with fire. My senses were jumbled as he overwhelmed every cell in my body.

His mouth was soft and warm and exploring. The kiss was so charged I was instantly sinking. My hands involuntarily traveled to the shoulders I clung to as the rhythm was intimate, deep, and familiar. I was lost.

I whimpered as his mouth left mine and he kissed my jaw.

His whiskers sliding down my neck sent tingles up my spine. One of his hands pulled my lower back into him while the other traveled up and held the base of my neck. He was lighting something that had been dead for what seemed like an eternity.

I wanted him to do all the things I shouldn't want him to do. I wanted him to lick my skin, and I wanted to watch him shake and sweat because of me. I wanted him to cage me against the mattress and satisfy every selfish need he had. I wanted to be everything to him.

His mouth found mine again as his hands held my bottom and lifted me onto the vanity. My legs instinctively wrapped around his waist as if they've always belonged there. His hand traveled, and I drew in a sharp breath. I held his hand as his fingers circled over my shirt causing my nerves to jump.

I couldn't get close enough as memories ran through my mind like a powerful storm; the backseat of his truck, me drunk and screaming with laughter as he tore off my thrift store wedding dress in a Vegas hotel room.

As I lost myself even more in his lingering kisses and taste, the memory of waking up in a hospital bed with him gone hit me like a bolt of lightning.

My blood ran cold, and I pushed him away. "Stop." I stood on my wobbly legs and ran my hands through my hair. "This can't happen."

"Allie—"

Confusion and anger tied a knot in my chest. "I don't know what's wrong with me. We are *over*. We've been over for a long time. Why in the hell am I kissing you?"

"I'm sorry, it's me. I just, after the ice and, well, I don't know." His hand touched my shoulder, and I batted it away.

"This is so bad. I don't want this. At all. You're the past. I have a life now and want you *nowhere* in it."

I exited the room and went into the hall so fast I tripped and landed on my knees before hopping back up.

"Are you okay?"

I stood. "I'm fine! I just like bleeding for fun."

I clearly seized the wrong effing day. I reached my room realizing there were three stages of life. 1. Birth 2. What the fuck is this 3. Death.

I shut my door and leaned against it. What in the living hell is wrong with me? That damn Levi made me like the Bermuda Triangle; smart thoughts go in and then they're never seen or heard from again. I was more confused than a chameleon in a bucket of Jelly Bellies.

I paced the room, slid open the window, and hung my head out in attempts to cool myself.

Okay, I needed to shove these negative thoughts from my mind. Yes, there was surely something positive I could reflect on at a time like this, right? Hmmm, something I could be happy and positive about?

Here goes. Uh, on a positive note, I'm not addicted to cocaine.

Crickets.

Yup, that was all I had.

My pulse rocketed at the quiet knock.

"Allie, are you okay?"

I walked to the door. "No, I am out of order until further notice. My stupid filter needs cleaning, and my give a shit batteries have run out."

"Langley—"

"I just, I want to forget everything. I hate that we, uh, I just hate it."

Silence as I rested my forehead against the door.

"Maybe this is just us saying goodbye." His deep voice was soft as I turned around.

"What?"

"Well, back then it was over in an instant." Through the door I heard him take a deep breath. "All because of me, and we didn't say goodbye or anything. Everything was left unfinished, you know? There was no end."

I just stared back at the door. There had been no end. One moment I was laughing and the next alone.

"We never had any kind of closure."

"What?"

"Like the chance to say goodbye to *us*. What we had. Maybe our kissing is just us saying goodbye."

His kisses made me want to do *anything* but say goodbye. Maybe my subconscious was thinking that? Although I doubted my subconscious was that smart.

"I think I once heard Dr. Phil talking about the importance of closure when people had a thing. Or some shit like that."

"I do like Dr. Phil." My brain was shaking her fist at me.

"I know, right? I think it's his southern drawl."

"Yeah. He's from Texas. Texas people are super smart."

"Well, I think his point was that people can move forward once they have closure. Then they can leave the past in the past."

Oh, this sounded like something that might bite me in the ass later. "So they won't kiss anymore after closure?"

"Nope."

You have a life now, don't go there.

"So what's closure look like?"

"Well, I think if we wanted closure, we hang out however we want and just have some time. Nothing has to happen, or maybe a little kiss might be okay, up to you. Then we say goodbye and it'll be good because the thing we had will have an ending."

"One day and we don't talk about anything now? Nothing about our current lives, just hang out?"

"Since nobody will be here until at least tomorrow, maybe we could give it a shot. Be close for a bit and then goodbye."

"One day. And after closure we be civil while in Colorado and never speak again once we leave this state."

"Yes. What do you think?"

My mind was attempting to compute and answer to his question.

Levi's pillow lips + my jankey heart / one day of closure x my mental health = fxubcrkgewd?%!

I walked over and sat on my bed thinking of his multiple female phone calls. "But if you have, well, someone you're seeing, or a relationship, I would never—"

"I'm not seeing anyone. I don't do relationships, and I guarantee I want nothing."

It felt like a kick.

He's not with anyone. How could that be? It didn't seem possible. "You see people?"

Pause. "To be honest, I don't date. Ever. I have, uh, casual things, but I don't do relationships."

"So, you and the people you date—"

"I don't date. I hang out."

"But you—"

"Allie, I'm not made for something serious. Won't ever have it. If we had closure, it would be a day of whatever and then nothing. It'd be done."

I was struggling to digest this new information. What happened to the guy who couldn't wait to marry me? The one who made me believe soul mates were real? How had he gone from one thing to completely another?

I never knew Levi.

But the thought of one more day in the house alone with him was an out of control high speed chase with no seatbelts. You know, the kind of ride that ends with body bags and a ten o'clock news story. I wanted to *not* want it, but if this was my one and only chance to be close for a hot minute, how could I say no?

What's the point of living if you don't take risks? I mean, if I had the chance to ride the highest roller coaster in the world and didn't because I was afraid, would I regret it forever and ever? Would I wish I'd taken the chance to feel the fear and adrenaline? To live a *hell yes* life for a little while? I'd likely live to see the end of the ride, right? I mean, people take risks all the time and walk out the other side just fine.

So basically, closure could be a goodbye to us without leaving my heart in pieces. Yes, no emotions, just the chance to hang out knowing it was over in a day. My brain put her hands on her hips with a raised brow, but I opted to ignored that crazy bitch.

"You in?"

I was in like a stripper dancing for her rent money due tomorrow, but my words were stuck. Maybe my body took away the English language to try to protect me? I didn't know how to make the decision.

"Maybe ask the magic eight ball?" Muffled through the door. "Then it's almost like we're not making the decision. We just do whatever magic eight says."

Maybe everything happens for a reason. But maybe the reason is because I'm a dumbass and make bad choices? Yeah, my decision-making skills are as successful as a squirrel crossing the street as of late. Maybe magic eight was the best one to choose between options A and B.

I gave it a good shake and looked into the window.

No fucking way.

Maybe she didn't understand the question, so I whispered. "Closure with Levi?" I shook her again as I counted to five and peeked.

Use your stupid ass brain.

Technically that wasn't really an answer; it was just a statement. I needed an *answer*. Shake, shake, shake.

Don't ask.

Again, not an answer so I shook her hard.

Yes, bitch.

There it was. A solid response from magic eight ball.

"Did you get the answer?"

I nearly jumped through the ceiling when I looked over to see Levi just inside the door leaning against the wall looking thoroughly amused. Scorching heat shot to my cheeks as I sat in silence while his eyes told me he'd seen me shake until I got the response I wanted.

"I, well, the little window was foggy." I nodded. "Couldn't see it."

I jumped again when he walked over and took it from my hand and read before his eyes found mine.

"Yes, bitch." The way his lips curled up at the edges made

my nether regions tingle. "So magic eight ball and the universe are okay with closure?"

I sat blinking.

"Are you good with closure?"

My voice cracked. "I guess so."

"You want to seal the deal?"

"Seal the deal?" Uh oh. My heart reminded me of the deep scars it had, but instead of using my intellectual mind, I told my heart to shut the bloody hell up.

He took my hands and pulled me to my feet while my nerves spun around like a pole dancer. Where would closure take me? What had I signed up for? As if reading my mind, he pulled me gently into his chest.

"What now?"

I squealed when in one swift move he had me over his shoulder. "Well, I believe you said Christmas cookies were on the agenda. Since the icy lake didn't take me out today, we should celebrate with homemade goodies. I am *very* serious when it comes to holiday baking. Well, more like holiday eating."

SIXTEEN
LEVI
CLOSURE

I stood staring down at her unable to comprehend what was happening.

She agreed to closure with me. She agreed to closure with *me*. If I'd told her what I really wanted, I'm pretty sure there'd be a Allie-sized hole in the wall. While I didn't know how this thing would play out, the obsession I'd had for her never left.

I owe you, Dr. Phil.

I carried her to the kitchen over my shoulder and a lightness I hadn't had in an eternity settled in my chest.

Best. Idea. Ever.

I set her feet on the floor, and she looked up at me. My hand went to her cheek, and her silky skin was begging to be touched. I'd been her person, her home back then, but I'd burned the bridge to Allie when I left. I was alive with hope for the first time in as long as I could remember.

"I believe it's holiday treat time." She walked to the stove.

After four dozen baked sugar cookies, I found out symmetrical sprinkles was a thing. Who knew?

I grabbed the bottle of tiny green Christmas trees. "Does it really matter if these candies aren't perfect?"

Her cheeks were a warm pink as her mouth dropped open. "Of course it does. Nonsymmetrical cookie decorating could actually *ruin* a holiday."

"That makes no sense, Langley."

She narrowed her eyes at me. "I don't want it to be this way, but it is. I mean if I'm opening Christmas gifts, and I know the cookies on the table are all wonky and stupid, it would take away from the Christmas spirit."

I poured a thick layer of sprinkles on one side of the frosted sugar cookie. "So this would make you crazy?"

"I'd like to say no, but that's all wrong."

I grabbed one from the cookie sheet on the stove. "So if I just put a blob of frosting here." I dropped a dollop in the corner. "And nothing more, would Allison motherfuckin' Langley lose sleep over this?"

Her eyes rolled. "No, Levi motherfuckin' Dawson, I would not." Her eyes dropped to the table. "Because I would sneak downstairs in the middle of the night to correct the problem." Her finger pointed. "And I think you'd be in trouble."

"I like trouble."

A giggle escaped her, and she remembered she liked it when they used to call us that. Teachers, parents, grandparents, along with the farmer at the edge of town who chased my truck out of his fields more than once because they were the perfect place for us to sneak off to.

She stirred some green food coloring into the frosting can.

"So tell me about your career." I used my knife to spread red frosting across my cookie. I'd gotten off Instagram years ago. I'd done some 'research' and saw her face in one post, and it sent me into a spiral that lasted weeks.

Her brow arched. "That's against the closure rules. We can't talk about our lives now."

"I think work talk is acceptable, don't you?"

"Fine. I'm a Biomedical Engineer."

"Wow. I knew from day one that brain of yours would take you everywhere."

She batted her eyelashes. "Yes, I'm still flirty, nerdy, and a little dirty."

Oh, this one could kill me. "I can see that. So what are you crazy biomed kids working on these days?"

"Artificial organ development."

"Whoa. So I don't need to worry about the crap I did when I was younger? You'll be able to replace all that stuff?"

She bit into a cookie. "You'd need like a whole new interior. Sorry to say you'll likely just die early."

"I knew all that fun would bite me in the ass eventually." She passed me the green frosting. "So for the smarter people who didn't ruin their body as a teenager, what are you doing for them?"

"It's kind of mind blowing actually. Artificial organs are one of the most groundbreaking innovations in biomed engineering. The devices are engineered to replicated a failing organ or assist in its function. It provides an alternative for patients who can't receive a natural organ transplant, or because of the severe shortage of donor organs."

"It's hard to believe any of this is possible."

"I know, it's amazing. But there are a lot of challenges with it also. The body's natural tendency is to reject foreign objects.

The whole process of the immune system and rejection can result in the failure of the artificial organ." She passed over the sprinkles.

"It makes me think of your grandma Dee."

She gasped. "I think of her all the time when I'm working on projects."

"If only this had been a possibility back then."

"I know, right? So many of the problems they couldn't fix even five years ago have possible solutions now."

I poured some sprinkles on my cookie. "She was the one who gave me a chance back then."

"Well, you were the one who'd come with me to her house and watch The Young and the Restless. Anyone who thought that was cool was an automatic favorite of hers." Giggles. "She made me promise to never tell my mother, but she thought you were incredibly sweet."

She hopped up, turned off the stove, and grabbed more cookies from the counter when I stood and pulled her to me. Her eyes sparkled and something in my gut squeezed tight when her arms wrapped around my waist.

"I think I'm digging closure, Langley."

She pulled me closer and our bodies were flush. There was a low murmur that buzzed through me, and I physically ached for her.

Her phone on the counter pinged and she grabbed it with a smile. "Looks like my gang will be here tomorrow late morning." She set the phone back down and her hands cupped my face. "So it's one day of closure."

I've never stopped loving you.

I shoved the thoughts of Rachel and Lexi and what their reaction to me would be out of my mind as she pulled me down and kissed my cheek. I lifted her and those legs wrapped around my waist without missing a beat.

When our mouths joined, it wasn't just a kiss. It was raw emotion and adrenaline that tore at everything in me. I barely survived this girl, could I make it out the other side of closure in one piece?

SEVENTEEN
ALLIE
CURATE'S EGG

I was so lost in the kiss I hadn't realize we were moving. His hands held my bottom as we made it up the stairs while a dangerous excitement surged through my veins like a river. You know, a river after a long winter when the snow melts and it's out of control. The kind that makes an entire community worry and fill sandbags trying to ensure all are safe.

The times I'd daydream about this was almost shameful. Breathing heavily, our faces an inch apart, my body aching, all catapulting into the rush that was Levi. The wild electrical current we'd never learned to control.

By the time we reached his bedroom our shirts had disappeared and feeling his whiskers on my shoulders was a reminder that closure would likely leave me with scars that would never disappear. My brain was screaming to stop, while my heart had given the key to this man long ago.

As he licked my neck, I realized maybe this was going to be okay. Yes, the difference was now I was a grown woman. I couldn't handle him back then because we were too young. So closure was *totally* okay. I would be able to get the key to my heart back, move forward, and all will be good. No, not good, we're talking effing great.

He set me on my feet and the last thread of control I had broke in an instant. I pushed him hard, and he reached out and grabbed me before his back hit the mattress. I was a shameless wild woman as I kissed his neck before my mouth returned to his as if we needed the connection.

The burn, the ache, and the heat of his skin were all feeding the fire.

Those hands found my hips as I sat up. My eyes soaked him in; the same as he used to be but better. My fingers traced my initials in his tattoo. As I leaned forward a tingle slithered up my spine when his hands slid around and touched my bra strap while his eyes locked with mine.

"This okay?"

My ability to spit out nouns and verbs had vanished so I nodded.

He unhooked and it slid down my arms as my stomach flipped while his hungry eyes traveled me.

"You're beautiful."

His words spurred something as he sat up and we were chest to chest. His hands and lips became reacquainted with me as my head dropped back.

He lay down and pulled me to his chest as fear and anticipation flooded me while his greedy mouth overtook mine, and his hands tormented me.

I'd never felt so desired in my life as his deep voice muttered cursing intertwined with my name. He licked and kissed my neck and chest as if marking his territory, which is all I wanted to be. His.

Those hands moved my hips as a panic made its way in as my knees clamped his hips.

"You know what you want." It was a husky whisper. "You're safe."

I felt safe which I knew was wrong as closure might be the death of me. But I was here now.

My body took over while the friction and closeness were overwhelming my senses. I moved against him and when I looked into his dark eyes the thrill I remembered was twisting everything.

He pulled me closer as his warm breath riffled through my hair. He had control of me, holding me, angling me. I thought I knew what my body was able to do, but he had it behave in a way it never had before. He had the knowledge of what it could do so much better than me as his body molded to mine.

The explosion of waves of pleasure derailed everything as life drained from me. The unbearable tension followed by a flush, deliciously slow recovery. I looked down and the expression on his face made me feel the high that Levi was. The lengths we'd gone to be together way back then because of the force between us. It was still there.

He pulled me into his chest and his skin against mine was filling a gap I hadn't known existed. A revived restlessness surged through every nerve ending in my body as my fingers explored and my lips followed.

I knew I'd always be a recovering addict when it came to him, and now I was having a taste of the one drug that I knew from experience was impossible to shake once gone. The smartest thing I could do would be to run as fast as my legs would carry me, but I knew an army couldn't move me from the spot I was in.

He growled my name as I made my way lower. The moan while he tousled my hair with his hands made me feel powerful and sexy as I took control.

After exploring he pulled me up by my shoulders and we were face to face as he wrapped his arms securely around me with our breathing loud. In one swift move I was on my back. He looked down at me as he placed his finger under my chin and slid it slowly down my body. The mattress sighed as he settled on top of me. His weight was solid and anchored me as the heat of his skin sent electric sparks to my stomach.

His teeth nipped my ear as his breath bathed my neck. "There's no one like you."

His lips moved slowly down my body. I looked at the man responsible for the temptation, the one who was in control of my every desire as he reminded me what only he could do to me.

He licked my stomach before looking up at me. His eyes were narrowed, searching my face with intensity as he slid my panties down my legs.

My heart hiccupped at the look in his eye. In a moment's time my leg was pushed aside and my breath taken away as I arched when he moved forward. We moved smoothly together, like a choreographed dance, with his mouth on my neck.

My hands trailed down his sweaty back, and I felt a new satisfaction as he said my name as he nuzzled against me, kissing his way to my earlobe. He was dominating and deep, and there was more than the action of our bodies, he was putting himself everywhere. Instilling visions that would be running through my mind in ten years, thirty years, forever.

His fingers dug into my hips as he rocked me against him and ran my body like he owned it.

"Look at me," he hissed, and I obeyed. "I want to see your eyes, and you to see mine. The one who makes you crazy."

He held me like I was a treasure making me powerful and wanting to give all I had to him.

His eyes burned into me, and I couldn't comprehend the emotion. I clung to him as he was rough, but somehow tender at the same time while my cries for more were muffled by his shoulder.

It was like nothing ever before. There was sweat and steam, and the heat between us was electric. We were both all in, and the desire to please the other was like an endless spiral. My body was trembling, restless, and we couldn't get enough.

Cursing, seething, and the primal sounds coming from me were foreign to my own ears as we both reach the place we haven't been to together in for so long.

He collapsed on me, and I wanted to never move again. I didn't want him anywhere but on me as I inhaled his scent trying to memorize him.

I gently tickled his back as we lay in silence for a long time and eventually dozed off for a little bit.

My eyes opened before I crawled out of bed, tiptoed to his closet, and pulled on a red and black flannel shirt. It was big and cozy and I floated down to the kitchen. I grabbed two cans of Coke and was heading back to my new favorite bedroom when my eyes landed on the guitar that sat in the corner.

I entered the bedroom and set our sodas on the nightstand as he came out of the bathroom wearing jeans and no shirt. Sigh.

"Hey."

"Hey." I set the guitar on the end of the bed. "I heard you playing last night."

"Is that right?"

"Will you play for me?"

"You don't want that. I'm a little rusty."

"Come on, please. Pretty please?"

A delicious grin slid across those lips. "Are you begging me right now?"

Eye roll. "No."

"That's a shame. I always loved it when you begged." He walked up to me.

"Stop."

He reached out and started unbuttoning my shirt. The shy me was no longer when near him. He still breathed life into every part of me. Made me bold and unafraid at a glance.

He pushed the shirt over my shoulders, and it dropped to the floor.

"Lay down."

I fought my grin and failed. "Are you being bossy?"

With one nod I lay on my side with my head on his pillow as he picked up the guitar and sat beside me. A new peace settled in as he began to gently strum the strings. My heart sighed at the song I'd heard so many times I still had each note memorized. It would always be my favorite, and hearing it now was almost surreal.

It took me to the day we ditched our last class, and his father wasn't home so it was an afternoon of Levi time. My favorite. I lay on his bed while he sat on the edge and listened to the song *Tenerife Sea* over and over again until he could play it because it was my favorite.

He looked over while his fingers danced across the strings and his grin sent little zings of electricity to my tummy.

"I like closure, Allison." He shot me a wink. "You good with it so far?"

My cheeks grew warm as I nodded.

"One day and we're done. It's good."

He looked back at his fingers on the strings while I hated to admit his words had my stomach doing a spinny thing. Not the good kind of spinny thing, but more like the dread kind of spinny thing.

As the beautiful music surrounded me, I had to check myself. I would not dread this when it came to an end. I was living like a wild woman for a day and that was that. There was nothing between us more than chemistry that could blow shit up. I just needed to keep my body armor on. I mean, I'd stay naked with him, duh, but I wouldn't let any little feelings creep in. This was a day of connecting and saying goodbye to us.

Before I knew exactly what was happening the guitar was leaning against the wall.

"I forgot some shit at home so I need to run into town." He walked over and pulled me to my feet. "You need anything from Walgreens?" He gave me a sideways glance. "Other than Dove chocolate? You still have a chocolate problem, right?"

I jumped up, threw my arms over his shoulders, and he held me against him as my feet dangled. "You remember my chocolate weakness."

He rested his forehead against mine. "I remember everything."

Be still my jacked up beating heart.

"Okay, I'll see you in about an hour."

After five more minutes of goodbye kisses, he left.

I took a hot bubble bath and let my mind relive every

minute in his bed. Not the bed of years past, but the bed of today. How could any of this be happening?

I jumped out of the bubbles and into the thick white robe that hung on the back of the door. I ran out and jumped back into Levi's bed and pulled the covers up just as my cell phone screamed and I grabbed it.

"Yo, Rach, what's up?"

"Well, holy shit, Allie. You sound happy. That must be one great vacation house."

I couldn't fight my grin. "It's an amazing place to be." Truth.

"Well, what ya been up to?"

A little nervousness hit my stomach as I painfully recalled she and Levi back in the day.

"Just, uh, hanging out."

"Emily is right here."

"Of course she is."

"I'm putting the phone on speaker."

Her scream almost blew out my eardrum. "The blizzard is wrapping up! You'd better have a big fat margarita waiting for me."

"Sure thing."

"Is Evan's cousin nice?"

I held in a giggle at the memory of him being *nice* to every inch of me. "He's okay. Pretty nice I guess."

Lexi's voice screeched. "You've been there with a man?"

Emily teased. "This is interesting."

"Stop. But I'm glad to hear you sounding a little calmer today, Em."

"Yeah, I've decided I'm letting all wedding stuff just roll off my back." She spoke in a fairytale whisper. "I'm done worrying. Yup, any non-RSVP guests will just be set on fire. That's all."

"Nice."

Lexi let out a dramatic sigh. "Okay, we're done hearing Emily talk about any wedding shit, thank God."

Emily laughed. "You're a bitch, Lexi."

"Yes, I am. I'm kinda like a finger in the ass. I'm either a wonderful surprise or just make everything awkward and uncomfortable."

After a mind-numbing conversation about whether you'd prefer to have no nose but really good smelling fingers, or be blind and have a kick ass body, I finally got off the phone.

I threw on black leggings and white hoody before I got to the bottom of the stairs to find the most handsome fella in Colorado, maybe even the world, wearing black pants and a steel blue sports coat over a crisp white button-down shirt that highlighted those pecs and biceps. What the what? He held my coat out for me. The sight of him made me realize I needed a hug. And maybe an orgasm. Yes, a hugasm.

"You're all dressed up. Have you been up to something, Levi?

"Well, picturing you naked is the most productive thing I've done all day. But things might be changing."

"They say a naughty thought a day keeps the stress away." Truth.

"You're my favorite naughty thought." He leaned down and kissed my cheek. "If you knew what was going through my mind you'd be traumatized or maybe aroused."

My cheeks grew warm, and I wondered if we should stay in.

"You ready?"

"For what?"

"It's a surprise."

I gasp. "You tell me right now or I'm not going."

He grabbed the magic eight ball from the coffee table and shook it.

"Should Allison motherfuckin' Langley go see a surprise with Levi motherfuckin' Dawson?"

His head nodded and held it out for me to see. "Hell yeah." He walked back over and helped me on with my coat. "We outta here."

Twenty minutes later he led me into a fancy boutique on the magical Christmas street in the beautiful ski resort town. "What are we doing?"

Two women approached. "Mr. Dawson?"

He nodded as they looked at me. "Are you ready?"

"I don't know."

"Follow us."

Levi's grin gave me a squeeze as we walked back to the dressing room area.

The boutique had a high-end flair, and the dressing area walls were wrapped in chic, high fashion wallpaper, crisp white doors, and three brown leather chairs close by a little pedestal in front of a large mirror.

"We have some items to get you started in the fitting room and can grab any others you might like."

Levi took a seat in a fancy chair and the woman helping me flashed him a whopper of a smile. Clearly, he was leaving all the women in the room a little toasty with that grin.

"What else shall we set her up with?"

My eyes darted back to the hot one.

"She needs a cocktail dress, short, that highlights those amazing legs. Maybe heels, and of course everything that goes underneath."

I swore the glint in his eye would make my bra burst open at any second.

"Levi, what are you doing?" I couldn't make my big old smile disappear.

"Closure ends tomorrow." He sat back in his chair. "We're going to live the hell out of today."

I stood frozen as the sales ladies buzzed around bringing all sorts of things in my direction. A man's head popped around the corner. "Who ordered pizza?"

Gasp!

My eyes met Levi's and he let out a chuckle.

"Are you Pretty Womaning me right now?"

"Bet your ass I am." He pointed to the dressing room. "Go."

As I entered the dressing room the memory of him sneaking in my bedroom window and us curling up in my twin sized bed watching Pretty Woman, my favorite old movie, had my heart doing a sexy salsa dance.

EIGHTEEN
LEVI

OH, WHAT A NIGHT

Yeah, I hijacked the boutique, but it had to be done. Well, I suppose the Cheesecake Factory delivery didn't *have* to happen, but how could the woman showing me each and every sexy little dress *not* have the Godiva Chocolate Cheesecake?

Did she sneak me into the dressing room and let me select the pink and white lacy bra and matching panties after a mind blowing make out session? That's a hell yes.

An hour later we strolled out onto the sidewalk with some shopping bags in hand as her soft giggles warmed the crisp air. Then I ran back inside and offered to pay one of the ladies if she'd drop the shopping bags at the house. Money talks.

We walked arm in arm and it truly felt like we were in a movie. But not a Hallmark movie, yeah, after what happened back at the house this was definitely NOT a "G" rating.

We passed stores and shops decorated with holly and twinkling lights while shoppers milled about. Christmas carols floated in the air and I wondered how we could stay there forever.

She looked up at me. "I can't believe you did this."

127

I kissed her forehead. "Our evening awaits."

We entered the Summit Bistro and were seated at the table I reserved in a small private dining room. Deep mahogany surrounded us in the room that was lit by a large Christmas tree filled with glimmering lights that sat in the corner, and the candles in the center of our table.

"Oh. My. Gosh." Allie clapped her hands quietly. "This is beautiful."

The waitress took our order and closed her little black book as a waiter set our drinks on the table.

I cleared my throat. "Gentlemen, would you mind leaving us, please?"

Allie squealed while the waitress popped a confused brow.

"You're still Pretty Womaning me! My turn!" She clapped her hands and eyed the waitress. "I'm just using him for sex." She burst out laughing and we had a glorious high-five as the waitress's eyes darted about before she exited and pulled the door closed behind her.

I stood, walked to the door and locked it before returning to her and extending my hand. "Dance with me."

"Did you just lock the door?" She smiled and slid into my arms. "This feels a little naughty right now."

I looked down at her. "Does it?"

NINETEEN
ALLIE
TEQUILA

I knew the life I had now and the people in it. Was being close to Levi for one day worth the risk? The answer was a hard yes. At least at this particular moment in time.

I couldn't resist. "*You could freeze ice on her ass. Love that one.*"

He looked down. "I think you are a very bright, very special person."

While it was my favorite line from the movie, something about the way he said it caused a pause as we swayed to the soft music.

His eyes were a little darker now, and he was the same kerosene he was when I was eighteen. He could steal my common sense away in an instant. I had been to him what he was to me; together we were dangerous. He instilled a deep fizz that soared through my body shining a spotlight on the weakness that remained after seven years.

He made me *not* me anymore. He made me strong. He was intoxicating.

His grin was absent when I pushed him into his chair, slid

my dress up, and climbed into his lap. Our eyes locked for a moment like criminals returning to the scene of a crime, determined to feel the rush once again.

His arm snaked around my waist pulling me closer. I kissed his neck and a low groan escaped him as I sucked and licked my way to his lips. The kiss was light, then more urgent as his tongue slipped into my mouth and my body reacted involuntary as my hips pressed against him.

His hands went through my hair and he held my head while his lips traveled to my jaw, and those whiskers slid down my neck as tingles tumbled down my back.

"You feel so good," he whispered.

He stood and, in a few steps, he held my back against the wall. His lips dominated mine, and I suddenly realized we might be christening the private dining room. His hands traveled and he took control of me as the sounds of the talking restaurant guests just outside the door filtered into the room.

"Good girl. Being quiet as I take over."

My new panties disappeared and he whipped them in the air as I clung onto his shoulders and pressed my lips together as he did what he does with ease.

Was there anything that could stop this? That answer came quickly when I opened my eyes to see my new panties on fire. Yes, they had landed on the candle and were now ablaze along with the bread basket.

"Shit!"

Levi pushed me aside and yanked the red Christmas tree skirt from the ground and started to smother the flames.

"Oh it stinks now!" I whisper yelled as he continued. After a frantic moment the fire was out.

Levi's eyes were saucers and laughter rolled out of me. "Holy crap!"

"Langey, I think the recipe for tonight would be one cup cluster, two cups fuck."

I grabbed my undies and tree skirt, dipped them in the ice bucket near the table before putting them in the trashcan in the corner of the room. I quickly took the bread basket and covered it with the one remaining napkin, set it on top of the burned area, and put my salad plate next to it so it was concealed.

Levi hopped over to the door, unlocked it, and we jumped back into our seats.

The waitress entered and her eyes narrowed. "Is everything—"

I cleared my throat. "I think we're ready to order."

He eyed my plate. "We're in a bougie bistro in a ski resort town, and you're dining on a grilled cheese."

I held up my knife. "Yes, but it's still super classy." I sliced my delectable sandwich and popped a bite into my mouth. "See how I cut it up? Top shelf."

He sliced his salmon. "You have to taste this."

I wrinkled my nose. "I can't."

"Now why in the hell can't you take a bite of this amazing fish?"

"I don't like fish."

"How do you know you don't like it?" He teased.

"Because I just do, that's how." Why did my eating habits encourage others to force food on me?

"When did you have seafood last, and why did it harden you to the entire seafood dining experience?" He reached over and stole a fry.

"I don't know." I took another bite.

"Was it in this decade?"

"OMG, why are you stuck on this topic anyway?"

"I'm just trying to get to the root of the problem."

"You're the problem. I just don't like fish."

"When was the last time—"

"Fish sticks, okay?"

"Fish sticks?"

I dipped a fry into ketchup. "Yes, the last time I tired fish it was in stick form."

He chuckled. "Are fish sticks really fish at all?"

"No clue, but they were mushy and disgusting."

"You can't swear off a whole world of ocean snacks based on a fish stick experience as a kid."

"Sure I can." I ate another fry. "I did."

"Come on, you have to have a bite. It's amazing."

"Nope."

"What can I do to persuade you?"

I spoke in a whisper. "Get off my back about aquatic eats, or I can guarantee you *won't* be on my back later."

"Wow." His brow shot up.

"Topic transition. So, you live in Brazil?"

"Yeah, a few years now. After two failed attempts at college, Evan made himself the boss of me and got me through it. I worked construction and liked it a lot. But once I finished school I knew I needed to get out of the U.S."

"Why?"

He looked down. "I was chasing ghosts and I needed to get away."

My heart clunked; was I a ghost?

"I knew you'd be good academically once you applied yourself."

"I don't know how you saw that through what I was back then."

"You were never bad." It shot out before I could stop it. "I mean, you were a little wild and reckless, but you had all the tools you needed."

He chuckled. "A little?"

My eyes rolled. "I'm sure somebody else concocted an experiment in chemistry that caught a desk on fire so they had to let us all out for the afternoon?"

"A little fire resulting in beautiful beach day in May? Hell yeah." He sliced his fish. "That's a talented student right there."

"And the pool hopping?"

He nodded. "Midnight swimming with you on the rich side of town? Totally worth it."

"I recall—"

"Don't you even say it, Langley. It happened once."

"Once is enough. You and me sprinting nearly naked through yards being chased by a police dog?"

He pointed at me. "Bottom line is we made it out of there in one piece, okay? Although Allie cupping her boobs while running was about the hottest thing ever. We were living on the wild side."

As my laughter subsided I was well aware I was there again. Sure, no scantly dressed running with boobs in hand, but I was presently living on the wild side with the wild one. We made it out of there unscathed that night, but my brain shot a warning flare. Would I make it out this time?

The waitress appeared. "Can I get you both anything else?"

While I was two margaritas in and officially buzzing a little, I raised my hand. "Two shots of tequila."

She nodded and exited as Levi sat back in his chair. The look in those beautiful eyes made me shiver. "Tequila?"

"Remember crawling out my window and onto the roof with a bottle?" I couldn't look away from his eyes. "Still your favorite?"

He let out a breath. "I can drink anything, but haven't had tequila in years."

"Really? It was your drink."

"Not anymore. Not for a long time now."

"Huh. Why?"

His expression was thoughtful. "That drink is tied up in my memories."

Our eyes locked for a long minute as my heart thumped.

I wanted to ask why he never came for me. Never called me. Never wrote a letter. His number no longer in service; he wanted me to never find him again.

I cleared my throat. "For me it's the opposite." My voice cracked as the liquor took over my sentence. "I don't drink often, but when I do, it *always* has tequila in it. Every time. Same reason"

Why did I say that aloud?

He let out a long sigh before leaning on the table and taking my hand in his. He grazed my thumb with his finger.

The waitress appeared and set two shots in front of us but

our gaze wasn't broken. I spoke without looking away. "Bring us another, please."

His head shook. "What're you doing, Langley?"

I batted my eyelashes. "Making up for lost time."

TWENTY
LEVI
IT'S A BAD IDEA, RIGHT?

W e stood at the bar, and I lost track of how many shots we had due to her cheering and jumping after each one highlighting her perfect breasts in that damn dress.

We bounced into a club next door which was packed. After much resistance the pretty girl got me on the karaoke stage. We belted out *What I want,* and we were fuckin' awesome, said tequila.

As we made our way to a table, a group of ladies grabbed Allie and in an instant she was back on stage yell/singing *I love it*. With some booze in her, those cheeks were pink and her curls everywhere while she laughed and danced.

It was the Allie of my memories. Me stealing a bottle of my favorite from the gas station and us heading to the railroad tracks. She'd carry a blanket, and I'd find an empty rail car. We'd watch the sunset, get drunk, laugh our asses off, and be wrapped up together for hours.

I sat back and watched her in the dress that hugged every curve to perfection while taking my mind to a place it shouldn't go. And the fact that I wanted a hell of a lot more than closure. I decided to look at all options to get my way. Sure kidnapping was illegal but not punishable by death, so I was keeping that in my back pocket.

A waitress brought over two more shots I didn't recall ordering. At this point, WTF?

Liver: You need to stop this.

Me: Calm your ass down.

She finished singing, took a deep bow, tripped down the stairs, and headed in my direction.

"Did you hear me up there? I'm like a mixture of Olivia Rodrigo and Taylor." She leaned in. "The audience loves me."

She downed her shot and pulled me to my feet before leading us outside where the crisp air slugged us.

The sidewalk was full of people shuffling between the bars and restaurants. The street was lit up by Christmas lights that seemed to be everywhere as *Holly Jolly Christmas* drifted through the air.

She stopped, turned, grabbed my coat, and kissed me as if she couldn't wait a second more. She pulled back and the way her lips curved into a smile with a touch of mischief and allure, is the reason I was a slave to her every wish.

She let go of me. "I just had to do that."

"We should be doing *that* often tonight. Like on every block."

Her laughter was quiet. "Okay!" She pointed across the street. "Look! I want a tattoo!"

"That might not be a good idea tonight."

Her foot stomped. "I want to get a tattoo."

"You can't get tatted up when you've been drinking."

"That's what everybody's always told me. That I can't get one."

I looked at her sweet face. People telling her what to do hit me wrong. All those years ago everybody in her life knew how special she was, and whether it was her family or friends, they all wanted to take care of her.

But she was an adult now and this was America for God's sake, why the fuck were they still telling her what she could and couldn't do?

"Are you sure, Langley?"

"I want a tattoo that stands for strength and a new beginning. Right now." She laced her fingers with mine. "Yes, I think after our closure is over I'm going grab life by the balls and not be afraid of anything." She squeezed my hand. "Yup, you'll be gone, and I'll be the new me and it starts with a tattoo! I can't wait!"

Well, that statement blows ass.

She yanked my hand. "Time to get going. Tonight's bad decisions aren't going to make themselves."

We entered and a woman in her twenties stood behind a counter. "Welcome."

"Thanks, do we need an appointment?"

Her head shook. "Not tonight, we have some openings."

Allie was beaming. "I'd like a tattoo that stands for new beginnings."

I pulled out my phone and we scrolled through some tattoos and she pointed to an infinity symbol. "I like that."

I read aloud as her head rested against my arm. "The infinity symbol can represent boundless potential, a reminder of all that lies ahead, and a celebration of life's unending opportunities."

Her giggle tickled my ears. "I love that so much."

She sat in the chair as the tattoo artist put her small infinity tattoo just below her collar bone as she squeezed my hand. Her eyes closed tightly as that smile shined like the sun.

Once complete I held up the hand mirror as she gazed at her new addition. "It's beautiful."

I looked at our new friend. "Is there time for one more tonight?"

Allie gasped. "What?"

"Maybe I need a new beginnings tattoo also."

She jumped up and down and chose a spot on my arm above my current tattoo and sat on my lap watching with an Eagle eye while the tattoo artist got to it.

She doesn't know it yet, but this tattoo is a new beginning for us.

TWENTY-ONE
ALLIE
FORCEFIELD

I insisted we check out a cigar bar where we shared a Tequila Sunrise and just one more shot.

I decided that it's not called slurring your words. Nope, it's called talking in cursive and it's fucking elegant.

We wove through the crowds on the sidewalk, and I would've sworn it was noon by the sheer number of people out and about, but it was, well, late. I looked at my phone to check the time, but my drinking vision wasn't cooperating. It was something o'clock.

With Levi at my side and liquor pumping through me, I was floating. And do you know what? When I ran into people and a parking meter, it didn't even hurt. Not a lick. Yes, tequila had put a force field around klutzy Allie, and I was protected from all ouchies.

I rested my head on his shoulder while the driver took us home. Once out of the car I walked into the house using my super model walk while Levi whooped and hollered.

But that didn't happen. Nope. Levi extended his hand to help me out of the car; I missed and ended up sprawled out on my stomach on the snowy ground as I laughed to tears. Once on my feet Levi wiped the snow from my tummy, and I made it to the front door.

He spoke in a dramatic whisper. "I'm learning you against the house while I unlock the door."

I cackled. "You're *learning* me against the house!"

He leaned in close, and we laughed so hard my cheeks hurt. Once through the front door he scooped me up in his arms and took me up the stairs while my head hit the wall three times. Again, no pain. Tequila = magic.

Once in his room he tossed me on the bed a little too hard, I bounced, and landed on the other side on the floor.

He was there in an instant and pulled me to my feet.

I giggled. "You kind of make me fall down a lot."

He laughed. "How can I ever make it up to you?"

TWENTY-TWO
LEVI

SHE FELT LIKE HOME

Once I helped her up after accidentally throwing her over the bed, I held her against the wall and her body pressed into mine as she pushed my jacket off my shoulders and her fingers traveled beneath my shirt. I leaned down kissing her neck while my hand found the hem of her dress and slid underneath as the sweetest sigh escaped her.

Her hands were shaking as she unbuttoned my shirt before pulling it down my arms. She was moving and restless. I fisted her hair and her eyes found mine. "I could have every inch of you pressed against me and I'd still say I wasn't close enough."

Her lips brushed against mine igniting fire that fed my hunger for her. But when she dropped on the bed her eyes closed, and she smiled. "I think the tequila just made me a little sleepy, but I want you to do all the things to me, okay?"

I chuckled as I pulled her heels off. "Is that right?"

She inhaled deeply. "Yeah, you go boy. I'm ready."

"Let's get you out of this dress—"

"Now you're talking."

"Why don't you sleep for a bit?"

She nodded, her eyes still closed. "But only for a few minutes. Then you'll do all the good stuff, right?"

"Right."

She spoke in a whisper. "Yeah, I like all of it."

I got her out of her dress and wrapped in the comforter, and just watched her for a bit. Not like a total stalker, just a medium stalker.

I crawled in next to her, took a good long peek under the covers, and pulled her close. I was home.

TWENTY-THREE
ALLIE

MORNING HAS BROKEN

I awoke to a sprained liver and the most handsome man in the world by my side. He was sleeping and next to me was a water and bottle of pain reliever tablets. I took two and lay facing him. My phone read it was six thirteen. I scooted as close to him as I could, and watched him sleep for nearly an hour.

My heart whimpered at the thought of closure ending. My mind wanted to relive every minute with him; the way he made love to me was nothing short of poetry and just left me wanting more. While I knew it was just a temporary state of being, in his arms I felt wanted and desired like with no other. I felt alive. Even the sound of his voice had a grounding effect; it took away the noise of my brain.

His eyes cracked open, and I smiled at his crooked grin and messy hair.

"Morning."

"Good morning."

I kissed his cheek and relished in the heat of his warm skin against mine, like a perfectly body blanket. "How's your head feeling?"

He let out a long sigh. "I don't remember all of last night, but considering I need sunglasses to look at the nightlight says something." He peeked under the covers and looked at me. "The best way to wake up."

His finger ran lightly under my collar bone. "I like it."

"What?"

He popped a brow. "You don't remember?"

"What?"

A boyish laugh bounced around the room. "Oh no. You don't remember dragging us into the tattoo parlor?"

"Oh my gosh."

"You *promised* you'd remember. Now don't be pissed, I tried to talk you out of it."

"I remember." I got out of bed and to the mirror on the wall. "Wow.

"So you're okay with it?"

I looked over. "I absolutely love it."

He let out a breath. "You wanted something to symbolize strength and a new beginning, you got it."

My eyes traveled the delicate infinity loop, etched in black ink just under my collar bone. As it curved around the tiny word *dream* in a beautiful font was on the second loop.

He held up the covers and I crawled back into bed. I looked at the new addition on his arm; identical to mine but larger.

He nodded. "I like it." He kissed the tip of my nose. "I guess we both needed something new."

We lay facing one another, my bare chest against his, while his fingers lightly tickled my arm. My phone pinged and he grabbed it from the nightstand and handed it to me.

"Looks like their plane will be here around noon." I set it back on the nightstand.

"Lexi and Rachel." His head shook lightly. "They are going to have a hot dip shit fit when they see me."

"You spit the truth." I scooted closer and our faces were inches apart. "But they won't kill you. Well, I'm pretty sure."

"The scary part is there are so many places they could hide a body in Colorado."

"Oh, they wouldn't have to. They'd make it an accident for sure."

"So steer clear of mountain hiking with your girls?"

"Oh yeah, don't even give them a cliff to consider."

We lay perfectly still while I knew our minds were doing no such thing.

He pushed a curl from my face. "They were scared. All of them. Your parents."

My voice cracked. "I love them, and things are good now, but I don't know. Maybe a part of me doesn't forgive them."

"Or me."

I shrugged. "It was all done by the time I woke up. I had no say."

"That day—"

"I don't want to talk about it." I pulled the blanket up to my chin.

"I do."

I didn't want to go back there. I shook my head, and he held me firmly; like he knew I was on my way out.

"I was responsible for you almost dying, Me."

"No, you weren't. The truck swerved into us."

"I was responsible for you."

"Things happen that are out of our control sometimes."

"I was out of control. You and me back then was raw energy that we didn't know what to do with. An all-consuming fire we couldn't control."

My chest tightened. "It was love."

"Hell, yeah it was. You were the moon and stars to me. And the lengths I went to have you—"

"Stop making it sound like that."

His eyes narrowed. "I stole my uncle's car, picked you up on your eighteenth birthday, and drove to Vegas to marry you. That doesn't sound a little bit unhinged?"

I traced my initials scrolled into his tattoo. "That day. Wow."

"We were like Bonnie and Clyde. Burning everything behind us so we could get where we wanted to go." He drug his thumb across my lower lip. "I've never seen anything more beautiful than you in that dress."

I giggled. "Never underestimate the treasures of Goodwill. Am I right or am I right?"

"You could've worn a trash bag, and I would've clawed my way through walls to get to you."

"I've never understood what happened. I mean, I know what happened, but I was stunned. All my parents would ever tell me is that you realized we were better apart."

His demeanor changed, and I felt his muscles tighten. "I was passing the truck on the interstate when he switched lanes. I saw him shoot over but it was too late. It was almost in slow motion. He swerved, my eyes shot to you sleeping in the passenger seat, and then it all went black."

He swallowed hard as his eyes became glassy.

"I woke up in the hospital. Your parents were there, and

when I saw you on life support, because of me, it tore me apart."

I fought the lump in my throat as I pulled him closer. "But it wasn't because of you."

"Because of my actions you were fighting for your life, and it didn't look like you were going to make it. You were this beautiful genius who'd fallen for someone who was a reckless thrill seeker. If it wasn't for me, none of it would've happened."

My vision blurred.

"I wanted to tell them to fuck off, but it was all true. You were weaved into my soul, a part of me, and there was no line I wouldn't have crossed to get to you. It was crazy, and I couldn't control it."

"What happened then? I want to know what really happened. Not my brother's version. Nobody was completely honest with me. I know it."

"It's probably better—"

"You started this, tell me."

His eyes bore into mine.

"It was a good four days you were on life support, and I was dying inside. Your parents let me have it on day one but held their tongues when I told them I wouldn't live without you. Would not. I was with you every minute."

His low voice was quiet. "The day they were able to take you off of the ventilator, my father brought in the annulment papers. He said it was time to let you go. To realize that while I hadn't killed you this time, it would be a matter of time before I'd kill your dreams and take you off track." He laced his fingers through mine. "That I was the dynamite and you were the match."

The apparatus in my chest caved and every part of me hurt. Ached for the past, ached for what could have been, and what should have been.

"I refused and told him to go to hell. I went back in your room and your mother was with you. She was holding your hand and her tears gutted me. You were the stars in her world too. It was the first time I thought I'd been all wrong. Wrong for letting you love me, wrong for taking you off of the path you were on. Everything they thought about me was true. I'd hurt you."

I rested my hand on his cheek.

"I told her how much I loved you, and said I'd do whatever she wanted me to do."

My eyes burned.

"She said she felt you'd be able to live out your dreams without me. That together we tested everything, but alone you would be safe." He wiped his eye with the back of his hand. "Once you were on your way to being stable, they asked me to leave. Forever. I signed the papers, went home, packed, and left to go live with my aunt in Wisconsin. Evan's mother. They'd been right about me all along, and I wasn't going to hurt you further. I asked my dad not to tell you or anyone where I went because I knew you'd be there, and as much as it killed me, you were better off without me."

All the air left my body and as hard as I tried, he held me while I cried. The trajectory of my life had been changed entirely that day, and I had no say in it. Time wasted, dreams twisted into different dreams, and my busted heart that eventually stitched itself back together.

He took my face in his hands. "I never wanted you to get

hurt." His deep voice had a velvet rumble. "I'm sorry for all of it."

My mind was a whirlwind of angst and desire. The sting of the reality of us, but his touch and skin on mine now were all I needed even if it was just for a day.

I did follow my dream. I had a good life. I was happy. Now closure was coming to an end, and maybe it was a good thing. I knew what happened, and now it was finally over.

We dozed off wrapped up together, and I awoke at nine forty-five to find myself alone. As I reached for the robe at the bottom of the bed Levi entered and my tummy did a flip. He wore jeans that hung low on his hips with no shirt. Yeah, there should be a law against Levi ever wearing shirts indoors. His body was a freaking piece of art.

"Whatcha got there?"

"Hangover help." He set a tray on my lap. "Chocolate chip pancakes still your favorite?"

"Bet your ass they are. A nice dose of chocolate will cure just about anything."

He plopped down next to me. "Yeah, if chocolate is the answer, who the hell cares what the question is."

"Amen. Chocolate is clearly God's way of saying he likes us a little bit chubby."

After a quick shower Levi dabbed ointment on my stitches and each of us swallowed two more pain reliever tablets which were working pretty well on my tequila brain. While a hangover lasts maybe half a day, the blurry drunken memories of my time with the hot one would last a lifetime.

Once downstairs we sat on the sofa next to the roaring fire and most beautiful Christmas tree in the history of time.

Levi went to the kitchen, and his phone pinged. It sat on

the glass coffee table. I casually grabbed a Skittle from the candy dish and tossed it under the coffee table. Yes, I'm a loser.

I bent down, basically crawling under the coffee table, and looked up through the glass at his lit-up screen. While I couldn't see all the words, I saw *birthday party next Friday*. In his life across the world, some woman named Martina would be attending a party with the hot one.

Yes, a reality check.

He entered the room as I flashed a smile. Well, whatever he had in his life wasn't happening today; nope, he was in Colorado with me.

He plopped down on the couch beside me before laying his head in my lap as I ran my fingers through his hair, I decided this was fine. It was all okay.

I grabbed my phone and read through messages. "Well, they're on their way here." I kissed his lips. "You were right. I feel like we finally had our ending and can now move forward with peace. I guess this is goodbye to closure."

TWENTY-FOUR
LEVI
NOPE

The hell it was a goodbye.

Not happening.

I wasn't leaving Colorado without her.

"Am I a puss if knowing Rachel and Lexi are on the way is making me a little jumpy?"

She patted my hand. "No. They can be some scary bitches for sure." She grabbed the magic eight ball from the coffee table. "Will Levi be okay upon the arrival of the girls?"

She shook it and held it out to me.

"Fuck yes." I threw my arms in the air.

"See, it'll be fine."

A short time later a horn blew from outside as Allie shot to the window. "They're here." She turned back to me and bit her lip, which made me want to bite her lip. "Maybe you should step away somewhere, and I'll announce you. Just so my girls don't drop dead."

I climbed the stairs so I could take in whatever the hell was about to happen. I wasn't sure if I should be saying prayers or stretching out my legs so I wouldn't have any cramping when I had to run into the forest to not be killed by Allie's crew.

The door opened and there they were. The friends who were scared shitless I'd ruin the brilliant Allie from the first time I spoke to her. They tried to reel her in and did anything to keep me away, but failed time and time again.

I always told them I'd never hurt her, until I did.

The pain I caused and witnessed in the hospital while she barely clung to life still eats away at me. I married her, promised to protect her forever, and she nearly died the next day.

All because of me.

Rachel and Lexi were with me by her side with every beep of the heart monitor machine and each sigh of the ventilator as air was forced into her lungs.

She looked so small in the hospital bed, and her swollen, bruised face was branded in my mind forever.

We'd sit for hours without a word being spoken, the quiet hum of the florescent lights overhead growing louder minute by minute. When they didn't know if she would make it her parents let me stay, maybe trying to respect what they thought was the dying wish of their daughter. They knew all she wanted was us and I'd always loved that, but it was a sword through my heart to know they'd been right about me all along.

Once they were able to take her off life support, my welcome was extinguished. Her parents, Lexi, and Rachel had me physically removed from her room and a security officer was placed outside her door.

My father showed up with the annulment papers and once he got me out of the hospital, he drove me to Evan's in

Wisconsin where he actually stayed sober for over a month. Who says hell can't freeze over?

Once my dad went home, I'd call, and he'd fill me in on what he could find out about her from the few people in town who still spoke to him after what I did. He was known for drinking, throwing punches, and sleeping with women, so adding father of the bastard who nearly killed the town sweetheart was the final blow to his tattered reputation. Phrases like *learning to walk again, significant weight loss*, and *won't leave her room* gutted me. A reminder that I hurt the most perfect person in the world all because she loved me.

"Hey!" Rachel hugged Allie as her eyes scanned the room. "Look at this place!"

Rachel was a die-hard friend to all she had. There was a quiet confidence about her that'd always left me to believe she could kill, bury a body, and arrive at a restaurant for lunch without anybody knowing better. Yeah, be afraid of the quiet ones. They sit back, observe, and plan while the rest of the world is normally bat shit crazy.

Lexi popped through the door pulling a suitcase behind her wearing a crocodile smile. "Allie!" Now Lexi was a one-of-a-kind person who had Beth Dutton flair to her and a long memory; don't mess with Lexi.

"So happy everyone is finally here!" Allie's smile lit up the room.

Lexi leaned in. "Oh my gosh, Allie! What happened to your face?"

"Uh, my car hit some ice."

Rachel took her by the shoulders and gawked. "Ice did this? Stitches?"

"Actually, the tree I ran into did this, but it's okay. The doctor said you won't be able to see the scar."

"Holy shit, Allison. You're sure you're okay? Does it hurt?"

"Nah, I'm good."

My cousin Evan entered with two suitcases in hand. We were the same height, and he had brown hair and sported his typical jeans and Nebraska Cornhusker hoodie. He dropped the bags on the floor while Rachel took everybody's coats and started hanging them in the closet next to the door.

Lexi did a little jump. "This place is awesome!"

Allie's baby blues shot up to me, and I could feel her nerves all the way upstairs.

Evan pulled Allie in for a hug. "Are you okay?" He examined her stitches. "Looks sore."

"Now Evan, you know I'm a bad bitch and stitches will not get me down."

His nose wrinkled. "I kinda don't know that for sure." He laughed. "When I texted my cousin, he said the pool was killer."

"It is." Allie ran her hands through her hair. "Just beautiful."

"Where is he?" Evan walked to the Christmas tree and looked up. "This is awesome."

Allie's hand went out as she looked at Rachel and Lexi. "Now I want everybody to stay calm, okay?"

Lexi's brow shot up. "Why do you say that? You know ya can't say *stay calm* and actually expect people to stay calm. It's like saying I have a drinking problem because you get on my freakin' nerves."

"It's just a *really* small world because we know Evan's cousin. It's like an unexpected coincidence."

Rachel's head shook. "I heard a quote once that said not to believe in meaningless coincidences. That we should believe that every coincidence is a message, like a clue that needs attention or action."

Allie looked up. The second Rachel's eyes landed on me I learned "white as a ghost" was a thing.

Lexi groaned. "What the fuck? The attention *this* one needs is death."

Allie put her arms out again. "Guys, it's okay."

Lexi looked at her as if she was speaking Bulgarian. "This is anything but okay." Her narrowed eyes walked back to me as I made my way down the stairs. "He needs to go."

Evan walked to me. "What's happening?"

Rachel grabbed Evan's arm. "*This* is your cousin?"

"Yeah. This is Levi. He's been in Brazil since we've been together."

Lexi slapped Rachel's shoulder. "Rach, how can you not know Evan is related to this son of a bitch?"

Yeah, this was going about as well as I'd anticipated. On a positive note, nobody had hurled knives or Christmas tree ornaments at in my direction so kind of a point for me.

Rachel's arm shot up. "We don't live in the same city as his family and there are Levi's everywhere. I guess you'd prefer I go to his parent's house and go through all the photo albums to ensure he's not related to a horrible person?"

Lexi's face was flushed. "Yes!" She looked at the group. "From now on anytime we meet new people we have to get the whole fucking family tree, do you hear me?" She shook her head. "Evan, we've always liked you, but this man this is unacceptable."

Rachel spoke in a whisper as if nobody else was in the room. "It appears your cousin Levi was formally *Allie's* Levi."

Evan's mouth dropped open as he looked back at me. The whole blood is thicker than water thing may have flown the coop as his eyes read he might be taking a place in the line of people wanting to murder me. "Wait, Allie was *your* Allie?"

Lexi's eyes killed me. "She is not *his* Allie. Oh hell no."

Evan was computing the situation in his mind. If anyone knew what me being in the same space as Allie meant, he did.

Lexi looked at Rachel. "How would Evan not know about Levi and Allie? Is he stupid?" She looked at Evan. "Are you fucking stupid, Evan?"

Rachel groaned. "We all agreed long ago to never talk about Levi or the accident. Remember? It was a pact we took to *not* talk about it or even speak his name, so I didn't mention any of it to Evan because what are the effing odds of this?"

Lexi spoke through gritted teeth. "Fuck! I don't think I can do this. Can I handle this?"

Allie flashed a tense smile, reached for the magic eight ball, held out her hand, and Lexi snatched it. She shook it hard with gritted teeth and looked into the window. "Fuck yeah."

Allie nodded to the room. "See?"

Lexi tossed it on the couch. "I don't see. I don't see how all this shit in one house is going to be a thing."

Allie took her by the arm. "Don't you have those essential oils for calming down?"

Her head whipped back to me. "Yes, I'll find essential oils. Rachel, which one calms other people down? Chloroform? It's chloroform, right?"

Through the door came Royce who was all smiles. He's two years older than me and started dating Lexi their senior year. He's also Allie's brother Will's good friend which meant he was a full-fledged member of the *Levi should burn in hell* organization.

He looked up at me and his smiled faded fast. It was nice to see resting *dick face* was still on point. I couldn't resist giving him a little wave, and I swore smoke was coming from his ears.

Allie held her hand out. "Everybody take a breath." She pointed to her Rachel. "You, take a drink. I know you have alcohol somewhere on you."

With that she yanked a silver flask from her purse and chugged. Clearly liquor was the word of the day.

"All eyes on me." Allie ordered. "Yes, Levi is here. Nobody knew he was Evan's cousin. Everything happened years ago, and Levi and I can be civil. The past is the past and we are all going to be grown-ups."

Rachel huffed "Well, I'm a firm believer in *burying* the past."

"I mean it. This is not a big deal. Nothing is like it used to be, this is fine."

Lexi's voice was sharp. "But Allie—"

"No buts, we're going to live by your golden rule. If we can't say something nice, don't say anything at all."

Her head shook. "That's never been my rule. I'd not be able to speak for days at a time if I followed that freaking rule."

Allie nodded. "And that would be okay, too."

Rachel's head shook. "I tell ya what, this blows ass."

Lexi mouthed *I wish you were dead* to me. It felt good.

It was then a woman I didn't know strolled through the door looking, well, either drunk or depressed. The gal was in her late twenties and sported Cookie Monster blue sweatpants and a white sweatshirt that either had spaghetti sauce or blood drops down the front of it. Her hair was tucked under a "Shit Happened to Me" baseball cap, and what I believed were mascara streaks ran down her face. I took a few steps to Evan who shook his head at me.

Allie sprinted over and pulled her in for a hug.

"Kristina, how are you?"

Her head shook in sorrow. "Well, Allie, I'm just waiting to die now."

Rachel cleared her throat. "Her divorce was final yesterday."

Allie kissed her cheek. "You're going to be okay. Better than okay. Your future is a bright, sparkly explosion of fucking awesomeness wrapped in glitter."

Before I could take a breath Lexi pushed me out of the way. That may not sound like a big deal, but she wasn't near me. Yeah, she actually took two big steps in my direction just to shove me. "You'll be better than ever after you adjust, Kristina, I can tell you that right now."

Kristina's eyes danced around the room. "I don't think so."

Rachel jumped closer to Kristina. "We will personally help you through this horrific time in your life." Her arm went over Kristina's shoulder.

I scooted closer to Evan. "What happened to her?"

He whispered, "Her hubby left her for the woman who lived in the apartment next door."

Rachel threw her fist in the air. "That's it, Kristina, we're taking you for a girl's night tonight. We'll all get settled and go for an early dinner before hitting the town. Yes, sireee, Bob. Women and whiskey are the answer."

Kristina's concerned voice filled the room. "I don't know if that's the answer."

Lexi pointed at her. "Of course it is. You're wearing something out of my suitcase, and I'll do your makeup. You currently look like something I drew with my left hand. We'll get your mojo back."

Kristina shrugged. "I don't know if I have any mojo."

Allie smiled. "This is a reminder that even Winnie the Pooh had mojo. He wore a crop top with no panties, ate his favorite food, and loved himself. You can too, Kristina."

I let out a laugh and all eyes shot to me. Some of the eyes looked like they wanted to shoot me. My bad.

Rachel pointed to the Christmas tree. "Kristina, it's the magical season. All things are possible."

My mind was whipping up a plan. "I'll be the designated driver for girls' night."

Lexi wrinkled her nose. "That's a hard no."

Royce pointed to the stairs. "I'm picking a room. And ladies, I can be the driver tonight. Last time Lexi drank she paid sixty dollars for the Uber home but somehow ended up tipping two hundred bucks."

Lexi slapped his shoulder. "I just get so damn generous when I drink." She battered her eyes. "You know all about that don't you, big fella?"

Groans around the room as Rachel picked up her suitcase. "Tonight, we're pretending it's Cinco de Drinko, bitchachos."

They all passed by me, but Rachel stopped. "Your being here is all wrong."

I just needed to stay quiet. "Rachel, I'm not going to do anything."

She dramatically gasped and whispered. "This is a Deja poo; the feeling I've heard this shit before."

I took a controlled breath. "I don't want to cause any problems—"

"Oh, here's the problem...you're a dickhead." She turned toward the stairs. "I hope you fall down with your hands in your pockets." She walked away.

That actually went better than I'd anticipated. Royce paused when he passed me. "You shouldn't be here."

I held his stare until he went up the stairs and Evan approached. "Dude, you knew she'd be here—"

"Not when you first invited me. I had my plane ticket and everything before I realized."

"You should've told me. Rachel's pissed and now I'm on her shit list."

"If I had you would've never let me come."

He nodded as his eyes shot open. "Correct. You shouldn't be here. This is all about the girls and the wedding. Not the heavy shit that went down between you and her." He let out a sigh.

"Come on, you can't stay mad at me." I leaned in. "I'll be good, I promise." I shoved him. "I can totally be the reason you smile today."

"More likely the reason I drink today."

"So you're not mad?"

"No, but I do look at you and wonder how nobody's hit you with a shovel yet. You seriously might die this weekend."

TWENTY-FIVE

ALLIE

Okay, Levi had survived everybody arriving. A solid win for him.

Since we had a little down time before dinner, I did some important things. Responded to a few work emails and thought about Levi holding me against the wall having his way with me. Sigh.

I jumped into my jeans, black wrap around top, and black boots. I applied every cosmetic in my overnight bag and even used the false eyelashes I never wear. After nearly blinding myself with the glue, I finally had lashes and the perfect cat eye thanks to a tutorial on YouTube. Cheers to me.

I roamed the empty downstairs, had a candy cane cookie, and shot of chocolate milk. I sat by the Christmas tree hoping to get a minute with Levi. Yes, closure was over, but what can I say, I like me some good eye candy.

Lexi came down holding a version of Kristina I hadn't seen in a long time. At the bottom of the stairs, she did a spin. Is flabbergasted still a word? If so, that was the vibe of the room.

Lexi sailed down the stairs like a super model in her

shredded jeans and red scoopy shirt, while Kristina sported black jeans, cheetah print shirt serving up some serious cleavage, and high heeled black boots. On her eyes she sported Lexi's signature false eyelashes and her make up pallet neutral except for the red lip.

She looked *nothing* like she did an hour ago. The way Lexi did a little jump at the astonished face in front of her told me her goal was achieved.

"Okay, I'm going to crack open a bottle of wine." She walked toward the kitchen.

Levi entered from the hall, and it was like the sun rose in the living room. He stopped in front of Kristina.

"Hey, I'm Levi. We weren't officially introduced earlier. You look nice." He winked. "Good to see you gave those Cookie Monster sweats a rest."

Like any woman standing before Levi, she giggled as her cheeks pinked up. "Thanks." She spoke in a hushed tone that I could barely hear. "Don't worry, I won't poison you."

Levi leaned in closer. "Is someone trying to poison me? Did you hear something?"

Why was this tickling my funny bone?

"Nah, I don't think they'd do that." She nodded and straightened her shirt. "Too traceable."

With that she turned on her heel and headed to the kitchen as Levi walked toward me while doing a quick peek over his shoulder.

"Your friends better not poison me. You tell them I'll haunt every one of them, and I'll be ruthless. I'll hide their mascara every day. I'll slam doors at two in the morning and crack all the eggs on the shelf of the refrigerator so they have messes all the time. And I'll have pure ghost glee when I toss a few red socks into the white load." He let out an evil laugh that made me want to run my tongue up the side of his neck. "Dead Levi leads to mayhem for their entire lives, they'll be praying for death by the time I'm done with them."

"Wow, you came up with that fast."

"Yeah, survival mode's kicked in."

"A man with a plan; I did not see that coming."

Once the gang was together Rachel grabbed her coat from the closet. "Where to for dinner? How about Italian?"

Lexi strutted over and grabbed her black coat. "Y'all, I have the perfect spot."

Evan helped Rachel with her coat. "Where to?"

Lexi fluffed her hair. "Oh, Cosco for sure."

Eyes darted about, and I cleared my throat. "Cosco? For dinner?"

"Oh, hell yes." She pointed to me. "Allie, do you know they have hot dogs for a buck fifty and a twelve-ounce soda for seventy cents? Can you believe that shit? I go there twice a week."

"So, it's just you and the geriatric patients out on a day pass from the nursing home?"

Rachel wrinkled her nose. "I don't know if I'm in a hot doggy kind of mood."

"They have Italian, Rach. And it's good pizza." Lexi whispered. "I was raised to be thrifty with my coins. We'll eat cheap and drink like queens later."

Who could argue with that?

The room was an inferno because with every glance in Levi's direction, I'd find his glimmering eyes locked on me.

But closure was over. It was time for new beginnings. Yes, we both agreed, got it freaking tattooed into our flesh, and it felt great. Did it leave me with a little hole in my being that would likely never be filled by another because nobody was him? Yup. Were the memories of being in his arms hijacking my ability to string two thoughts together? Yes. But the bottom line was I'd leave Colorado in a few days with a peace throughout me. The past was reconciled, and I could go home and live my life never looking in the rearview mirror again.

You can build a teepee with your lies...

"Y'all, I'm starving. Let's get dinner and we can check out some clubs."

K ristina's blinking eyes clocked seventy-five an hour. "We're going to a club?"

Rachel shot her arm in the air. "Bet your ass we are. And there's no worrying during drinking hours so turn up your smile. As a matter of fact, I think I'll skip my meds and stir things up a bit."

Allie placed her hands on Rachel's shoulders. "No. You take those meds. I don't want to have to dig up bail money later."

Rachel gave a sarcastic grin. "You won't need bail money, I promise. I've learned that sarcasm and attitude are so much cheaper than bail money. I'll be good."

"Yeah, in life laughter is the best medicine." Lexi flashed one of her evil grins. "Unless you have diarrhea."

Allie ran her hands over her curls. "I can't go to jail. I haven't memorized a phone number in years. Who could I call? Then again, a good friend will bail you out, but I know my true friends would likely be sitting beside me."

The words inspired a group hug that even I had to admit was pretty damn cool.

They'd been friends forever and would walk to the ends of the earth for one another. Back in high school the only people in my life other than Allie were the thugs who taught me how to hot wire cars and score booze. Until after the accident and moving to Wisconsin with Evan's family, I'd never had people in my corner like that.

Allie was the first woman to show me what that looked like. I barely remember my mother. She found my father to be intolerable but left me behind. WTF, right? My dad, at the time, could've been summarized as a functioning alcoholic with a short fuse. If I had a problem, he was the last person I would've taken it to. I'd always just solved shit myself. Sure some solutions would've been frowned upon by police officers and the authorities, but when you have nothing, you have nothing to lose.

That's how Allie flipped everything in me. She was caring, patient, and wanted to hear my thoughts on things. She'd question my questionable decisions but not judge me. She wanted to understand and showed me different ways to see things. If it wasn't for her, I know with everything in me I'd be in prison somewhere. No doubt.

When I left and lived with Evan and my aunt and uncle, Allie had somehow instilled the tiniest seed of trust in me, and when Evan's family wanted to help me find my way, I let them. All because of her.

Rachel eyed Evan and Royce. "Now if you fellas are going to actually be our designated drivers, we need to lay down a few ground rules."

Evan crossed his arms over his chest. "Go."

Rachel pointed at me. "First of all, this one steers clear of me and Allie."

I gave a nod that said yes while trying to control the grin that screamed *hell no*.

I spoke to the hostile room. "I clearly remember you all hate me."

Her eyes rolled. "I don't exactly hate you, but if you were on fire I'd make smores."

I gave her an impressive nod. "Noted."

Lexi glared. "Levi should just stay here."

Evan slapped my back. "Come on. It's been years since all that happened. I invited him to be here, and he's traveled halfway across the globe so he's going."

Lexi's eyes dramatically rolled.

Rachel clapped. "And my second point was that *I* say where we're going tonight, me. No chiming in or thoughts from anyone. It's a night to take Kristina's mind off of dickhead Dale. We might be going to the dark side, and I don't really give a tiny "F" what you guys think, got me?"

Lexi pointed to the men. "Either agree or stay here and introvert tonight."

Rachel gave Kristina a hug. "Come on girl, I forgot I have the perfect necklace for this shirt." She looked at the group. "Give us five minutes."

With that everyone scurried away, but I hung back. I walked to the Christmas tree, and I could feel Allie's eyes.

"Looks like you survived introductions."

I plopped down on the sofa. "You had doubt?

She leaned against the chair. "Yes, many."

"Never underestimate me, Langley. I know more than I

say. I think more than I speak and notice more than anyone realizes. I'm like the new and improved Levi."

Her giggle filled the space between us. "I think I'll always be the same weirdo who runs into things, spills food, and laughs at random stuff. What can I do?"

"Do nothing. Never change." I rose to my feet, strode to her, grabbed her hand, and pulled her behind the Christmas tree.

"Mr. Levi, I believe closure is over." Her dirty grin was a gut punch.

"They could see us."

"One farewell kiss?"

I pulled her close as her perfume floated around me. She went up on her toes, and when I leaned in her breath blended with mine as her fingers went into my hair.

Everything about Allie was warm and soft, and a need from deep inside shot through while I closed the distance between us. Her hair brushed against my face tugging at the desire to have her everywhere. My house, my bed, and every other place I go. I was lost. All my defenses fell away, and for an instant I don't care who might walk in.

Her lips melted into mine for the softest kiss that I hoped to explore more later.

She pulled back and rested her forehead against mine. "You better get away from me before one of the girls come back."

I nodded and we walked back around by the couch.

"I'm getting my phone." She walked toward the stairs. "I can feel your eyes on my butt."

"I hoped so."

TWENTY-SEVEN
ALLIE
HERE WE GO

I made it into my room when Rachel shot in from the hall and shut the door.

Her eyes were question marks. "I can't believe Levi is here."

"I know."

"You've been *alone* with him and that's all you're going to tell me?"

"It's been somewhat awkward, but, uh, we, sorta had some closure." Not a lie, had lots and lots and lots of closure.

"But when you first saw him?"

"Yeah, I was a little pissy, but it was a long time ago."

"Pissy? He left you in the hospital with signed annulment papers and you were *pissy*?"

"Okay, maybe psycho bitch would be more accurate, but we came to a truce I guess."

"I can still feel it."

I looked over. "What?"

"The electricity between you guys. It's the same as back then. I don't like it, Allie. He needs to go."

"We're grown up now. I think we both now realize that

kind of electricity is the equivalent of tossing a toaster into a bathtub."

Her examining eyes made me twitchy. "I see. So, when you were in this big old house all alone, you guys were, uh, cool."

Damn she and her questions. "We were good."

What? It wasn't a lie. We were super-duper good.

Yes, our gang may have been a tad over dressed for Cosco. While my favorite has never been hot dogs, Rachel doesn't lie; good grub for $3.50. I even ran over to the bakery section, grabbed a white cake with flowers on it, and we had ourselves a delightful dessert. I am now a proud card toting member.

TWENTY-EIGHT
LEVI
WIENERLICIOUS

While I'd like to say I revolted against our first stop, Rachel and Lexi scare me a little. Edit— a lot.

They decided the initial destination for Kristina was The Wienerlicious Male Review Club. Was that anywhere on my fucking radar ever? Hell no, but again, scared of the girls and fairly certain they could successfully dispose of my body. The only silver lining to this shit show was the pretty girl with who seemed to take a peek at me from time to time. She was a magnet so where she went, I would follow.

She stood around a tall table next to the stage sipping on something; I was jealous of her straw.

What made her even more irresistible was the fact that she had no idea how beautiful she was. Her auburn hair and out of control curls framed her light skin and made her baby blues almost glow in comparison. Her shirt was nicely filled out, sue me, and those jeans hugged the good stuff to perfection. As if feeling my eyes on her, she glanced my way and a little grin made its way across those pink lips that made me want to throw her over my shoulder like a caveman and take her away from here.

Evan and I took a seat at the bar, and Royce sat a few stools away from us. Ruby red lights shined a devilish glow on the room as drinking and laughing seemed to be on like Donkey Kong.

I'd never been in a male dancer situation before, but the jam-packed Colorado club had a literal pulse of its own with women as far as the eye could see hootin' and hollerin' for the gent on the stage thrusting to *Million Dollar Baby*.

Lexi walked over next to us and ordered a round of shots from the shirtless fella behind the bar. As she waited her glare settled on me.

"You're the designated driver, quit drinking."

Evan shot her a grin. "Lex, We drove the rental van. I'm driving so a beer or two for Levi is fine."

She leaned in close. "I mean it, don't you go near Allison. You hear me?"

I sat back and held her eyes for a moment. "I do hear you."

"Good. Because I've watched so many Criminal Minds episodes, I can make your death look like Santa Clause did it."

She walked away with a tray of shots in her hand as Evan leaned over. "I still can't believe you came here knowing what Colorado had in store."

"I realize I should've told you."

"This whole thing went completely sideways back then. You're keeping it cool, right?"

I took a long drink of my beer. "Oh yeah, totally cool."

"Really? Because I feel like your survival rate has decreased significantly since the arrival of our group." He clinked his cup of water against my beer bottle. "Here's to you, because if you don't keep your damn eyes off Allie, this whole thing unravels tonight. I'm sure you don't want your last stop ever to have been at The Wienerlicious strip joint."

Evan sounded cool, but he knew better than most what she could do to me. He'd literally put me back together when I went to live with his family.

"I hear you. And I won't be dead tonight."

My eyes found their table through the crowds of crazy ladies to see Lexi flipping me the bird before Evan roared with laughter. "Ya sure about that buddy? I think the only focus tonight should be on keeping the peace."

"If Coke and Pepsi can't even be in the same restaurant together, there's no chance of peace anywhere."

"Come on, Levi. You need to keep everything in check. Just embrace the attitude of a child and play nice."

"You knew me as a kid. If I try to embrace my inner child the little asshole will bite me."

"You just need to stay away from Allie."

"Don't worry. I'm putting together a plan."

"To stay safe and healthy?"

I leaned up and awaited his reaction. "A plan to get her back before we leave Colorado."

He groaned. "No. Terrible idea." His eyes were intense. "Rachel's a sweetie, but I know what she's capable of. You back off right now. If you still feel it in a few months, go to her then."

I took another long drink while holding his eyes which seemed to wrangle up a little panic in my cousin. "Levi, I need your promise you won't fuck this trip up."

"Fine, I promise not to fuck up anything."

I felt there was at least a seventy percent chance I was spitting the truth.

TWENTY-NINE
ALLIE
FUN?

After two shots Kristina loosened right up and was giggling nonstop as Rachel passed out crisp one-dollar bills.

The fella on stage made his way to our table when Lexi hopped on her chair hollering while waving her cash in the air like she just don't care. Kristina's cheeks turned neon pink as the dancer slithered in her direction.

I sipped my tequila sunrise as Lexi scooted her chair closer.

"Please tell me you're using your brain."

I crossed my fingers beneath the table. "Lex, I promise there's nothing to worry about."

"So you'll steer clear of him? Because my head hurts today. I think my horns are coming in, and you don't want any part of that shit."

I nodded as the left side of my brain laughed. *Not likely to comply.*

An hour had passed, and I could feel Levi's eyes on me. Maybe it was my two drinks and a shot, but I liked it. He was what the overthinking smart girl needed more than oxygen back in the day. He still made me feel sexy and beautiful, and maybe it was nice to have that again, even if only for a few days. Closure was over and we were kinda friends now, but knew I had to leave that friendship in Colorado when I left. He was my past.

To my right Kristina was shoving dollar bills into the G-string of a dancer. It was then the lights dimmed, and a spotlight hit the empty stage while *Pony* pumped through the speakers. I have to admit, I was a little curious to see what was about to go down. As I glanced over Kristina was now seated in a chair receiving a heated lap dance while Lexi giggled like a schoolgirl, I wondered how "down" this night might go.

Once the lap dance ended Rachel pulled our group in close. "Let's have a toast!" We all grabbed our glasses. "Here's to you ladies. We may not be athletic or super young or smart or talented or wise." Her eyes narrowed. "I kinda forget where I was going with this." She shrugged. "Here's to us!"

Like idiots we all cheered and slammed our drinks.

In a blaze of glory, a man walked onto the stage. It was a fog-filled space and he sported jeans, work boots, a bright yellow construction worker vest, sunglasses, and no shirt. Even though it was winter in Colorado, he was tanned, muscley, oiled up, and open for business.

The construction fella started his performance, and I must admit he was very entertaining with his shimmying and smiling; the crazy bitches around me were losing their effing minds.

He stood at the edge of the stage, and his hand went up shielding his eyes from the light as he looked into the audience. My heart clunked when he hopped off the stage, walked to me, and in an instant, I was being led onto the stage. While I wanted to run, I had to be a good sport, right? This was all in good fun. As I was set in a chair, it was safe to say it would not be the *clean* kind of fun tonight.

The place went wild as he circled me before giving me an up close and personal lap dance. He had shed his vest somewhere and placed my hands on his oily chest as the music and screams were pounding my eardrums.

I wanted to get the hell out of there but sat frozen in the chair as he continued his slick moves. I was playing it cool until a millisecond later he was on his knees, had pushed my legs apart, and was simulating *some actions*, if you know what I'm saying. A panic went through me, and I pushed his shoulders, but he firmly held my legs in place.

THIRTY
LEVI
PROTECTOR

My fucking eyeballs were about to blow. My throat felt like I drank kerosene and swallowed a match.

Evan touched my arm. "Levi, it's okay—"

"Oh, hell no." It was so far from okay I wondered if a jail cell might be in my future. She was being a good sport, but the second I saw that look on her face and she pushed his shoulders, and he didn't let her go, I knew this was over.

I don't remember storming the stage, but I'll never forget the relief in her eye when she saw me shove the guy aside and get her the hell out of there.

I took her hand and somewhat aggressively pushed my way down a crowded back hallway toward an exit sign. I knew the girls wouldn't be able to catch up. The most important thing was how tightly she held my hand. She may not know shit about my true intentions, but that one fact showed me all I needed to know.

I pushed open the door and we were in an alley. I grabbed her waist and pushed her against the cold brick building. No words needed to be spoken as I looked into those ocean eyes. I pulled her closer and leaned down. The expression she wore told me closure wasn't over for her either.

Her arms wrapped around my shoulders as she whispered. "I know with all of my soul that you need to back away." The gentle caress of her lips against mine fueled the hunger for her.

"Being in the alley behind the Wienerlicious strip club kissing your face off is *not* what I want." The soft pressure of her lips ignited a fire. Kissing her is indescribable. This is where I belonged. This was beyond lust; she was my addiction. She'd always been, and I needed to be with her even if she didn't know she needed to be with me yet. Okay, that may be a phrase used by a stalker, but that's not me.

Well, maybe me a little.

She broke the kiss. "Okay, one more minute and this is *so* done. No more kissing, this is it."

Her mouth led mine while I pushed her further away from the door into the darkness.

She spoke through the kiss. "Just one more second, then I mean it. It's done. You go back into the past."

Her words twisted something, and I pressed myself into her as she drew a quick breath before my mouth dropped to her ear. "Do you feel what you do to me? One look and you have me on my knees. And I sure as hell know what I do to you."

She growled my name while my hands traveled. The little moan going from her mouth to mine nearly undid me as I gave her what I wanted to every day. Forever.

I pulled away and she stood dazed as I pushed curls off her face. "You go in ahead to ensure Rachel and Lexi don't hurdle the bar and strangle me, okay?"

I ushered her through the door. "Go."
She wore a tiny grin and disappeared down the hall.

THIRTY-ONE
ALLIE
THAT HAPPENED FAST...

Whoa, my mind was holding on tight to the train wreck that seemed to be me coming in hot from the alley out back. I took another cleansing breath that didn't do shit and decided this was okay. Sure, closure was over, but maybe this was just a quick goodbye. Again. Maybe I'm not a total train wreck?

Then my brain laughed. *Toot Toot mother trucker*.

Screw you, brain. I'll just be an out-of-control fun train for a bit. Like one filled with cheeseburgers, sparklers, and glitter. Bottom line, this would be okay.

I don't know exactly how long we were in the alley, but when I returned to the table Rachel and Lexi were laughing and Kristina had turned into a dancing machine.

While I sipped on a drink I realized it was *not* mine, gross, but finished it anyway, my mind was still in the alley. *I know what I do to you*. His words made my stomach sink like a rock.

I needed to stay away from those damn pillow lips because one look turns me into a kitten high on cat nip.

Pull your shit together!

I kept my eyeballs toward the thrusting fireman who just lost his trousers on the stage, BTW, and wished I wasn't as tipsy as I was. I needed to *not* see Levi's glorious eyes that had the ability to steal my words and make my clothes fall off.

I stood up at the same moment a woman with platinum blond hair was throwing a drink in the face of the woman to my left, but instead got me. Yes, burning alcohol up my nose and over my hair.

The woman glared at me as if I'd done something wrong as she slurred. "Sorry, you were in the way."

I ran my hands over the top of my head and knocked off a few ice cubes as Rachel sprung to her feet. "What in the hell are you doing?" She grabbed a napkin and dabbed my face.

Drunk girl let out a huff. "She was just in the wrong place."

Lexi gasped. "You aren't even going to apologize?"

The girl tossed her hair as Rachel tossed her drink in the stranger's face. "There you go, how does that effing feel?"

Clearly not well as she shoved Rachel who fell back into Kristina.

"Don't you touch my friend!" I pushed the assaulting mean girl away. I looked back at the same time the unbelievably ballsy gal grabbed my hair and pulled. Before I could blink twice my fist was in her face and she fell to the floor.

I looked up just in time to see one of the two armed security guards grab me. Lexi grasped at the man's arm. "You don't touch her!"

"Ma'am, remove your hand from my arm or you can accompany this one out of here."

Kristina bolted over. "You're not taking her anywhere!"

With that security officer number two had Lexi's arm in one hand and Kristina's in the other. Yeah, I don't half ass anything. I fuck it all the way up.

THIRTY-TWO

LEVI
YUCK FOU FOTHER MUCKER

Evan's eyes shot a dagger in my direction. "Did you just make out with Allie?"

I shrugged and took a swig of my beer.

"You have fucking lip gloss on. Come on man, you promised you'd leave this alone and keep me happy."

"I don't recall. And you know to *never* put the key to your happiness in my pocket. I don't even trust myself most days."

His head shook. "When you be anything in the world Levi, an asshole seems like and odd choice."

"Calm down. It's a pretty good night. We're not in jail, not in a hospital, and not in a grave."

"YET. Yet is the key word." He pointed behind me. "What the hell is going on with the girls?"

I spun around in my seat to see Allie, Lexi, and Kristina being led somewhere by two security officers. Clearly in the past ten minutes this thing had gone off the rails.

We followed as they were led to an office inside the front door.

"Get your hands off me." Lexi glared at the security officer.

I walked in. "Lexi, it might be a good time to keep all thoughts to yourself."

She shook her head at me. "Your *check asshole* light is on again, Levi. And just so you know, I hope a bird shits on your face today."

One of the security guards sat behind a desk. "Wow. She's a little ray of sunshine, huh?

I nodded. "I wish they made shut-up spray."

Lexi snarled at me while the second security officer stood at the door.

"And you are?"

"I'm Levi Dawson."

"Are you with these three?"

"Yes."

Lexi's head shook. "Not me. Yuck fou fother mucker." She laughed and nudged Kristina with her arm. "See, I told stupid Levi off in a secret language."

"Lexi, here's a reminder before you lose your shit. They don't serve alcohol in prison. Watch it." I pointed to her. "Sir, please ignore this one. She's crazy."

Her gasp was dramatic. "*Me* crazy?"

Kristina nodded. "Oh, for sure. But honey, I don't care if you lick windows, run into doors, or even pee on yourself. You're my favorite crazy person."

"Awww." Yes, it was a cute yet annoying hug.

The security guard cleared his throat. "Well, the ginger punched a woman in the face, and the lady in leopard tried to punch me."

Lexi flashed a tense smile. "I apologize about that. Y'all, it took me a second to realize what was going on."

"She's a little dim." Why was I trying to push her buttons?

"You shut your face, Levi."

Allie raised her hand. "May I speak? Would that be possible?"

Her shirt was wet, and the outline of her bra was on full display. The security dude nodded.

"I was just standing there when that woman threw her drink at me. All Lexi did was tell her to get away, but then she pushed everyone around."

As if in a play Lexi leaned forward in her chair and held her back. "Oh yeah. She pushed me hard. *Real hard*. Knocked the wind right out of my lungs." She coughed dramatically.

Eye roll.

Allie nodded. "I just wanted her away from my table, but then she grabbed my hair and wouldn't release me. It really hurt and before I knew it, I hit her to make her let go."

Lexi's arms flew in the air. "Your honor, this is clearly a case of self-defense."

The security officer shook his head. "I'm not a judge."

She flashed a ginormous smile. "Ya should be, Sir. You look like a real smart fella."

I stepped forward. "Excuse me, may I say something?"

He gave me a nod. "By the way, thank you for what you do. I imagine it's not easy to keep things under control around here."

"I'm a police officer by day and this whole city is nothing compared to the clientele at this club."

"Yeah, half clothed men, liquor, and ladies don't mix well. But I can promise you that what Allie did here was because these girls are so special to her. She'd walk to the ends of the earth to protect her people. You know what I mean?"

"I do."

"Well, I didn't have many people there for me growing up, but you did. You know about the instinct to protect." I pointed to Allie. "And this one. She is an angel. She's brilliant with that brain of hers. She believes in people and sees the best in them without judgment even when they're a little jacked up." I met her eyes and knew there had to be a way to get her back. "She's sweet, kind, and anyone she has in her life is lucky to have her. I know things went sideways here tonight, but these women would never be out to just hurt anyone."

The security guard leaned back in his chair. "Listen to this guy talking you ladies up."

I scanned over to Lexi and for the first time in, well, probably forever, her eyes were a little softer. Like not raging hate toward me, maybe just bubbling fury at the moment.

The security guard stood up. "You all had better get out of here before I change my mind."

THIRTY-THREE
ALLIE
EXTENSION?

W e grabbed Rachel and a shocked Royce when he heard what had happened before and flew out the door. Peace out Wienerlicious.

"I think Kristina could use some fresh air anyway."

Rachel elbowed me in the boob. "Yeah, she's probably had her fill of liquor and wants to forget the last hour."

Kristina gasped. "Are you kidding me? You punched a chick, and we almost went to jail? I love tonight."

As we all scrambled out onto the sidewalk I locked arms with Lexi. I knew she would keep me thinking clearly, especially after Levi's words with the security guard which were sweet. The best thing for me would be to go back to the house and lock myself in the bedroom until sunrise. Nothing good happens after midnight. Enough todaying for today.

Lexi walked ahead of us and screamed. "An ice rink!"

In the distance was an ice rink with people skating around. There was an enormous Christmas tree in the center of the ice lit up with red and white lights and giant silver ornaments while *Jingle All The Way* drifted through the air.

I cleared my throat. "It's getting kind of late." I looked at my watchless wrist.

Rachel spun around. "Jeeze Allie, you're younger than me. Don't be a fuddy duddy."

"By three months, crazy lady. I just think some people might be sleepy and maybe don't want any more craziness." I pulled down my coat, almost feeling Levi's laser eyes a few people behind me.

I peeked over my shoulder and my eyes met Levi's and his brow arched. I clearly needed to get away from this man. "But Rach, you should care about how the rest of us feel."

She laughed and started skipping. "I actually cared earlier but you missed it."

Levi's crooked grin reminded me that I needed to be anywhere he was not. "And it's cold." I threw my arm around Kristina. "I think this little lady might be chilly."

Know it all Lexi pulled out her phone. "It's unseasonably warm, it's like a heat wave for Colorado."

"Well, I don't feel super skatey. I'm just going to watch."

Rachel pinched my arm. "Just *try* to be happy. If I give you a straw, will you go suck the fun out of someone else's night?"

Royce yelled from behind me. "Rachel, you can't make people be happy. You're not vodka."

I was losing patience. "Warning to all, I'm having a moment where I just really need some therapeutic stabbing. Don't push me."

Lexi did a little jump. "There she is!"

Our crew got skates, and I found a chair sitting on the ice across the rink. Perfect. I planted my butt in it and watched Rachel laugh and hold hands with Evan while I pushed images of hot Levi from my cerebrum.

Rachel and Evan; the perfect pair. She was the sun to his shine. The cheese to his macaroni. The dirt to his gutter. The booze to his hangover. The vomit to his party. I should probably stop here, you get it.

My eyes skipped over to Lexi skating hand in hand with newly divorced Kristina who was laughing her ass off. She was Kristina's answer. Isn't it weird how one person being put into your life can flip the script? I pulled on my gloves and inhaled the crisp Christmasy air and watched our crew for ten minutes in peace.

Then my chair moved.

I looked over my shoulder as Levi's chuckle hit my ears.

"What are you doing?" I held on. "You stop this right now or I'll tell Lexi on you!"

I felt his breath on the top of my head as he laughed. "I know you really don't want to sit in a boring chair. You need a little thrill."

His words cranked my tummy tight. "No, I don't *need* a thrill. I'm an adult, and I don't want any of that."

"Wasn't it Hemmingway who said when you stop doing things for fun you might as well be dead?"

I held on tighter as we picked up speed. "You quoting Hemmingway is shocking enough to provoke death. But I don't need thrills or fun."

"Are you trying to convince me or yourself?"

Good question. With that he whipped the chair, and I sailed across the ice while screaming with laughter. By the time I slowed he was right behind me and whirled me in the other direction but even faster as I clung to the chair. "Stop it!"

He skated over, placed his hands on the chair beside each

of my legs and leaned down. "You don't want me to stop. Do you?"

I needed to stop all of it. My brain had the clarity of a muddy water after a storm.

"You ready, pretty girl?"

I went sailing past the Christmas tree and suddenly wondered why my ladies weren't stopping the shenanigans. I turned my head, and the girls were entering a little gift shop next to the ice rink. That was when my chair was pushed again, but this time to the end of the ice arena and behind a wall.

I stood and planned to walk away, but the intelligent organ inside my thick skull stopped working. It had too many tabs open and just froze up, leaving me standing there chewing on my lip.

He took a step closer. "Hi."

"Hi."

"I'm sorry about what happened in the alley at Wienerlicious." The corner of his mouth turned up. "Now there's a sentence I never imagined coming out of me."

I nodded at the eyes that held the promise of forbidden pleasures. Forbidden pleasures I knew were over and done with but still made the little hairs on the back of my neck stand on end.

"You'll always make me crazy. But we agreed to a day of closure. We both have our lives to get back to." He grabbed me by the front of my coat and pulled me to him. "So this is it."

Relief washed over me; we were on the same page. This was what I wanted. *Farewell Allie and Levi forever. Adios. Au revoir.*

Forever. Yes, I'd leave Colorado and never see him again just as it was supposed to be.

While I waited for a sense of calm to fill me, it did not. Instead, a rigid strain in my upper chest cavity arrived.

The flirting, *my* flirting, the kisses, and longing to be as close to him as possible was something I had to release into the universe and move forward with a new sense of peace in my life.

THIRTY-FOUR
LEVI
PLAYING IT CHILL

I held her close while *I need Allie* was intertwined with my blood. How to make her see it should be us? I had to keep it light.

"Ya know Langley, it might make more sense if we just tie closure to Colorado."

Her grin squeezed me. "Did you say you want to tie me up?"

My laughter bounced off the wall behind her. "I did *not* say that, but I'm a firm believer in being open to all options." I kissed her forehead. "I was just saying, especially if rope is on the table, that we let closure linger until we head out of this great state."

Her eyes were blinking in Morse code. "So?"

"I'm wanting to get your thoughts on hanging out a little longer." Should I cross my fingers? Toes? Locate a wishing fountain? Find a dandelion and blow?

Her eyes locked with mine and her wheels were spinning. "Hmmm."

I brushed my lips against hers. "Once we leave Colorado it's all done."

"That might not be a smart option for me."

"Come on, intelligence is living life for today."

She stood completely still.

"Come on Langley, a few more days? You up for some risky business?"

She inhaled deeply. "Risky."

I threw on my best New Jersey accent. "I'm about to get into some trouble. You comin' doll?"

I didn't want to push.

"We should probably get back."

I took a step, and she pulled her hand from mine. "I'll go. You stay here for a few minutes."

I had no confirmation of anything. After a few ticks of the clock, I found the bench and took off my skates as Evan and Rachel skated toward me.

"Where is everybody?"

"There're some gift shops still open. Odds are Lexi is stocking up on wine."

Rachel nodded. "It seems many solutions in life are found at the bottom of a wine bottle."

They got out of their skates and Evan scooped them up. "I'll take these back."

He walked away as Rachel pulled on her boots. "I still can't believe you're here."

I nodded.

"It's taken her a long time for her to work through all that."

"I should *not* have listened to my dad." I looked over. "Or any of you. I'll never forgive myself for leaving her there."

She let out a long breath. "You were young, and it was probably for the best in the long run. You guys being together made you both go off the rails a bit."

"I should've stayed with her."

"Levi, the way it happened sucked. But she would've never left to go to Columbia if you were together. She would've only been focusing on you. Look at what's she's accomplished. She's literally saving lives on the daily." She put her hand on my arm. "In a way what you did that day was allow her to achieve a dream she had."

The thought of her missing out on anything because of me turned my blood to tar. "I would've supported her in everything she wanted to do. I should've never walked away."

"I know *you* would have. But she wouldn't have gone for it, would have never put herself first."

I looked over to see Lexi, Royce, and Kristina talking to Allie just off the ice. One glimpse of her and it was difficult to take a breath.

Rachel let out a sigh. "Levi, please tell me you're leaving this alone."

I stood and stretched my arms over my head. "Okay. I'm leaving this alone."

I started toward Allie at the same time Rachel's voice drifted in the breeze. "Levi, you leave her alone. Do you hear me right now?"

I shot her a wink. "I hear your words."

I took another step. "But are you *listening* to my words?"

I put my hand to my ear. "What?"

"Are you listening to my words?"

"What?"

"Levi Dawson, you'd better listen to me or somebody's going to be dead soon."

Kristina's arm waved in the air as her voice echoed across the ice. "Hey guys, we're going to the town square to have hot chocolate before we head back to the house!"

I got closer to find Lexi and Kristina each carrying a tray of red and green striped cups topped with thick whipped cream. I took a tray in each hand.

"Allow me, ladies."

Allie was trying to hide her grin while she stared up at me. I noticed Evan's eyes darting between us, and I quickly stepped away. "Are we ready?"

Lexi pulled on her gloves. "Where's the town square? Close enough to walk?"

"Yeah, follow me. We saw it the other day."

Oh, shit entered my blood stream as Lexi and Rach stared at me as if I were speaking Turkish.

Lexi pointed. "You and Allie saw it?"

I swallowed hard as panic shot through Allie's eyes.

Evan slapped me on the shoulder. "Me and Levi saw it when I got gas earlier."

Lexi squinted her eyes at my cousin who was attempting to save my ass.

"Gas?"

"Yeah, while you gals were doing shots at Wiernerlicious we got some fuel and gum." He pulled a pack out of his pocket. "Hubba Bubba?"

Lexi took a piece, popped it into her mouth, and chewed angrily as she glared at me.

We made it to the town square to find a scene that belonged in a Christmas book or some shit.

A large white gazebo containing a man playing a guitar and a woman slapping a tambourine against her hip. Above them hung greenery and white twinkly lights that lit up the space. To the right was a large Christmas tree filled with lights.

In front of the microband were white benches where people sat and sang along to *Deck the Halls*.

Kristina squealed. "Is this the most beautiful thing you've ever laid your eyes on?"

THIRTY-FIVE

ALLIE

SECRETS

We all found seats and sipped on hot chocolate. While everyone's eyes were on the little band, mine were stuck on the hot one as he laughed with Evan.

I am literally insane to let myself think of him. Well, "insane" sounds a little mean. Maybe I prefer the phrase "mentally creative" when referring to my sanity from this moment on? I needed to grip.

A grip on his tushy. *Stop!*

Kristina pointed. "Hey, a candy shop."

Lexi let out a yell. "Let's do it."

Rachel tossed her cup into a trashcan. "I'll come."

Royce slapped Evan on the shoulder. "Let's find some cigars." He eyed me. "Levi, come with us."

It wasn't a request. It was a *we don't trust you out of our sight* thing.

"I'm good."

His head shook. "You're being here is all jacked up."

The delightful town square that was magical ten seconds ago was now a little darker.

I touched his arm. "Royce, it's fine. It's in the past. Nothing to worry about." Was my nose growing?

My cheeks warmed as he examined my eyes.

Evan stepped between the two. "Let's all calm down. It was a long time ago."

Royce let out a huff. "Evan, you weren't around. What he did—"

I stepped to Royce, the one who came to my house with Lexi every day after school to help me with my walking. My parents installed a long ballet bar in the hallway where I'd practice. When I'd feel sorry for myself Royce would stand at the end of the hall hurling insults at me until I finally made my way to him and he'd allow me to punch him in the arm.

"Royce, I promise you I'm fine." I flashed my toothiest smile. "Today was fine, right?"

He glared at Levi. "I feel like today is The Fuckening. A day when things are going too well and you don't trust it because you're suspicious some shit is gonna go down."

Levi's voice was quiet. "Nothing is going down. I live in Brazil. I'm leaving in a few days." He spoke as if talking to a toddler. "Do you know that Brazil is on a different continent, Rocey?"

I bit my lip to conceal a smile while Royce's eyes bulged.

Evan patted Royce on the back. "Come on, let's get those cigars."

He pointed at Levi. "Anything shady and I'll—"

Levi let a sarcastic laugh out. "You'll have to get in line behind Rach and Lexi for that." He whispered, "I've heard through the grape vine that poisoning is on the table.

Evan gave Levi a weak smile as Royce flipped him the bird before they walked away.

"This is not good."

A moment later Levi extended his hand. "Dance?"

"Bad idea. Too many eyes around here."

The little band played *Have Yourself a Merry Little Christmas* and he took my hand and led me behind the Christmas tree, hidden from all eyes.

He pulled me close, and I did the very last thing I should have, I melted into him. His eyes held mine and not a word was spoken, but so much was said. I was well aware that my mind was the Devi's playground at this moment in my life.

We'd extended closure. Extended the time the most handsome man in the universe would wrap his arms around me. For better or worse I was in.

Once home in the quiet house everyone scattered. My first thought was how long I'd have to wait to be in Levi's arms. Yes, I was chucking common sense into the fuck it bucket and living like a wild child until I exited Colorado.

Lexi leaned against the wall. "My back has been buggin' me all night."

"I have Tylenol—"

She stretched her arms over her head. "I think I'm gonna just crash on the sofa in the sitting area by Allie's room." Her head nodded. "Yes, it's firm. Really good for a sore back."

"What? You can't sleep on that. It's not comfortable." Well, it appeared the evening wasn't ending in an orgasm as I'd anticipated.

She flashed a transparent smile. "Yeppers, that's what my back needs. A firm couch. That's the ticket."

At that moment I saw my ticket to Levi hop on a broom and zip off into the forest.

Or did it?

Rachel gave me a hug. "Night Allie." She glanced at the hot one. "Levi."

Evan slapped Levi on the back. "See you in the morning guys."

The hall emptied and it was clear as an air raid siren that Lexi was my gatekeeper.

I watched Levi and his fine self disappear down the hall, and when I turned back around Lexi's eyes were boring into me.

"What?"

"Allison, you are a smart woman. Do not—"

"I *am* smart. Remember that. And you're crazy by the way.

Her eyebrows screwed together. "Me, crazy? I should get off this unicorn and slap you right now."

"Ya know Lexi, you're really starting to piss me off. I'm a grown ass woman and capable of good decisions." It would've been a strong sentence, but some giggles fell out of me and ruined it. "You're kind of being a bitch. I mean not a huge one, but sort of a medium one."

"I will keep you safe, my Allie. As far as being a bitch, all you have to remember is that I'm ten times the bitch you could ever hope to be." She pointed to my room. "Now run along."

I turned on my heel and went into my room feeling as unsmart as one could be.

I changed into my pajamas with the candy canes on them and squirted a little perfume on my wrist as I looked out the window. It was a slanted roof. A good roof.

The one thing I could count more than the sun rising from the east was the fact that Levi would get to me tonight.

The past and the present swarmed together like a pack of pesty mosquitos as I sat on my bed just like I did every night we were together and waited.

Back in the day his dad normally worked late and either went to a bar, his girlfriend's, or straight to bed. There was nobody to stop him.

My parents caught Levi in my bedroom once and the memory of him jumping out the two-story window with shoes in hand still made me giggle. (He landed on the hood of my car so no real damage to him, just a dent my father pounded out while busting out some colorful language). That was when my parents, Roxy and Jerry, invested in a high-tech security system so they could sleep at night knowing hooligan Levi couldn't get to me.

Two days in, I used a nail file and loosened the sensor on my window so it appeared fine, but nope, it wasn't. He was in like Flynn. He'd come over after ten when my folks went to bed, parked around the block, and would watch Pretty Woman or old Friend's episodes with me. I'd set my alarm for five thirty and he'd be out of the house before anyone awoke.

It was perfect.

So I waited tonight in the big old house in Colorado, knowing with everything in me he'd get there.

Fifteen minutes later I jumped at the quiet tap. I had to fight my laughter as I slid open the window and Mr. Handsome crawled inside. Yes, this man was like Spiderman on a roof. Now a snow-covered roof may have been tricky, but the look in his eye said it could be no other way.

I closed it and immediately found myself caged against the

wall. We were finally alone, no need to extinguish anything now. Well, except for the fact that Lexi was ten feet on the other side of the door. But we'd managed this predicament before. I could almost say we were experts.

Ice was under my skin, but I was burning on top. Our lips moved in tandem as he cupped my face and kissed me like I was the only thing that could keep him alive. He tipped my head farther back as his fingers slip down to the base of my neck and his lips went below my ear while his whisper sends tingles dancing up my spine.

"You were waiting for me?"

I nodded.

"What do you want, Allie?"

To be with him forever and ever and ever? Not possible. His whiskers slid down my neck awakening every nerve ending in my body.

"What do you want?"

"You." It came out as a broken whisper.

His teeth grazed my collar bone before he kissed my fresh tattoo as his hot breath bathed my skin. "What?"

"You, I want you."

His hands curled around my biceps, and his lips overtook mine while leading me to the bed. He sat and pulled me to him. While there were no words, his eyes told me what was about to happen and my skin heated.

I held his gaze as I pulled my pajama top off and dropped it to the floor. He sucked in air and let it out. The way his eyes traveled my body made me feel strong, like a powerful queen who can bring him to his knees because I'm what he wants. *Me*. It was exhilarating.

I was restless as he stared at me; Again. How could he bring me to this place so many times in the past day? Even the tiniest of muscles in me were pulsing. His grin told me I was in control, and he didn't move an inch as I shimmied out of my jammie bottoms. I stood before the man who knew me to my core left only in my purple lacy panties.

I climbed onto his lap facing him. He was still as I kiss his forehead, cheeks, and finally his lips. I pulled away and pushed his shirt up and over his head while my hands traveled. My fingers traced the lines in his biceps before moving to his chest. Our old tattoo, and the new one.

My eyes caught his for a second and he was watching me so intently it tightened my stomach. His muscles jumped when I touched his abs as he remained still. I trailed kisses down his neck and chest. His warm breath was on my face as I kissed the tattoo.

My head was swimming, and I pushed him back on the bed. I placed his hands on my chest and as if I was handing over the "I'm in control" key, and he came alive. His mouth and hands were everywhere as my aching body moved against his.

In a split second he flipped me on my back and hovered over me as air caught in my throat. His lips nipped and kissed down my body, his steamy breath on my chest, stomach, and lower leaving pleasure coursing through me like a raging river while I pressed my lips together to remain quiet as he was painstakingly slow as if trying to torture me.

As he moved north, I wrapped a leg around his hip as he pinned me to the bed and pressed against me while his tongue ran up my neck. He'd tossed the match, and I was suddenly a wild woman clawing and holding him as close as possible. I was consumed and restless as he pulled the strings like he always had. Being under his control was a mind-bending excitement that had my heart palpitating. Yes, it could kill me, but what a way to go.

A little moan escaped me before his hand covered my mouth and he picked me up. My legs wrapped around his waist, and he carried me into the bathroom before the door shut, the little lock clicked, and he set me on the vanity.

His hands pushed my hair back and a mischievous smirk appeared. His lips hovered closer before his mouth met mine. His fingers were in my hair as my arms wrapped around his waist. His mouth and the reaction of his touch rushed through me pushing heat to every vein in my body.

Lust was humming through me as I pulled him closer. I gasp when he bit my lower lip playfully before stepping away, turning on the shower, and then back to me. I scooted off the vanity and dropped to my knees in front of him. His eyes were dark when he looked down as I unbuttoned his jeans before he fisted my hair while I took a little control of my own.

I was pulled up by my biceps and led into the large walk-in shower. Before I could turn back around, he was all over me as steam rose and hot water showered over us.

My hands glided over his slippery skin, and it was somehow taking it to an even higher high. He kissed and teased me while I pressed into him. He grabbed my wrists and held them above my head while his other hand traveled leaving me whimpering.

"Can you stay quiet?" His deep voice speaks low in my ear.

"Yes, I promise."

Stars explode in front of my eyes as he nudged forward while holding onto my bottom. His breathing quickened and it was an electric strike as I tried to catch my breath. My skin was crackling while his head nuzzled my neck. "I'm lost in you."

The ability to speak the English language had vanished. I forgot where I was. Everything was just a fuzzy dream.

His body was made for mine and through the silence we both knew exactly what the other needed. I clung to his shoulders as he whispered my name again and again while hot water poured down on us.

He turned off the shower and as I stood on the rug, he used a towel and dried every inch of me.

Back in my bedroom I grabbed my pajamas from the floor when he caught my wrist and pulled me into bed with him. He lay on his side, and I curled into his warm chest as he wrapped those arms around me. I listened to his soft breathing as I had so many times before.

This was perfect. Was it because we were in a beautiful vacation home in the Christmasy mountains of Colorado? Because we hadn't discussed anything about our current lives? Because he wanted a few days of action and then would be wheels up on a plane?

He wasn't in a relationship in Brazil. He didn't do relationships. I would've been certain someone as perfect as Levi would've been scooped up by now. Probably multiple times. So the single Levi was in my bed and every part of me today. This was okay.

Then I dozed off and slept like a baby.

But that didn't happen. First of all, my freaking brain wouldn't shut off. I rolled over and faced the sleeping man beside me. The moonlight shined in on his thick, messy hair and those amazing lips. I scotched closer so we were nearly chest to chest and eventually fell asleep.

I woke up feeling on top of the world. Maybe that's because I spent some time on top of Levi at two in the morning. Either way I crawled out of bed and into a hot bubble bath in the soaker tub. I touched my lips still a little swollen from my midnight make out maneuvers and couldn't remove my dorky smile.

My mind was running endless laps around Levi.

I hopped out of the tub, into my Agolde jeans that make my bum look nice, white American Eagle tee topped off with my fuzzy black cardigan and candy cane earrings. Yes, the holiday spirit was alive and well.

I entered the bedroom to find Levi hopping into his Levis, which I found to be hilarious, before he pulled me into him. "I've got to get out of here." He laced his fingers through mine and spoke quietly. "Let's get some ointment on your stitches, okay?"

THIRTY-SIX
LEVI
AT IT AGAIN

I cleverly fought every arch of that damn roof and made it to my window without breaking my neck; would not recommend.

I'd left my sliding window opened a crack and locked the door just like I had as a teen when I went to her. I'd made a lot of bad decisions back then, but she was the one right turn I'd taken.

I took a hot shower with the only thing wrapping around my brain was my shower last night. I chalked up a "W" in the closure column; she'd extended it. It wasn't just me feeling all this shit I didn't know what to do with. Edit; I knew exactly what to do with it; get Allie back.

I turned the corner to see Lexi sporting jeans and a black sweater with a cheeta print Christmas tree sitting at the table with Royce.

Oh shit, ran through me as we were alone. All four eyes shot to me with a look of hate with a dusting of disgust.

"Morning."

Lexi let out a huff. "Not anymore."

I hopped behind the stove figuring they couldn't totally hate me if they realized my cooking was kind of the bomb. Right? When I lived with Aunt Nora, she had an addiction—the cooking channel. And through it all I ended up with some sick culinary skills.

I pulled a pan from under the stove. "Eggs Benedict with bacon?"

Royce lifted a brow in inquiry. Maybe a point in the *don't kill Levi* column?

"We'd all eat anyway. Just pretend I'm not the chef."

Lexi rolled her eyes and grabbed her phone just as Kristina strolled in.

She quickly read the room and walked to the stove. "Levi, are you the chef this morning?"

"Yes, ma'am."

I grabbed the eggs as she sat at the table. "Morning." She patted Lexi's hand. "I slept like a baby for the first time in weeks."

Lexi winked. "That's what The Wienerlicious and drinks can accomplish."

Kristina pointed to me. "We are in for a treat this morning. Levi gives off the vibe of being a great cook." She looked over her shoulder. "Levi, what do you do for a career?"

I grabbed a spatula. "Construction."

She scooted her chair so she could see me. "So you build houses or what?"

"I've built houses and commercial projects. Worked on job sites all over the place. I've moved around a lot."

Lexi's eyebrows drew together. "So, you're a drifter? Going from place to place wherever you can get a gig?"

Evan walked in. "Morning everyone." He sat at the table.

"Am I a drifter?" I tossed bacon into a pan. "Maybe, I guess in the big picture of things I am."

Lexi shook her head and spoke quietly. "I called that a long time ago."

Evan sat back in his chair. "Levi? A drifter?"

Kristina nodded. "Well, it's nice to go from place to place. A big career isn't important if you're happy, uh, seeing lots of places. Everybody should live their dream."

Lexi nudged Royce with her elbow. "Yeah, seeing places is cool. As long as you have enough to get a hot meal it's all good."

Evan leaned forward. "Levi?"

Royce took a drink from his coffee cup. "Yeah."

He looked at me and laughed. "A drifter? Is that what you call a guy who started a construction company in Kansas City, then expanded to Brazil? Contracts in place for the next two years? The guy never sleeps."

An unexpected satisfaction hit me as Lexi's smile fell.

"Construction company?" Her tone dripped doubt.

Evan nodded. "Oh yeah."

Lexi crossed her arms over her chest clearly not happy I wasn't a thug. "Huh."

Royce shifted in his chair. "Glad he pulled it together before ending up in prison somewhere. That would've been my bet."

"People grow up." Evan scooted his chair in. "He figured it out."

Did you just see that? Had a plan happened on its own to help me maybe shift the needle when it comes to Lexi and Royce? *Thanks, cuz.*

As I flipped bacon Rachel entered and took seat at the table.

My eyes kept going to the door awaiting the most beautiful woman in the world to enter with those baby blues, perfect ass, and amazing breasts. The one that had twisted me so tight I didn't know how to deal.

THIRTY-SEVEN
ALLIE

SIGH

I floated down the stairs attempting to remove the cheesy Levi smile from my lips but was failing. I needed to pull my crap together so nobody, AKA Lexi and Rach, figured out the hot one had kept me warm last night.

I entered to find Levi at the stove wearing jeans and even through his Minnesota Wild hoodie, I could see those muscles.

"Morning."

"Good morning."

I sat next to Kristina, and she leaned over. "I drank so much vodka last night I woke up with a Russian accent."

"Exactly what you needed."

Her eyes went wide. "Maybe I need a Russian?"

Lexi flashed her a whopper of a grin. "Maybe? It's a beautiful day for a Russian."

Rachel raised her coffee mug. "It's a beautiful fucking day to start over and be a kind, badass, get-shit-done, happy little caffeinated mother truckers. Here's to you, Kristina."

After stuffing ourselves with breakfast cooked by a man who resembles a Greek God, I helped clean up. But the way

Levi looked at me made me realize I needed a reason to cancel this day and return to my bedroom. *Levi, do me a favor and get in my bed and cuddle with me all day.*

Rachel stood. "I picked up some of that delectable hot chocolate we had in town last night, and I insist y'all join me by the Christmas tree." Her smile disappeared when she looked over at Levi. "Don't feel obligated."

Levi gave her a smile. "I wouldn't miss it. Hot chocolate is the bomb."

Her eyes rolled as she mumbled. "I wish I had a bomb."

THIRTY-EIGHT
LEVI

AN UNEXPECTED TURN

It couldn't have felt more Christmasy when we all sat around the tall Christmas tree that made the room glow even in the daylight.

As Lexi handed me a cup of hot coco, the whole poisoning thing ran through my mind. Odds are they'd use a sneakier method of offing me anyway.

I sat in the furthest chair away from them and after a little glaring, Lexi seemed to almost forget I was there as she told crazy college stories. The whole time Allie and I were sneaking looks, and I realized I wanted this time in Colorado to never end.

In her presence the air was thick with the scent of desire. To watch her move reminded me that her body was a temple of temptation, and she instilled a hunger that could only be satisfied by her hands on me.

I needed to make it happen.

The laughter got pretty loud when Rachel switched the music from Jingle Bells to Beastie Boys and the ladies started dancing around.

Evan jumped up and joined in while the familiar gratitude for a pretty cool cousin was there. Since my mom ran off when I was too young to really remember her, being in a house with Evan and a woman like my aunt who wanted to cook and make sure I had enough blankets at night, was what I needed when trying to pull my shit together after Allie.

I'd grown up with a man who drank a lot. I mean a lot. He tried but was not a natural parent. By the time I was seven I was taking care of myself for the most part. If I had a Christmas program at school or a blizzard was coming, I'd ask a friend to ask their parents if they could pick me up. If there was something I needed, I'd have to figure out how to get it on my own.

It always sucked with money being tight, but when you've been on the bottom and come from nothing, it instills almost a fear of being there again as an adult. Likely responsible for my work ethic which has helped me excel in business.

Lexi pulled Allie to her feet when Taylor's *Bad Blood* filled the room. *but* when *Crank That* hit the air, Evan and I were unleashed, and it was a full-blown dance party in the living room. While Royce sat on the couch with his eyes shooting daggers in my direction, the girls who hated me didn't seem to mind my presence. It was nice.

Evan handed me the guitar that sat in the corner. In high school Allie dabbled in everything and loved a good throwback. When she entered her *Violent Femes era,* I couldn't help being sucked into that shit.

When I started *Blister in the Sun* the girls scream/sang while dancing around the room. From Rachel using the coffee table as a stage, likely frowned upon by the Vrbo owner, to Evan accidentally swinging Kristina into the Christmas tree, it was the best morning I could recall in forever, and exactly what the doctor ordered.

What the doctor had *not* ordered was a knock at the door.

Kristina danced her way past me while I made sticky eyes at Allie. I needed to be alone with her like she needed fucking Dove chocolate. I had to make this happen ASAP.

There was a commotion at the door, and I looked over to see a guy, my age, dark blond hair and a little shorter than me.

Kristina gasped. "Oh, good Lord! Clint!"

I set the guitar down and stood.

The new dude chuckled as Rachel sprung to the front door. "Clint! Oh my gosh!"

Clearly everybody loved this guy. Somebody's relative?

Evan walked over. "Who's that?"

He gave me a look. "Oh buddy, you're not going like this."

It was then I glanced in Allie's direction to find her frozen.

"What's going on?" I asked Evan who seemed to be a fountain of knowledge.

Royce, who now stood by the sofa on my left, nodded. He walked toward the door where he and new guy had a weird man hug. Evan stepped closer to me. "Clint and Allie had a thing."

My throat was suddenly as dry as the fucking Sahara. "Say again?" Please, for the love of anything good in the world, let me have misunderstood. "Had?"

Evan spoke in a hushed tone. "They were together about a year when she got the dream job on the East Coast."

"So she dumped him?" Please.

"Not really, I guess they just put it all on hold because he was up for junior partner in his law firm and couldn't really leave."

My eyes landed on Royce who was all smiles as he spoke to Clint. Had he called the old boyfriend because I was there? WTF? I realized it was one of those days that might end with a torched body in the fire pit out back.

My heart was grinding like metal on metal. "So it's basically over, is that what you're saying?"

"That's *not* what I'm saying. They put it on hold."

There was a weird twitch at the base of my neck. "We all know that's always bullshit. You're either together or not. So they broke up. That's what you're saying."

Evan shoved me. "I did not say that. Are you hearing me at all?"

"I have selective hearing. And you're not selected."

Allie stood to her feet, and I'd know her forced smiled anywhere.

"How long ago?"

"What?"

"How long since she and dickhead put it on hold?"

"Maybe six months."

My windpipe pinched shut as he made his way over to Allie. His stupid toothpastey smile made me want to barf. I didn't want to hurt him, just to be clear. I wanted to kill him.

Evan leaned in closer. "I'm just saying you need to relax."

"Fun fact, I don't care."

Before she could do anything, Clint pulled her in for a hug as Lexi was literally beaming and clapping her hands.

WTF was happening?

I don't know what expression I wore, but Evan elbowed me. "Take a breath, man. Relax."

Relax? Clearly Evan wasn't as smart as I'd given him credit for.

As I watched cockbag Clint hug her *too* long and *too* tight, rage was bubbling just below the surface. Me and bubbling rage don't mix well. While I was an adult and used common sense almost every day, something about this situation was waking the "old me". The one who went to great lengths to get what he wanted. The one who'd burn shit down to get what he wanted. What he needed.

I needed her.

I took a deep breath reminding myself they weren't really together anymore. And he wasn't worth the jail time.

Clint pulled back. "You look beautiful."

She smiled up at him, and I suddenly couldn't tell if it was a *happy you're here* smile, or *how the fuck to I get away from this dude* smile. Either way, I hated her smiling at any man but me.

"Thanks." Her eyes darted around the room but not in my direction. "I am, uh, a little shocked to see you."

While it wasn't funny, the room burst into laughter, and I wondered how Clint wasn't going to die today. WTH?

Buzzkill Clint chuckled. "I wanted to surprise you."

Suddenly Rachel nodded like a stupid bobble head. "I think you accomplished that goal there, Clint." She turned to Royce. "That guy, man, he is something."

Royce shot me a cocky look. Could he see the fuck you in my eyes? I hoped so.

Asshat nodded as he looked at Allie. "You'd shown me this Colorado house and talked about the wedding last summer. After some soul searching, I had to be here." He looked at Lexi. "I hope it's alright with everybody."

A giggle came from Rachel. "Clint, seeing you here has made my little old heart completely full." She shot me a glare. "You are welcome anywhere."

Shithead's slimy stare returned to Allie. "I can't keep away from this girl."

WTF?

Her eyes went wide as his words wrapped around my neck like razor wire.

Dickweed took a step in my direction and extended his hand. I'm so lucky people can't hear what I'm thinking.

"I'm Clint."

"Levi."

While I assumed there would be some reaction as I'm sure my story would've come up at some point, he just nodded like a jackass. NO reaction at all. "Nice to meet you."

She'd never mentioned me? Not once?

Whatever, I just needed to focus on staying calm. Maybe this wasn't as big of a deal as it seemed?

Lexi grabbed Kristina by the arm. "That's it! I know Clint is a cheesecake lovin' bastard so I'm whippin' up something in your honor! Or a chocolate cream pie, Allie loves her chocolate."

I hoped it was a pie.

Fuck off pie:

1 cup of no one cares

A pinch of kiss my ass

Throw in some fuck you's

A dash of blow me

Stir and shove it up Clint's ass.

You can only say "WTF" so many times in an hour before you

decide to start day drinking. I had a sudden desperation to get up close and personal with Jack Daniels.

Lexi and Rachel disappeared into the kitchen to create some magical culinary treat for fucknugget, while Evan and Royce spoke to him.

Kristina pointed to Evan. "Maybe you could show Clint to an empty room." She winked at Allie. "And not too far from you know who."

My ears burned off while Allie's face flushed. He could *not* be close to her. Couldn't happen.

Before I knew what I was doing, my feet sprung toward the front door. I grabbed Clint's suitcase from the floor and headed toward the stairs. "Follow me."

I looked over my shoulder as Royce glared at me. No way in hell was his room going to be next to hers. I'd burn the fucking house down before that'd happen.

Evan followed us. "So Clint, how's everything going?"

My head nearly exploded when I looked back to see him grab Allie's hand. "Not as good as it should be. I find my new life is missing something."

While I was certain my head would explode at any second, my only hope was that after the explosion, a sharp piece of my skull would pierce through dickhead's heart like a sword ending him.

At the top of the stairs, I turned left; he was going to be in the room next to mine, about as far away from Allie as possible. That'll show the bastard who shows up unexpectedly trying to get her back.

Well, technically that was me too, but whatever.

At the very end of the hall, I opened a door and there was a room nearly identical to mine except for the bedding which was baby blue and white. Seemed appropriate for the pussy behind me.

"Here we are." I walked over and tossed his suitcase on the bed and pointed to the window as if I were a tour guide. "And look at this view. Just splendid."

Evan popped a brow.

"Thanks, Levi."

As I looked at the smiling jerkoff in front of me who acted like he didn't know who I was, it hit my gut wrong. Allie dated this guy and never mentioned us? Like ever?

We all know when we start dating someone the questions are asked about the past. And she left me *entirely* out of the discussion? The husband she had for a hot minute? Sure things crashed and burned in the most horrific way possible, but not even in the discussion?

Allie stood in the doorway, and he took her by the hand, *again*, and nodded as Royce and Evan walked toward the door. He wanted everyone to leave them, and it was happening as panic swelled. "Uh, Evan, weren't we all going to do some paintball gunning out back?"

Evan stopped and turned back to me. "We were?"

I enthusiastically nodded. "Yeah." I motioned to Evan. "Look at this guy." I slapped him on the back. "He forgets everything." My laughter was solo. "So, uh, why don't we all meet downstairs in five minutes?"

Cockalorium Clint looked at Allie and back to me. "I think I'll pass. Paintballs hurt."

I took a quick step toward him. "Nah. I saw they had jelly balls so no pain. Rach and Lexi even said they'd play."

They had not, but I was 110% certain they'd be up for anything involving guns and me.

"I don't—"

I couldn't stop my legs from stepping closer. "Come on, you're not a pussy, are ya?"

He looked bewildered. "Well, no—"

I slapped him on the back with a little more force than I'd intended. "Alrighty then, see you two downstairs in five."

My eyes slid over to Allie who quickly looked away. No sooner had my feet hit the hall than the door shut behind us. What in the living hell had transpired in the past twenty minutes? This was some raggedy bullshit.

While a part of me wanted to be as far away from whatever was happening behind the door as possible, my legs weighed five thousand pounds as I grabbed Evan's arm.

"She can't be in there with him."

Royce's eyes rolled. "Says the guy who snuck into her room every night back in the day."

I ignored the true statement as Royce walked away.

"You have to relax, buddy." Evan shrugged. "The Vrbo guy said there were coveralls in the garage somewhere for paint-balling. Come on."

Finally, something that regulated my breathing; my gun pointing at Clint.

C lint hung up his jeans on a hanger in the closet and then his navy suit. He had enough clothes to stay through the entire Colorado thing.

I didn't think I liked that. Or did I? My life was currently going at 13 WTF's a minute.

"I still can't believe you're here." I sat on the edge of the bed.

He zipped up his empty suitcase and set it on the floor of the closet and turned to me.

"Royce and I touch base now and then, and when I found out you were here, I wanted to be also."

"But when I left, we kind of let everything go." Yes, I took the new job and left because I have trouble when things get to a certain level. If you'd like to see me do a beautiful swan dive out the window, say *Allie, should we move in together?*

She's outta here!

He walked over and pulled me to my feet. "It took letting it go for me to see how much I need you."

I stood silently looking up at his handsome face awaiting

feelings of some sort to follow his utterly romantic statement. Helllooo? Swooing...are you in the house? Take-my-breath-away...anywhere?

Crickets.

Clint grinned and a panic shot through my veins as he was about to kiss me. The last lips on mine were Levi's. I quickly jumped back. "Oh my gosh, ten minutes have already passed? They're waiting for us to paintball."

His hands grabbed my waist. "Maybe we skip the paintball and stay here."

"Oh, uh, well, it's kind of planned. Yeah, before you arrived." I shuffled to the door and pulled it open. "You know, magical friend time."

"Let's fuckin' go!" Lexi shouted as "magical time" wasn't really her thing. Yeah, some girls may be a delicate flower, but she's like the claw end of a hammer.

We'd all jumped into our white coveralls which were big enough to fit right over our coats and approached the forest beside the house while I kept my eyes peeled for the crazed wild turkeys that were gobbling in my mind.

Evan yelled. "Okay, here's how this is going to go!" We all gathered around. "I loaded everybody's guns with jelly balls so it won't hurt. Every man and woman for themselves. You can get hit five times before you're dead."

Levi, who stood across from Clint and I, narrowed his eyes at Clint. "Dead."

Clint looked around as if to see if anyone else heard the

comment as I scolded Levi with my eyes, but the glimmer in his sent a little tingle cartwheeling down my spine.

Evan waved his gun in the air. "Okay, when I say go, everybody gets five minutes to hide, and when you hear me yell, it's on!"

Rachel grabbed his arm. "Damn straight it's on, you sexy son of a bitch!"

Kristina giggled as she scurried into the forest. "I'm going to shoot all y'all up, watch out mother hubbards!"

Clint gave me the thumbs up sign. "You know how to work the gun okay?"

While Levi was out of sight, his deep voice bounced around us. "Bet your ass she can work a fuckin' gun!"

Clint's eyes locked on me as I shrugged. "I think I'm good."

I jogged through the crunchy white beneath my feet into the forest where the snow-covered trees glimmered in the sunlight. I kept going until I heard no other running close by. I hid behind a huge oak tree and looked at my gun.

"Hey."

I spun around to see Levi behind me.

"You scared me, I didn't hear you coming."

His brow popped up. "You never will. You remember hunting with me?"

"You track like no other."

He took a step closer. "While I hunted because my old man wasn't one to ensure we had food in the house, I knew I could get what I needed."

I nodded as he stepped beside me, then paused and leaned against a tree.

"What do you need, Allie?"

226

My temperature shot up five degrees and he leaned in closer, so close his lips were just inches from mine and his breath was on my face. I opened my mouth but only an odd little squeak came out. Yup, that was all I had.

"I can almost feel your heart beating right now." I stood frozen as his lips brushed against mine. "What I can do to you with a few words, nobody else can."

With Clint here and Levi saying words that were burning my skin, I was attempting to figure out my mood about any of this. Happy? Sad? Ready to bolt? Yeah, my moods don't just swing anymore, they appeared to bounce, recoil, pivot, fluctuate, oscillate, and occasionally pirouette.

I was almost in a trance as he continued to speak in a husky whisper. "I don't give a fuck who's in that house. I'm coming to you tonight."

His gun dropped to the ground before his hands went to the base of my neck. He tilted my head up before his lips were so tenderly on mine the forest melted away leaving me soupy.

Could he be thinking of more, like after Colorado? Sure, we'd agreed to closure and that was where it ended, but was there a possibility of more?

He pulled away and rested his forehead against mine for a moment when Evan's voice rang out in the distance. "Everybody, go!"

He picked up his gun, gave me a nod, and walked off as I stood with *WTH* running through my mind like the two-hundred-meter dash at the Olympics.

As I leaned my head against the tree in front of me with a swirly brain, I didn't think I could take the past out of the past. That was where it was supposed to be forever. The untamed and wild Levi and Allie love story had to stay buried; it couldn't be anything but in the review mirror.

Right?

I mean I had loved Clint. Maybe I still did a little? He was a steady guy. He had his future all figured out and now he realized he wanted me in it. If I had to trust someone again, he was a fairly safe bet, right?

Well, that is true for the most part. Clint wanted to move things forward, but when things move forward, it means throwing all your trust into the hands of one person. And that's like bungy jumping off a bridge with only that little cord keeping you from being squished and dead. Logically you know there's an overwhelming good chance it will keep you safe, but what if it doesn't? It would be impossible to live through that shit.

I peeked around the enormous tree in front of me and saw nobody. I moved to the right as Rachel tore through the trees after Kristina. I put my gun up and got Rach in the back and a second later hit Kristina in the arm.

This was a little more fun that I'd anticipated. I jogged through some evergreen trees before I was pelleted twice in the back. I whipped around to see Royce take off, but Lexi was in my sights. I aimed, fired, and got her right in the ass while she let out a scream. Once she saw me, she waved her weapon in the air.

"I'm gonna kill you, Allison!"

"Clearly not with a gun!" I had to admit she was a scary bitch at times. You couldn't let her cute look fool you. She may appear like a lady, but she could fight, pull hair, and break bones. She's like the total package that got fucked up through shipping and handling.

I trudged through the snow and hid behind some thick shrubs as quiet as a frickin mouse. I held my breath until she passed.

"Pppst."

I looked up to see a rugged smile looking down at me while he extended his hand. I bit my lip to conceal my smile as hunting memories filtered in.

In high school I'd gone deer hunting with him multiple times. While "normal" deer hunters had tree stands, Levi lacked the funds for that. So in the summer he got some plywood from the Surburban True Value Hardware Store on Robert Street's dumpster, and we dragged it into the woods where he screwed it to a solid branch and that was where we'd sit in silence for hours. I'd read a book or just stare at him as his eyes awaited any movement in front of us.

Did I mention we never once left the forest without a deer? The boy had mad skills.

I climbed up a few branches when he reached down, got my hand, and pulled me up beside him. While there was no plywood for our asses today, the branch was big enough to be fairly comfortable. From our high perch we had a wonderful view, and I already saw Evan and Kristina sneaking around.

Levi pointed, and I took two shots and got them both as he chuckled.

From our location above, we pulled a full-fledged jelly ball attack on our housemates for ten minutes while colorful language and frustration floated through the forest like fairy dust.

"Allie! Where are you?"

Lexi's voice bounced around me.

"I better go." I dropped my gun to the ground and started down the tree.

Once on solid ground I picked up my weapon to hear pops from above as he pelleted my bottom.

"Levi!" I whisper yelled.

He shrugged. "You know I can't resist.

I whisper yelled, "You're a handful, and I don't like it!"

"I know I'm a handful. That's why you have two hands."

I shot him a dramatic eyeroll before I took a few steps.

"Allie Motherfuckin' Langley."

I spun back toward him, and he shot me in the left boob leaving a purple streak.

I whispered yelled. "You stop that Levi Motherfuckin' Dawson!"

With that he shot my other boob. While annoyed, it did even out my look.

Twenty brisk minutes later Royce's voice floated through the forest. "Is this thing over? Is everybody dead?"

One by one we all appeared with our white coveralls now rainbowed up a bit. A few moments later my heart skipped a beat as I realized Levi and Clint had not appeared yet. I knew Levi could easily stage a horrific accident, but of course he wouldn't.

A minute ticked by and Clint came into sight as gasps from all cut through the air. His white coveralls were not white. *At all.* Every inch of him had been assaulted with jelly balls, including his blond hair that was now purple and green.

Rachel laughed. "Holy shit, Clint."

He flashed a tense smile as he rolled over to me. That's when Levi walked out of the forest in his white coveralls. Completely white. Not hit once. He shot me a wink as the rest of the group was silent. My eyes met Lexi's and there was still pissiness there, but underneath I could see she was impressed; even she couldn't resist a badass who could shoot shit up.

Once back at the house and after Clint took a quick shower, Kristina clapped her hands. "Alrighty y'all, I thought since we're in a ski town, maybe we should hit the bunny hills this afternoon?" She put her arm around Clint. "I haven't been on a pair of skis ever, but when in Rome, right?"

I stood at the kitchen counter and Clint made his way over to me as everyone was grabbing snacks.

"Hey." He nudged my shoulder with his. "Maybe we hang back here while they hit the slopes? Have some time to talk?"

I went to the fridge and grabbed a bottle of water, opened it, and held my finger out as I took a long drink while trying to gather my thoughts. He came here, I should stay and talk.

"You're really thirsty."

I put my bottle down. "Yes, this air is, uh, dry."

He took my hand in is. "So, we're staying?"

"Well, I really think we should go with everybody. I mean, it's a ski town, we should probably ski for a bit. Right?" My armpits were sticky.

FORTY
LEVI
HERE WE GO

I hadn't realized "over the moon" was an actual thing until it registered with me that there would be no alone time for douche nozzle and Allie if we were at the slopes. Yes, I heard the news from the walk-in kitchen pantry where I hid eavesdropping like an obsessed lunatic.

A new low for me.

We all piled into the van and a few in Evan's car.

Once we all hopped out of what I was certain looked like a frickin' clown car in front of the ski lodge, we made our way to the rental area where everyone rented proper ski attire. In a few minutes I'd jumped into ski pants, jacket, and had my skis in hand.

The women appeared one by one. Lexi and Kristina wore matching hot pink ski outfits, Rachel in black, and then it happened. Allie strolled out of the dressing area looking like a fucking snow angel. Her ski outfit was bright white and fitted, while her auburn curls bounced as she walked.

I shoved my hands in my pockets as she passed, afraid I'd grab her before my frontal lobe could kick in.

She had no idea how beautiful she was. She joined Rachel as they were getting their skis.

It was when jerkoff Clint approached and his arm went over her shoulder, that I realized I needed to knock off Clint even more than I needed H2O in my lungs. A collision with a boulder? Could he hit a cliff instead of a slope?

Evan appeared by my side. "Dude, unclench those teeth or you'll need a dentist."

I turned away and took a controlled breath. "If he doesn't remove his arm, I deliver cockolorum Clint to the dentist right through the fuckin' window."

"Okay, we need to get a grip. Come on, let's hit the slopes."

I sounded like a toddler. "I'm not going without her."

Evan leaned in. "Pull your shit together. If you want to see if there's anything with her, just play it cool until after the wedding. He's here for now and Lexi and Rach will castrate you if they find out you're trying to get back with her. Don't rock the boat."

"You know what they say. You *have* to rock the damn boat sometimes. If someone falls out obviously, they weren't meant to be in the boat in the first place."

"Nobody says that."

I looked over my shoulder to see dumbass's arm still around her. "Yeah, they do. And you know what? If you blink you sink."

"What does that even mean?"

"Think about it."

He shook his head. "This conversation is hurting my brain."

"So you're saying you want to hurt Clint, too?"

"I'm not saying that. Don't go off the fucking rails, Levi. Keep your head on straight."

"Well Cuz, I'm beginning to realize that banging my head against a brick wall is surely imminent on a day like today."

Everyone headed out of the resort toward the ski lift where Christmas was on full display. There was Santa and an elf skiing by, and a large Christmas tree decorated with shiny bulbs that reflected the sunlight surrounded by chairs and outdoor heaters. Huge red and white candy canes were sticking out of the snow and a hot chocolate stand with a small line of people was to my right. Kids and families were everywhere.

I looked over to see Clint say something to Allie and she smiled.

It's beginning to look a lot like fuck this. Come on, sing along.

FORTY-ONE
ALLIE
WONKY

Kristina tapped the bag hanging from her shoulder. "I got us all some snacks to have before we ski so our tummies are full. There's an empty table by the tree." She grabbed Allie and Lexi by the hands. "You girls have made the dark cloud of my divorce disappear for a few days. Being here with you all has been exactly what I needed. I love you guys so much."

Rachel smiled. "Friendship is being there when someone's feeling low and not being afraid to kick them if you have to."

Lexi burst out laughing. "We've been friends so long I can't remember which one of us is the bad influence."

I kissed Kristina's cheek. "You know what they say. Friendship is like peeing on yourself. Everyone can see it, but only you get the warm feeling that it brings." I pulled back. "Speaking of that, I'm going to hit the ladies room real quick." I took a step away and Clint caught my hand and kissed my cheek as Lexi giggled. My eyes did a spin around our group to see Levi absent; probably good.

I hung out in the bathroom a little longer than normal

trying to figure out what I was doing. Clint was there and I had no clue what to make of it. I wanted to want him there. Or not? Shit, I was as confused as a baby in a topless bar.

I washed my hands and no sooner had I taken a step out of the bathroom that my arm was being pulled by handsome Levi.

"Come on."

"I should get back to everybody."

His eyes rolled before he pulled me around the corner, and I was in his arms. I looked up at his devilish grin before he gently kissed me. "I knew you needed a little Levi time."

While he was correct, everything was wonky. Sure, I stood, and we kissed for many more minutes, but still, Clint's arrival made my mind circle around the past and future. *What am I doing?*

Seriously, what am I doing? Yeah, I'm talking to you.

"So Allie—"

As much as I didn't think I should, I pulled him closer. "I'm not talking about anything. Closure is—"

"It was the *whole* time in Colorado, remember?" He rubbed his nose against mine. "I *need* you in Colorado."

"Levi—"

"You guys ended things like six months ago. If he's here to try to get you back, he hasn't yet. So you kissing me isn't wrong."

"So, you think it's right to be kissing you now even if I decide Clint and I should have a second chance?"

His jaw clenched and he looked away. "We're just a weekend thing, I get it. We don't want more, but I can tell he's not your type."

"You don't know him."

"He's vanilla. You need a hot fudge Sunday with M&Ms, crushed Oreos, chocolate shavings, and a shot of caramel. You'll die of boredom with that one."

I just stared into the face of the self-proclaimed bachelor for life. We would never be and that was how the universe planned it. It was simply a weekend fling before I moved on with my real life.

As our lips melted together in the back hallway of the ski resort, I reminded myself that Clint is a good kisser, too. I mean, like a solidly good kisser. Probably four out of five stars. I'd definitely recommend him to a friend.

I pulled back and looked at my phone. "Shit, we've been here for twenty minutes?"

"Time flies when you're having Levi." He lifted a brow.

"Did you really just say that? I'm going out to find everyone."

He yanked me to him. "Maybe we should go and do some *we shouldn't be doing this* kind of things."

I pushed him back. "I'm going."

He walked after me, and I turned back. "You know Levi, you don't have to ski. I mean, if you haven't—"

"Awww, you're worried about me?" His eyes twinkled.

"No, I just, well, if you haven't skied maybe today isn't the best day to learn."

His arms folded over his chest. "Are you concerned about me making an ass of myself?"

"It's not that. It's just that everybody else has, and I know sometimes you—"

"Get frustrated and beat the shit out of douchebags?"

"Kinda."

"First of all, I'm a grown ass man now. I only beat up

237

mother fuckers who deserve it." He pointed to his face. "Secondly, if you're worried about bodily harm to this handsome mug, don't. I spent a month in Austria last winter and got learning to ski off my bucket list."

What the what? "You spent a month in *Austria*?"

He nodded.

"Wow, that's cool. I suppose construction workers get time off in the winter?"

"You think a laid off construction worker could afford to vacation for a month?"

"I don't know. If you did, I guess so."

"There's always work available in construction. All seasons. I went to Austria to hire construction employees and stayed in a chateau for a month to learn how to ski. Got that bad boy off my to-do list."

Is dumfounded still a word? "Oh. So you were hiring for the company you work for?"

"My company."

"Your company?"

"Yup. I worked for others and didn't like some of the ways people ran their businesses. Got sick of the shit so started my own."

"You started your own?"

"Yes. It's been a wild ride, and I learned as I went along, but it's good."

"Huh. I did not see this coming."

We walked outside and saw nobody from our crew. No one at the table, nobody in line for hot coco, nada.

His phone screamed out and he grabbed it from his pocket as I turned my head, but not my eyes. He silenced it, but not before my supersonic vision caught a glimpse of his screen and the blond woman who popped up and disappeared quickly before he shoved it back in his pocket. How much Brazilian action did this man get? It appeared I was just one of them now. Yup, a notch in his belt, but I agreed to this so I needed to suck it up and let it go.

Levi pointed. "Maybe they hit the slopes."

"I'll call Rachel."

"Let's just go up. We'll likely find them there."

It'd been a few years since I'd hopped into some skis. Emily, Lexi, Rachel, Kristina, and I had gone on a ski trip in college to Breckenridge, and I forgot the enthusiasm of knowing you're about to be carried two miles up by a rickety bench hanging from cables above. As we started our journey up, the skiers below me appeared at a leisurely pace as they reached the bottom, but as we went further up the mountain, I chuckled as skilled skiers whipped by others who were on their asses.

As our chair reached the top and became even with the surface of the mountain, we slid off and turned to the trail with none of our gang insight. "I wonder where they are."

He zipped up his coat. "Let's go and maybe we'll find them along the way."

We approached the trail we were planning to take, and I'd be lying if said a few butterflies didn't take flight in my tummy.

"Langley, you okay?"

I nodded. "Yeah, it's just been a hot minute since I've zipped down a mountain." I gulped as I looked at the hill in front of me. "Just give me a second."

"Are you procrastiskiing?" He nudged my arm with is. "Get it?"

"You're not funny, Dawson." I inhaled deeply. "You

remind me of my pinky toe. Sooner or later, I'm going to bang you on a table."

His laughter boomed. "Okay, replay that sentence and see why I'm a little aroused right now."

"Okay, you've done it. Due to personal reasons, aka you, I'm evil now."

We got our skis clicked in, and I pulled down my goggles. The sun had dipped behind some clouds, and the view was breathtaking. I unzipped my pocket and grabbed my phone to take a picture. I peeked at Levi as he pulled his goggles down while looking out at the horizon. Right, wrong or otherwise, I quickly snapped a photo that I imagined I would stare at for decades to come. Yes, I'm such a loser if there was a contest for losers, I would get second place for sure.

As we started down the slope, gliding on the powder, my blood and muscles came alive with the thrill of adrenaline making me nearly forget everything else.

We zig-zagged down the first slope and after I fell on my ass three times, I finally found my groove. Levi kept at my speed and every time I snuck a look his smile smacked me.

Maybe it was the crisp day with zero wind, whitest of white beneath my skis, or the man sliding down the hill beside me, but it felt *magical*. As we were getting close to the ski lodge, I was wondering if there was anything that could ruin this perfect moment in time as we slid down the mountain.

The universe answered that question a mili-second later when I passed Lexi who was *not* skiing. Nope, the lady was facing a tree just off the slope and as I slowed, she appeared to be *taking* to the tree with one ski on the ground beside her, and the other hanging from a branch above.

"Lexi!" I got out of my skis and walked over. "What happened?"

She let out a huff as she spoke to the tree. *Spoke to the tree.* "I think I killed him."

"Who was killed?"

Levi joined us. "Shit. She killed someone?" His head shook. "I can't say I didn't see this coming."

I inhaled. "I just always assumed it'd be you."

FORTY-TWO
LEVI

GREMLINS?

Allie grabbed her arm. "What did you do?"

Lexi's head whipped to Allie. "Royce?"

"Uh, no, it's me. Allie."

Her eyes narrowed. "Well, sure as shit you're right." She pointed to the slopes. "Welcome to Disney World."

Allie's eyes shot to me. "Lexi, did you fall and hit your head when you were skiing?"

She roared with laughter. "How in the hell would I be skiing with my damn ski in the tree?"

"That was my next question. Why is your ski up there?"

She leaned in close. "Before I got to Disney World, there was a demon cowboy after me."

Levi stepped closer. "Langley, is she drunk?"

Lexi let out an annoyed huff. "I'm not drunk ya asshat!"

Allie touched my arm. "Lexi, please continue. About the cowboy?"

She nodded. "Sugar pie, it wasn't a cowboy. It was a *demon cowboy*. That fucker came up behind me out of nowhere. I was shakin' like a leaf as terror I've never known filled my veins."

Her eyes were bulging. "I had no choice but to kill him." She leaned over to me. "It's been a long time since I've seen a man take his last breath."

Was she confirming what I always suspected to be true?

Allie let out a long breath. "You killed a demon cowboy?"

She pointed to her ski. "I'm afraid so. He climbed the tree planning to jump on me, so I threw my ski up there, hit him square in the heart, and he died."

Allie threw her arm up. "What in the hell is happening?"

I couldn't resist and leaned in. "Lexi, what did you do with the body?"

"Well, asshat, I planned to burn it but just when I was fixin' to find some wood, a gremlin shot out of the fucking forest and drug his body away! Can you even believe that?"

"Wow."

"I know. That's when I knew I needed to get my tushy to Disney World." She pointed down the hill. "I was just about to look for that flyin' Dumbo ride I love so much. Ya know, to keep my head off the demon cowboy and all."

Allie's mouth dropped open as she looked at me. "What do I do?"

"Steer clear of gremlins, that's for damn sure."

"Come on, Lex. We're almost to the ski lodge, we can walk."

Lexi patted Allie on the head. "Don't you worry. I'll be cool as a cucumber. Nobody will ever guess I offed a demon cowboy today."

I grabbed everybody's skis, and we walked down the slope just next to the trees so no fellow skiers nailed us.

About twenty feet down, I looked over as Rachel skied past

us and Allie gasped. Yes, Rach gave us a wave as she zipped by wearing her ski pants and purple bra.

Allie screamed, which made Lexi laugh. "Rachel is skiing in a bra? What the hell is going on?"

We finally reached the bottom of the hill where the normal people were hanging out. Rachel was stepping out of her skis as onlookers gasped.

"Levi!" I looked at Allie who had shock written across her forehead.

"I got it." I left the skis on a table, pulled off my jacket, and jogged over to Rachel. "Let's get this coat on you."

She looked up at me while her hand went to my cheek. "But it's just so warm out. I don't think I need it."

"You do, trust me."

She patted my face. "You're still a hottie like you were back then. Don't tell Lexi I said so."

"Uh, thanks."

"But I still hate ya, just to be clear."

"Got it."

I grabbed her arm and led her to Allie who had Lexi seated on a chair next to the Christmas tree. Rach sat on Lexi's lap.

"Hello my beauty."

Allie clapped her hands. "Okay, what is going on? Did everybody do shots or what?"

Lexi shrugged her shoulders. "No. But I think *you* could use a shot." She kissed Lexi on the cheek. "Allison has a stick wedged up her ass, I think. She's a party pooper and didn't even let me ride the Dumbo ride."

Rachel waved her arm in the air. "Boo!"

Suddenly Evan shot out the ski lodge. "Thank God. Please tell me you both aren't stoned?"

I glanced at Allie. "Nope. But after the last ten minutes I sorta wish I was."

He was out of breath. "Turns out Kristina bought some—air quotes—fundraiser baked goods from some fraternity in the parking lot. By the time I figured out what was happening our crew had inhaled every last one and vanished."

Allie shook her head. "So they're all high?"

Evan laughed. "Sky high in Colorado." He pointed to the ski slope. "Clint disappeared up the mountain so not sure where the hell he ended up."

My heart did a cheerleader jump for the first time ever as the thought of clusternut Clint never returning. "I'm sure he's fine."

Allie held her arm up. "And Kristina?"

That's when Kristina's cackle shot through the air. I followed it and ended up in front of the hot chocolate stand and there she was. Behind the counter. I cautiously approached.

"Kristina?"

She looked up. "What can I get you, dear?"

I leaned down. "Uh, you don't work here."

"Well, I have an apron." She pointed. "So I'm pretty sure I do."

We finally had everyone together but Clint and Royce. While my idea was to just leave them, and like dogs, I was certain they'd find their way home, Evan and Allie did not agree. After a bit more discussion, our crew seemed to be coming down from whatever kind of high they were on.

There was a yell, and I looked up just in time to see Clint fall from a ski lift and into a pile of snow as a little bit of glee registered in my brain. *Bad Levi*. The good news was the fall was only about ten feet. The bad news was he was still alive. I just could *not* catch a break.

Evan tore over and helped Clint up. His hair was sticking out in all directions as he was pulled to his feet.

"Did you see that?" He let out a laugh. "I fell off the damn ski lift!"

Allie reached him, and I hated the concern in her eyes. "Are you okay?"

"I fell off the ski lift! Did you see me?" He put his arms around Allie and lifted her so she was level with his face, and I suddenly wished I had a level to beat him with. "Look at you."

My hand balled into a fist as he gave her a quick kiss, and I could hear Lexi clapping in the background. Evan put his hand on my shoulder. "Uh, we'd better get everybody back to the house."

Lexi yelled. "Where's Royce?"

As fuckity fucker Clint still had his hands on Allie, and I knew I needed to disappear. "I'll look for him."

I roamed through the enormous ski lodge that seemed to be throwing up Christmas. Every place my eyes landed there were wreaths, candy canes, and twinkling lights. I'm a full-blown Christmas lover, but it was too much.

He wasn't in the bar, but beer was, so I ordered one to assist with my search. I checked out the men's bathroom and gift shop but nada. I then roamed through the restaurant and didn't see him anywhere. As I was leaving, I tripped over feet sticking out from under a table covered in a red tablecloth. I sighed as I couldn't think of another visitor in the lodge who might be under a fucking table.

Dear Life,

When I said, "Can this day get more fucked up", it was a rhetorical question, not a challenge.

I peeked down to see a sleeping Royce. Or a dead Royce. *Please be dead, please be dead.*

I pushed his leg with my foot. "Royce, wake up." I pushed harder and he rolled onto his side appearing to want to continue his slumber.

Clinking silverware was in the distance as I assessed how to get this guy out of there. I flipped the tablecloth up, leaned down, and shook his shoulder. "Royce, we have to get you out of here."

His eyes popped opened, and he jumped at the sight of me. "Where am I?"

"Well, you're sleeping under the table in a fine dining establishment."

"Huh." He looked around. "Maybe I just wanna stay here for a while."

What in the hell was in those baked goods? Clearly our group was standing on my last freaking nerve. "Get up, we're leaving."

"Why?"

"Dude, I don't have the time or crayons to explain this to you. You're stupid, Royce."

He rubbed his eyes. "Don't call me stupid."

"Okay, let me put it another way. Wisdom has been chasing you but you're running too fucking fast to catch at the moment."

"I—"

"That's it, I'm billing you for this conversation. Get your ass out here."

I stood, grabbed him by the ankles while the table next to

us seemed fascinated with our effed-up situation. I pulled him out as a waiter stopped dead in his tracks.

"It's a boy!" My laughter was solo. Royce looked up at the faces peering down at him and quickly scooted back under the table. I took a deep breath reminding myself he was not worth the prison time.

I leaned down and whispered. "Royce, get out here right now."

"I just need a minute."

"You're being a jackass. I'll stab you with a fork if you don't cooperate. Got me?"

He spoke through gritted teeth. "Don't you fucking insult me."

"I'm not insulting you I'm just *describing* you." My patience is like a gift card, you never know how much is left. At this time, I found out I had a zero balance. I grabbed his ankles, yet again, and pulled him out from under the table, and kept going right out of the restaurant to gasps and pointing.

He was squirming as I pulled him through the hall. I didn't even try to control my laughter as I dragged him down three stairs.

"Ouch!" He held the back of his head. "Let me go!"

"No, you've proven yourself as a runner, and I don't have time for this shit."

"I'm fine. I'm just a little loopy. I'm not going anywhere."

I let go and he got his feet. "Where is everybody?"

"Well, we found Lexi talking to a tree and killing demon cowboys."

"Shit. She's okay?"

I nodded.

"I don't know what was in those snacks."

"Everybody has been found."

We stood for a second. "You called Clint, didn't you?"

He nodded. "He and Allie had a good thing—"

"To cut a long story short, you're a dick."

"Allie is a good friend."

"And you wanted to make sure I—"

"Yeah. I was around for the last episode of *Levi and Allie*, and it was a disaster. I won't let that happen."

"So you called someone to—"

"They're good together. She left for a job opportunity, and it was just a matter of time before they got back together."

"So you took it upon yourself to decide things? Who do you think you are?"

"I'm one of the people who put her back together after you. The one who stood at the end of the hall every day when she *relearned to walk*."

"I didn't want it to be like that! A truck ran into us, and I had no control."

"Yes, you had *no control* of yourself. When you were with her all hell broke loose and she almost didn't make it out alive. I'll call in the fuckin' cavalry to make sure that doesn't happen again."

With that he walked away, and I suddenly came to realize I was at the point in life where I needed a stronger word than fuck.

Allie had gone against them all back in the day for me, and here I was again. Wanting to push her for more than closure in Colorado and I'd be asking her to do it all again.

FORTY-THREE
ALLIE
IT'S A CLUSTER

Once back at the house I went to the bathroom and when I opened the door, I was suddenly pushed right back into the bathroom by Clint.

"Hi."

"Hello."

"We haven't had any time to talk between all the people in this house and the whole baked goods thing." He chuckled. "Can you even believe today?"

"I know. It's been a cluster."

He pulled me close, and I looked into those brown eyes that were warm and familiar. "Can we chat tonight?"

He had a twinkle in his eye, and I was as nervous as a snowman in July. Levi had announced he would be my night-time visitor this evening. What in the bibbity bobbity shitballs was happening, and how would this thing play out?

Option one: see Levi under the cover of night. Option two; see Clint? Yeah, I might be going to hell for this.

I glanced out the window and wondered if I'd break any pertinent bones if I just jumped now.

"Ya know Clint, I think Emily has something planned for the girls tonight. She's been busy with her family today. I should probably keep my calendar open for bridezilla." Maybe true, it seemed like something she'd do. "How about in the morning?"

He kissed me, and I froze as my heart drummed a rock solo. While Levi and I were just a closure thing, Clint suddenly felt wrong. And *that* was wrong. I would be outta here after the wedding with Levi off to another continent; there would be no us. And he made it as clear as a nuclear bomb that he doesn't do relationships. And the dozen women callers was a reminder that he was a good time guy. Fun and done.

I could see it now; even as a forty-year-old man Levi would still have the charm and sexiness that would have women of all ages hoping to catch his eye. Yeah, he'd bounce from the beaches with Brazilian beauties to the Austrian Alps and snow bunnies; the man would have a life normal men would only dream of.

I needed to get my head on straight because I couldn't walk out of this broken. Again. I didn't want to have to get over Levi. Again. The "missing him" reaching the center of my bones, and the ache that I knew was the equivalent of being beaten by a spiked baton.

Clint was a solid option that would never hurt me. While it was a question mark, maybe I should leave the door open for something now or in the future? But I didn't need anyone either; it was safer for me to just count on myself.

While I wanted to push him away, I let him kiss me. I kissed him back, and it was a nice kiss. Really nice, actually. So why was my stomach going like a popcorn machine?

I focused more. Yes, focus on the man who came to

Colorado for me. The one who didn't leave me in a hospital with signed annulment papers on the little table beside the bed.

I dove deep into concentration mode. I pushed myself to experience Clint's kiss, and it was still nice. Yes, I just needed to concentrate *more*.

I did a quick recap to find I'd used the words concentrate, forced, and focus when kissing someone. Time to regroup. I pushed his chest. Clearly, I needed a 500 mg dose of Fuckitol to deal with whatever the hell my life had become.

"We'd better get back."

He opened the door, and I stepped out to see Levi in the hall. Are you kidding me right now? He smiled until Clint stepped out behind me. His jaw instantly clenched, and his eyes burned me before I quickly looked away. Just when things couldn't get more awkward Clint wiped his lips of my lip gloss and let out a little chuckle. UUUGGGHHH.

"Sorry if we kept you waiting."

Clint took my hand, and I sort of wanted to die as we walked into the kitchen.

FORTY-FOUR
LEVI
TAKING CLINT OUT

I stood in the hall for a good five minutes attempting to put out the wildfire that was jumping through my veins.

They were in the bathroom.

Together.

Kissing.

I was quickly running of reasons to not grab the frozen leg of lamb that sat in the kitchen sink, bludgeon someone to death with it, and then eat the murder weapon to get away with the perfect crime.

Somebody = Clint.

Because he had to die, right? There was nothing else that could happen if he stayed in this house one more hour.

I walked into the kitchen while everybody was chomping on cookies. Even though the room was filled with symmetrically decorated treats, red and green Christmas tablecloth, and more damn holiday carols ringing through the air, my blood ran like mud through my veins.. The only thing that didn't suck was the beer pong table and cups set up in the corner of the room.

She only wanted closure with me, nothing more. Did she want Clint back? I'd burned the bridge to any relationship with her long ago. What if I pushed the closure thing more, keeping her "okay" with me, while working on warming her up to the idea of me forever and ever and ever? I'd make her see she didn't want to be with dickhead. She wanted me.

Three of the four voices in my head thought this was a winning plan. The fourth said murder was the only way. I'd attempt to ignore that bastard.

I went to the cabinet next to the sink and had the first sense of calm hit me as my eyes wrapped around Jack Daniels. Yes, he could get me through this, right? He was loyal and always did what he promised; make me numb.

The room was too loud. The overabundance of talking and smiling made me want to whip up a salad with a side of cyanide. *If you all would shut the fuck up, that would be just lovely.*

I hadn't realized the force I'd used to shut the cabinet door until I turned around and all eyeballs were on me.

"Sorry, did I hit the door too hard?" My laughter was lonesome.

I held the bottle with one hand and grabbed two glasses with the other. Whiskey would help me deal with Clint.

I sat across from assface and filled a glass as Kristina babbled on about something.

"Anybody like a happy hour drink?"

Royce grabbed a wreath cookie topped with green frosting and red sprinkles from the tray in the center of the table. "After losing a few hours of my memory today, I think I'll pass."

"What about you Clint?" I filled a glass. "You're not a pussy, are ya?"

A hush fell over the room as his brow rose. "I'll have a drink."

I slid the glass over to him as I held mine up. "To you." He clinked his glass against mine never knowing his evening was about to end early. There would be no repeat kissing for dickhead.

"Clint, how about a little pong with Jack?"

My eyes shot right to receive a warning glare from Allie which I ignored.

Kristina clapped. "I'll play, too!"

An hour later Royce entered the room to learn, along with Clint, that I don't lose at pong. Ever.

It was his turn, and he leaned sideways to get out of the kitchen chair he was on and fell to the floor with a thud. He was done and victory was mine.

Allie leaned toward me. "This is *not* cool, Levi."

Kristina did a dance around the table. "This is totally cool!"

Evan walked in while his head shook. "Clearly we shouldn't have left the room unsupervised."

Clint slurred and pulled himself up by the chair. "I'm fine."

I shrugged. "Some guys just can't hold the whiskey," I whispered. "He might have a problem."

Allie huffed. "He doesn't have a problem. Except for you, you're the problem. He's solid."

Evan came over and we got him to his feet.

"Evan, does this look like a fella who's solid?"

"I'm solid." Clint slurred and narrowed his eyes at me. "But I fuckin' hate you."

I nodded. "Ya know Clint, you can fuck straight to fuck off

mountain while riding your fuck off horse to the land of Fuck-tardia for all I care."

Allie let out a huff. "Real mature."

Evan chuckled. "I'll help you get him upstairs."

"No, I've got him." Allie came around and Clint put his arm over her shoulder.

Allie led him through the living room as Lexi and Rachel gasped.

I followed Clint and Allie. "Nothing like a lush. Right ladies?"

Clint turned, let go of Allie, and pushed my chest. "Fucking shut up, man."

"I'm not saying anything we all can't see."

Allie stepped between us. "Everybody, just go, okay? I'll help Clint upstairs."

The room cleared, and I reluctantly followed Lexi toward the kitchen. As everyone walked inside, I hung by the door wondering what Allie was saying to Clint. He was bent down and my pulse ticked up as his mouth was only inches from hers in what appeared to be a heated conversation.

He grabbed her hand, but Allie turned and walked toward the stairs. What was happening?

What *wasn't* happening was me staying in the kitchen. Because a second later Clint reached out and grabbed Allie by the upper arm and yanked her to his face. I don't remember flying out of the kitchen, but before I could lasso my brain, I had grabbed Clint by the shirt and shoved him into the wall. By that time Lexi and Rachel had torn into the room.

"Don't you ever grab her like that again!" I pulled him to my face. "Do you fucking hear me?"

He pushed me back. "You're just some ex-boyfriend trying to stir shit up!"

I let out a laugh. "Ex-boyfriend? Try husband."

Clint was stunned as he looked at Allie who let out a groan.

Lexi jumped forward. "That was a long time ago. A mistake."

Allie held her hands out. "Everybody, shut up!" She grabbed Clint by the hand. "Please, just go away."

FORTY-FIVE
ALLIE
THE UNRAVELING?

We made our way to Clint's room in silence. Yes, I'd never mentioned I'd been married, and yes it was clearly a bad decision. When it comes to terrible life choices, I'm pretty sure if I make one more I'll own the whole set.

We reached the door.

"I knew about the accident, but you left out the part about you and Levi being married?"

"It's just a painful memory I never wanted to think of again."

He was slurring slightly. "You didn't feel like you could talk to me about it?"

"It wasn't that. I moved on after everything with Levi. It was a long time ago. I didn't know he'd be here or knew Evan."

I crossed my fingers behind my back. Technically closure wasn't a relationship, so when I said *it was a long time ago*, that was basically true.

He stepped closer and took my hand in his. "So you and Levi?"

It was a good question I didn't have a solid answer for. But there was nothing after Colorado. We both agreed. "There's nothing with Levi."

Why did those words put a restless ache in my tummy?

His face was red and hair everywhere. "You should sleep this off."

I pulled down the comforter and when I turned around, he was right in front of me and pulled me into his chest. "Stay with me?"

"I really need to touch base with Emily on some wedding stuff. There's so much to do as a bridesmaid. But I'll see you at breakfast, okay?"

His lids were heavy. "I love you."

I froze and flashed the strongest smile I could muster. "Is that the liquor talking?"

"No. I believe in you, and us."

Heat went to my face. "I, uh, believe in you, too." Awkward silence and a giggle from me. "But I also believe in Bigfoot, so not sure what to do with any of this."

His blinking was slow. "You rest and I'll see you in the morning, okay?"

I went downstairs to find the living room empty except for Kristina, and I plopped down next to her on the couch. The space was lit only by the white twinkling lights of the Christmas tree shining a warm glow. She took my hand in hers. "How are you doing? Lots of surprising stuff in one day, huh?"

"Yeah. My brain hurts. I'm 500% done with today, and like 72% done with tomorrow already."

"What can I do?"

"Well, if you can make it so vodka could come out of my shower head that would be a great first step."

She giggled. "I'll work on that." She turned to me. "I didn't know you back when you were with Levi, but I'd be blind if I didn't notice how he looks at you."

"You have a wild imagination. And maybe you're crazy."

"I'm not crazy. I prefer the term mentally hilarious."

I put my head on her shoulder. "Then make me laugh. Do it now."

"Ooh, a joke. What did the hurricane say to the coconut palm tree?"

"What?"

"Hold onto your nuts, this isn't any ordinary blow job."

"That's awful. You are *not* the jokester of our crew."

She gasped. "I take offence to that statement. I'm the chaos coordinator, mischief manager, and supervisor of shenanigans in our group. I wear many hats, you know."

"So you're the brains of our gang?"

"Hell, yes." She reached to the bowl of Skittles on the coffee table and popped one in her mouth "Did you know the phrase "never odd or even" spelled backward is still "never odd or even"? I'm super-duper smart like that, Allison."

"You took learning some new shit off of my to-do list today. Thanks Kristina."

She tossed a red candy into her mouth. "Let's cut through the crap. I'm not telling Lexi or Rachel anything. Let me be here for you."

"Honestly, I don't even know if I'm playing an active role in my life right now. Shit happens and I'm like "oh, so this is what I'm doing now?"

"It'll be okay." She nudged me with her shoulder. "I promise."

"Yeah, next week I'll totally get my shit together, right?"

"My lips are sealed, but I have to ask as your friend. Is something going down with Mr. Levi?"

Going down...giggle.

"Not really."

"So that's a yes." She inhaled sharply. "I'm not going to say a word but be careful. Sparks can fly when people are trapped in a vacation house together outside of the real world. You both have a lot of history. But it's been dead for how long?"

"Seven years."

"So neither of you had contacted the other in all that time? If you hadn't ended up in Colorado for a wedding, you likely would've never seen each other again. Do I have this correct?"

I nodded. "You do. The fact that things went down how they did, and he just left me there was unforgiveable. No letter or text? His phone number was disconnected and he just cut me out of his life. He wasn't the person I thought he was." Sigh. "It took me a long time to find the yee to my haw after him."

"So you two have talked about it since you've been here?"

I looked down and nodded.

She pushed my hair off my face. "And held hands?"

I nodded.

She whispered, "Maybe he kissed you?"

Heat hit my face as I nodded again feeling like a child being busted for stealing gum from the gas station after shoving it down my pants. Not only did I do it, but I was well aware it was the wrongest of all wrongs.

Kristina lifted my chin. "So it's just a casual thing?"

"Yeah. We kind of said we could hang out in Colorado but then it's done. It's like closure."

"And both of you want nothing after that?"

"Yes." I spoke as quietly as I could. "But I think it was all a mistake. And now Clint is here and everything is messed up."

"You took that job because Clint wanted something a little more with you."

"Yeah, but if I acted like a grown up instead of being afraid maybe there would be something there with him. I don't know."

She sighed. "Since we've been friends, I've seen you bolt the second a guy seems like he might be a good one."

"Maybe. But I think I'm just better on my own, you know?"

Lexi and Rachel bounced into the room.

Rachel sat on the coffee table in front of me. "Emily texted and said we have to meet her at the caterers place at nine tomorrow morning."

Lexi sat in the chair next to me and scrolled through her phone. "The caterer is a friend of hers and she's just started her business and doesn't have a van. We'll have to drive all the food to the reception ballroom."

I looked over to see Rachel examining my face. "What?"

"You look stressed."

"I'm fine."

"Clint being here is a lot. I can't believe he came. How do you feel?"

"If you could look inside my brain, it would appear as if I'm losing a game of Jumanji."

Lexi wore a grin that was a little too happy for me at the moment. "Royce said he's been missing you so much. I hope you guys will give it another go. He's so hot."

"Time will tell."

"Time? But you were bummed when you guys split."

"I was. But once I moved away, I was good. I mean I missed him, but maybe not as much as I should've if he was the one for me. I just don't think—"

"You run every time you get into a relationship that's good for you." Lexi's head shook. "That fucking Levi screwed you up."

"I was my dream job. I was given a great opportunity and wanted to take it."

Rachel's eyes narrowed and my arm pits were suddenly sticky. "That's a load of garbage, Allison. Instead of discussing the options or ways to make it work, you got scared and ran the first place you could."

"Don't judge me. I said it didn't feel right, get off my ass."

Kristina's jumped in. "Girls, relax. Rachel and Lexi, we know you just care about Allie, but you have to calm down. Just because Clint showed up doesn't mean Allie has to jump into his arms. This is her life. Maybe we should realize that she might be feeling a bit overwhelmed at the moment?"

I kissed Kristina's cheek. "Thank you."

Rachel took a breath. "You're right. I just wish stupid Levi wasn't here. He's history, but I know this is hard for you."

"It's been okay. We're existing together here, and I'm not plotting his murder, so it's really a win/win situation."

Kristina giggled. "Levi's smoking hot. Yup, every part of him."

Rach and Lexi shot her dead with their eyes.

"We don't talk about him, Kristina. *Ever*. He was responsible for almost killing Allie."

Kristina's smile was warm. "I get it. But sometimes you can't just cut people out forever."

Lexi kicked her feet up on the coffee table. "Can't cut

people out? Snippidy, snip mother fucker. He was bad for Allison from day one. It just took all hell breaking loose for her to see it."

Kristina grabbed Lexi's hand, squeezed it hard, and she yelped. "Let's focus on expanding our vocabulary to include encouraging words."

"I actually have a really big vocabulary for someone who says fuck so often."

Kristina continued. "You're acting—"

Lexi flipped her hair. "Yes, I know I'm insane. We all know that, Kristina. But my intentions are gold and my heart pure. I love all you witches, and I just want Allie to open her mind to how amazing Clint is."

Kristina took a breath. "I'm just saying it's okay if Allie has doubts—"

Lexi stood up. "Allie, you need to be done with doubts and insecurities. You're fucking amazing and that's just what it is."

Rachel leaned forward. "We love you, Allie. How are you feeling?"

"Right now, I'm feeling that feeling when you don't know what the hell you're feeling."

"That's okay. You need to *not* think for a while." Rachel stretched her arms over her head. "I'm going to bed. Let's meet down here at eight thirty, okay? Everything will feel better in the morning. I'm sure the whole food thing won't take too long and then we can all chill."

Once in my bedroom I called Emily.

"Allie."

"How are you doing? You're last text was unclear."

She let out a sigh. "It's nothing." Sigh. "I'm just maybe having wedding jitters or something."

I plopped onto my pillow. "I think that's normal. I mean you've been planning this and now it's almost time. Just take a breath. You have hearts in your eyes whenever you speak of your soon to be husband."

We sat in silence for a minute. "Speaking of hearts, how are you feeling with Levi there? *And* Clint?"

"Well, it's totally cool. Really."

Her giggle hit my ear. "You lying bitch."

"Shut up."

"I've never met him, but after the descriptive words of Lexi, I kinda can't wait."

"Enough about the shit show over here, you focus on you and relax.

"Thanks, Allie."

I disconnected the call, pulled on my jammies, and when I turned around, I jumped at Levi's face that was pressed against the window. I slid it open, and he climbed inside.

"It was not cool what you did with the drinking earlier."

He nodded and shoved his hands in his pockets. "Maybe a little cool?"

"I just think it'd be best to end closure now. I mean we're all leaving in a few days and, well, we just should."

"You don't want to do that."

"Everything is weird."

"Well, the way I see it Clint came here but you guys aren't back together. We're doing nothing wrong by finishing closure."

All I wanted to do was be in the state of closure forever and ever and ever, but I wanted to pry.

"And for all I know you have some Brazilian chick waiting for you."

His head shook.

"So no lady for you?"

"There's been some here and there, but nothing special. I'm just not interested in a relationship. It's not my thing." He reached out and took my hand.

"So, you mess around with women but want nothing? Like fun and done?"

He nodded and my brain had a quick reality check that felt as good as a swift punch to the boob. He meant what he had said. So what he'd been telling me all along was completely true; he wanted closure with me, sex with me, and steaming up the windows good times with me. But he didn't want me.

He laced his fingers through mine. "I know you want to hang out a little more. And you don't have to worry about me after this is over. I just want to be close to you while we're here and then we go our separate ways."

I should totally be relieved, right? It was a reminder that he's lived seven years without me and wanted to live all the rest of his years without me.

There was a knock at the door, and his eyes went wide.

"Allie, let me in." Lexi knocked again. "Royce has pissed me off so I'm sleeping with you tonight."

I pushed him to the window and whispered, "Go!"

FORTY-SIX
LEVI

While pretty and all, the new dusting of snow was nearly the death of me as I scaled the roof back to my room.

I tossed and turned most of the night missing her beside me. If I could just keep her in closure mode I could work on getting her to give me a second chance. I just needed a little more time.

Once up I showered and roamed downstairs to find an empty kitchen with Lexi at the stove making omelets.

"Good morning."

"It was."

I grabbed a cup and poured myself some coffee. "You know, it's okay to not entirely hate me."

Her head shook. "But I've put so much time and energy into the rage thing, it'd be a shame to let it go now."

I leaned against the counter. "I'm not going to hurt her."

Lexi's eyes met mine. "I promise."

She held my stare. "Please just leave her alone."

Luckily my response wasn't confirmed as Royce and Evan entered and sat at the table.

"Breakfast served in five," she sang.

Royce scooted in his chair. "Since you girls have to get the wedding food, I thought the guys could check out the indoor golf place in town and get lunch." He took an irritated breath. "Levi, you should come."

Allie entered the room and stole every bit of oxygen from me. Everything from her jeans hugging that perfect backside, to the gray shirt that made those baby blues pop, and the auburn curls I wanted to run my fingers through, made her perfection shine like a diamond.

While nobody in the room knew yet, I would not be golfing. Or lunching with the guys. Nope, I was going to be with the girls starting my plan to make Allie realize she can't live without me.

"Thanks for the invite, Royce, but I have some emails and work to get to. I'll just hang back while you all go."

The room seemed to accept this answer. One point for Levi.

Let the games begin.

FORTY-SEVEN
ALLIE

I SWEAR ON MILLER LITE

We pulled on our coats by the front door when Kristina grabbed my hand and looked at our gang.

"Girls, I just want to thank you. I know none of us were thrilled with Emily's decision for a Christmas Eve wedding, but with the divorce so fresh, if I wasn't here with you, I'd be a blubbering mess at home alone. The first holiday by myself. I'd be having such a terrible Christmas somebody would seriously have to shove a rainbow up my ass to prevent me from flinging myself out the damn window."

Lexi giggled.

"You all are giving me energy so I can start a new life after this."

I hugged her. I knew what starting over without the love of your life was like shared glass slicing and dicing your flesh.

"I'm glad we're all together. And Kristina, you're going to be great. A new life and adventures ahead."

She nodded. "I just hope to find a nice, sweet guy who will love me, and occasionally handcuff me to the bedpost."

Rachel nodded. "Your Prince Charming will come. He

may not come on a horse though. He's obviously riding a turtle in a different land, really confused. But I feel like he's about to ask for directions and will be here before you know it."

"Awww, we'll always be friends because y'all match my level of crazy."

A giggle bounced out of me. "Finding friends with the same mental disorders." I squeezed them tighter. "Priceless."

We piled into the van with Rachel behind the wheel. The radio blared *Feliz Navidad* and we sang our freaking hearts out. Next came Applebottom Jeans. I must admit that is a song that awakens my inner stripper, and I'm okay with it.

We drove down the magical Christmas street and passed the ski resort as memories of the day before danced in my mind. There were some kids having a hot chocolate stand on the sidewalk so we stopped, and I got everyone a cup topped with whipped cream and red sprinkles. I hopped back into the van and we slowed when Maps said we'd reached the caterer's place.

I scrolled through what felt like a zillion wedding messages from Emily. "I kinda wished we'd brought the guys. How much food do you think there is?"

Rachel gave a nod. "Yeah, we should've brought the men. Some muscles are needed right now."

"I got you."

I jumped and whipped around to see Levi who had appeared out of nowhere in the back row of the ginormous van.

Lexi groaned. "What in the hell are you doing here?"

He flexed. "I believe I'm an answer to your muscle prayers."

Kristina's nose wrinkled. "You've been hiding in the van?"

His perfect eyes rolled. "No, I just wanted to come into town and thought I'd hitch a ride with you ladies."

Rachel rolled her eyes. "You should be at the house—you can't be here. That's how it's supposed to be."

Levi huffed. "Oh look. Nobody gives a shit."

She hit the steering wheel. "That's it, I'm taking you back."

Kristina reached up and patted Rachel's shoulder. "Let's be the bigger person here."

She growled. "Fuck being the bigger person. I'm going to start slapping people around, so help me God I will."

Kristina held her hands up. "Let's all take a breath."

Rach whipped around and glared at Levi with gritted teeth which I found to be hilarious. My laughter was *not* well received.

"Levi, I'm like five people packed into one body. I'm warning you right now, you don't want to spin that wheel to see what you're gonna get. I *do not* play well with others."

Kristina shrugged. "Truth."

"Here's the deal." Levi put on his sweetest grin, and the way his hair dropped over his brow made me want to tear off my shirt. "You can work me like a dog when it comes to whatever you have to get from the caterer. I promise I'll be on my best non-fuck up behavior." His hand lifted. "I swear on Miller Lite."

FORTY-EIGHT

ALLIE

THAT WAS UNEXPECTED

We entered to find a little coffee shop. The tables were topped with red and green table clothes, wreaths on the walls, and a Christmas tree in front of the large window. We stood at the counter when a woman wearing jeans and a red shirt popped through a door.

"Can I help you?"

Rachel nodded. "We're here to get the desserts for Emily's wedding."

She motioned for us to follow her through a door.

"It's been a catering day from hell."

The kitchen was small with a long stainless-steel counter, two large stoves, and three refrigerators.

"Something happened after I closed up yesterday and both freezers quit working. That's where a majority of Emily's items were."

I stepped forward. "What can I do to help?"

Lexi sighed. "Kiss ass."

"Well, the café next door let me put some trays in their freezer, but there's no more room." She pointed to several boxes on the counter. "If I don't find a freezer to store these for the next hour or so until we have access to the reception kitchen, we're screwed."

Kristina nodded. "Is there anywhere else on the block we can ask about freezer space?"

She shrugged. "Well, there's a guy who rents apartment seventeen above us. I don't really know him, but he seems okay."

This was my chance to be a superhero and solve the day's problems. "I can go ask him. Just a few hours, right?"

"Yes, even one hour would be amazing." She beamed up at me. "I've just started this business and the last thing I need is a wedding debacle to ruin it."

I grabbed two boxes and Allie took the other. Her ocean eyes twinkled as she looked up at me.

As if sensing something, Lexi jumped between us. "Let's go."

We climbed a flight of stairs and Rachel knocked on the door as she adjusted her boobs. "This is for Emily. I'm pulling out the big guns."

Allie elbowed her in the arm. "Big guns?"

"Okay, a strong set of mediocre guns, but I'm in it to win it."

The door cracked open, and I could see one eyeball looking out at us.

"What?"

I cleared my throat. "Hello, sir. I'm Levi Dawson and these are some friends of mine."

Rachel mumbled. "Playing fast and loose with the friend thing."

"You're not the cops?"

"Uh, no. Not the cops." This was taking an odd turn. "We have a friend getting married tomorrow and the caterer downstairs had a freezer issue. We wanted to see if there's any way we could store these little boxes in your freezer for an hour?"

The door cracked open further to show that this man was in need of a comb. His light brown hair was shaggy and shot out in every direction. "You want to store wedding food in *my* freezer?"

"Just for an hour." I developed a quick incentive. "And I'll give you one hundred dollars for helping us out."

Rachel nodded. "That's a good idea, Levi. I'll pitch in twenty-five."

Finally, I had a thought that didn't make Rachel want to stab me. Score.

The door opened further to show our new friend wore a green SpongeBob sweatshirt that appeared to be in need of a spin around the wash cycle while his brown eyes darted about.

"You want to put wedding food in my *freezer*?"

Allie flashed her amazing smile that made my heart do a dirty tango. "Yes, please."

His hands went through his hair. "Uh, I don't know about this."

Rachel shimmied her shoulders and oddly thrusted her bust at him as his brow popped up.

Kristina stepped forward. "Sir, could you please help us. It's just an hour and you'll even get some cash out of the deal. The boxes are small, and we would be so grateful to you."

The guy ran his hand over his forehead; he appeared to be suddenly sweating. What was happening?

"Umm, well, okay."

I nodded. "Thank you. We can follow—"

"No!"

We all jumped.

"I mean, I'll take them." He grabbed my box. "Just set them on the floor, and I'll get them."

I reached in my back pocket to grab my wallet when he let out a yell. "What have you got there? Is that a gun?"

What the what? "I was getting your cash."

He flashed a tense smile. "Oh, okay."

I set the cash on the box and tried to get a peek into his apartment, but he pulled the door closed.

"We'll be back in an hour."

He nodded as the rest of the boxes were set on the floor and he disappeared into the apartment. We all exchanged a WTF look and headed downstairs.

We got the most of the food in the van and when the girls were still inside getting items, I pulled Allie into a little hall off of the caterer's kitchen.

"We're supposed to be stopping this." She pretended to be irritated before she threw her arms around my neck and kissed me.

"Nope, not until we leave Colorado."

She rubbed her nose against mine. "I don't think I totally agreed to this."

"You want this."

"Levi, I do not want—"

"I know. You want nothing. I get it."

We entered the kitchen to find ourselves in Lexi's cross hairs. She marched over and grabbed my arm. "You swore on Miller Lite you'd behave today. *NO* talking to Allie alone, not happening. Now you get your ass to that van and load in the rest of the frickin' wedding food. You got me?"

I saluted because it felt right. "Yes, ma'am."

Her eyes squinted at me, and I got the hell out of there.

Food loaded into van: check. Hot cup of coffee in hand: check. Allie giving me hopes I had a shot at something more than closure: check. No, wait, not a check. Well, sort of a check? A light check that could be erased? Yup, no fucking clue, I couldn't read her.

The caterer walked out behind us. "Whew! Thank you all for your help on this. The last thing we need is an upset bride coming for us." She laughed. "I called and you can get into the reception kitchen now. If you're okay getting the items upstairs and heading to the reception hall, I'll stop by in a few hours."

Allie nodded. "Absolutely. We're good."

She gave us a wave. "Thank you."

As she left, Lexi pointed. "What's going on?"

To the side of the building was an alley. And parked inside were two cop cars.

"Do you think everything is okay?"

The answer came swiftly as the door flew open and two officers led our freezer friend out of the building in handcuffs. He saw us and yelled, "You got the wrong guy! They did it! They're crazy!"

He was put into the backseat of the car before we went inside and hauled ass upstairs. The hall that was now filled with yellow crime scene tape and an officer was standing guard outside the door.

A door across the hall opened and a woman stepped out.

Allie walked over. "Do you know what's going on?"

"I don't know for sure, but that guy seems a like a nut job." She whispered, "There's always weird sounds coming from his place late at night."

Kristina whispered, "What kind of sounds?"

She leaned in closer. "Like maybe an electric saw or something?"

Lexi's gasp nearly sucked the fire extinguisher from the wall while Kristina's eyes were softballs.

The stranger looked around before continuing. "And on December 13th, which is Taylor Swift and author Mary Lee Painter's birthday by the way, he had a ginormous deep freezer delivered." She nodded. "I think he's the Super Saver Serial Killer."

Now I was leaning in. "The what?"

"Several months ago, some people went to the Super Saver grocery store and were never seen again. They went in for Goldfish crackers, and vanished. I think it's him."

Rachel's grabbed Lexi's hand. "And he chopped them up and put them in his freezer?"

She gave a knowing nod. "I wouldn't be surprised."

"Shit." Allie looked up at me.

The lady waved her hand in the air. "I'm going to check my police scanner to try to get some dirt." She disappeared back into her apartment.

Allie shook her head. "Emily's wedding food is in the freezer with dead people? She's going to kill us."

Rachel stomped her foot. "What are we going to do? Emily's desserts are in there with feet or arms? I need alcohol, stat."

I clapped my hands. "Everybody calm down. First of all, that lady may be crazy."

"I'm not crazy." Muffled through the door as we all jumped and quickly moved a few feet away.

The police officer took a step towards us. "I'll need you all to leave."

Lexi looked at me. "What do we do, Levi?"

I shrugged. "How would I know?"

"Well, you had some experience with this kind of shit back in the day. I believe you're the only one here with a criminal record. I thought you might have a clue."

"I never dealt with murder."

She shrugged. "We don't know that."

"Yes, we do." I walked to the police officer. "Excuse me sir, the man that lives here had let us store some wedding reception food in his freezer an hour ago. It looks like you're really busy here, but we just wanted to get our desserts real quick."

His head shook. "This is the scene of an investigation and nobody will enter. The detectives should be here soon to proceed."

Kristina flashed a smile. "Hello officer. Thank you for your service. Our friend is getting married tomorrow, and due to a freezer issue at the caterer's business below, we were allowed to store some reception food there for an hour. We really need to get it because it's for a wedding. Super important stuff."

"I see. Looks like you're in a pickle."

Lexi nodded. "Yes. So you'll let us get the food?"

"No can do. And I need you all out of this hallway pronto."

Rachel leaned in close. "Please, please help us. Our friend Emily will be crushed. And then she'll likely crush me, her

Maid of Honor. If you want to avoid another crime scene at the Whispering Pines ballroom tomorrow, you have to let me grab them real quick."

"I'm unable to help you. Please kindly leave or I'll haul you out of here."

FORTY-NINE
ALLIE
SUPERHERO?

U nless we could become a pastry chef in the next hour we were screwed.

Kristina groaned. "There has to be a way out of this."

We walked around to the backside of the building and could see the balcony just two stories up of the possible Super Saver Serial Killer.

Lexi eyed me for a long moment. I did not like it.

"Levi, there's a fire escape."

He looked up. "Yeah?"

She cleared her throat. "We all know you did some shady shit back in high school. The only one here with a mug shot."

He put his hand out. "That was way back. I've been an upstanding citizen for a long time now."

"I hear you, and, uh, that's good. A real good thing. But I'm about to ask you to return to the dark side for a hot minute."

His head shook. "Won't do it."

Rachel pointed at the balcony above us. "You can't climb

up there and get our shit from the freezer before the detectives arrive?"

A sarcastic laugh. "Of course I could. But I won't."

Lexi stepped toward him. "This is our *best friend*, Emily. We can't show up without her wedding desserts or she'll kill us."

He grinned at me. "Maybe you need more understanding friends."

Allie held my eyes and Rachel stepped between us.

"You stop looking at each other that way! Stop it right now."

He looked at Lexi. "I will *not* do this for you." His eyes walked back over to me. "But I'll do anything Allie asks me to."

His words tickled my tummy and then I suddenly wanted to tickle him. "Do you want me to do it?"

I nodded as a swirl of heat circled the back of my neck when Rachel waved her hand in front of my eyes. "Stop looking at each other. Right now!"

"I'll go if Allie comes with me." He wore that flirty, dirty grin that always made me crazy.

Kristina squinted at him. "She can't climb a fire escape and break in that place!"

"She's done it before."

All eyes shot to me, and I shrugged, maybe feeling a little badassy.

Rachel's voice was filled with irritation. "Allison, you did not break and enter. I don't believe it for a second."

Levi's brows raised. "It's true. Allie told me she wanted Dairy Queen ice cream one night at midnight. I made it happen."

Rachel's eyes cut Levi. "You made a lot of shit happen that shouldn't of."

He leaned his back against the building and crossed his arms over that muscly chest. "I don't get your wedding food if she isn't with me." He looked at his watch. "Tick tock. The Po-po will be inside any second."

His green eyes lit up something in me I knew nobody else ever would.

"Fine!" Rachel spoke through gritted teeth. "Go get our damn food."

Levi walked over and stood in front of me. "You ready pretty girl?"

Lexi whisper-yelled, "You stop talking to her like that Levi!" She punched my arm. "You keep your eyes to yourself, Allison!"

I didn't listen.

His hands touched my waist and every nerve in me jumped. "I'm going to lift you and grab the fire escape. Then step on my shoulder to get up there. Okay?"

I nodded and a second later pulled myself up on the fire escape. I looked down to see Levi jump and get a hold of the ladder and pull himself up. Hot *and* strong. Be still my horny heart.

I climbed up and felt him behind me.

"Have I told you that you still have the sweetest ass in the history of the world, Allison?"

I looked down at him. "I don't think so."

"My bad then."

Lexi whisper yelled up at us. "I see you looking at him! Stop it right now!"

We made it to the balcony and climbed over. Once at the

door we looked through the glass door to see it empty. Levi knelt down and examined the lock.

"This is good. It's old."

He pulled out his keys and flipped through and held up his little screwdriver tool.

"Is that the same one?"

"Yup. While breaking and entering isn't my jam anymore, it's nice to know it's here to help in sticky situations."

He went to work as I leaned over the rail and flipped off the girls below. Did I mention it still felt good to be bad?

A few minutes later Levi pulled open the door and whispered. "You stay here. Let me check out the place real quick."

I nodded feeling a weird sense of calm considering our predicament.

A moment later he waved me into the apartment and down a hall. I followed his fine ass to a bedroom, and there it was. The ginormous deep freeze the crazy neighbor lady had filled us in on. We approached and my pulse spiked. We stood for a second.

"Well, here we are."

"I don't think I can look in there."

"Okay, you stand with your arms out, I'll pile on the boxes, and you just keep your eyes away. Are you ready?"

"I don't think so. I'm about ready to just stick a fork in the outlet and call it a day."

"We got this."

The freezer top was lifted and Levi piled boxes onto my arms without a word.

"Levi, do you see anything?"

"I'm focusing on the boxes. I'm not looking at anything else."

"Good move."

I kept my eyes up high until I heard the freezer close. "We're good?"

He took two boxes from my arms. "I believe so."

We scurried through the patio door and onto the balcony. Below us were the girls jumping up and down at the sight of us and the boxes.

I climbed down one story on the fire escape and Levi handed me the boxes. I dropped to my stomach and passed the boxes to the girls below. Levi then climbed down to the balcony I was on. But before I started down the ladder, he caught my wrist and pulled me to him.

"Do you want to freak them out?"

"Always."

With that he gently kissed my lips. Whisper-yelling came from below as a rock hit the building before I pulled away. "You're still so good at pissing off my friends."

He popped a brow. "It's a gift."

We climbed down and as soon as Levi's feet hit the snowy concrete Lexi slapped his arm. "You stop this shit right now!"

With that we all grabbed boxes, jumped into the van, and got the hell out of there.

"What is happening today?" Rachel laughed as she sped down the block.

Kristina clapped. "We did it! Levi you were amazing!"

"I'm here to serve."

Rachel met my eyes in the rear-view mirror. "This is killing me but thank you."

I looked up. "And not a single flying pig?"

"But if I see you two talking or having sticky eyes, I will kill you, Levi Dawson. I've been washing bloodstains from my clothing for decades so I have enough knowledge to pull it off."

"Wow."

Kristina turned to me. "Forget her Levi, you saved the day."

Allie punched her arm. "What about me?"

Lexi turned around in her seat. "The smart girl can break and enter."

Allie pointed. "Say it!"

Lexi threw her head back and laughed. "No!"

"You say I'm a badass right this minute or I'll throw you from the freaking car!" She flexed. "We all know I can do it!"

To see her laughing, those pink cheeks, and wild curls everywhere shined a blinding spotlight on how much I adored her. I freaking adored this woman. The thought of next week and every week without her was suffocating me. I'd lived a hell being without her, and I couldn't do it anymore. I didn't want to scare her off, but I needed to work fast as time was not on my side. And Clint. Fuck.

FIFTY

ALLIE

ARE YOU FREAKING KIDDING ME?

Emily met us at the reception venue, and we got all the food into the high-tech kitchen, and had a group hug. She wore jeans, pink sweater, and her long brown hair was in a bun on the top of her head. We opted to *not* share any details about the possibility of her wedding desserts rubbing elbows with, well, elbows.

Once the food was all taken care of, Emily leaned against the counter and looked up.

"Well, it's nice to meet you, Levi."

He cracked a smile and pointed at Lexi. "Don't believe a word she says about me."

Lexi grabbed Rachel's hand. "Levi, you are dry humping my last freaking nerve today. We'll meet you in the van, Emily."

They exited as Emily and I walked arm in arm with Levi beside us.

"So you're the grown-up Levi."

"Yes," he whispered. "But being grown up is a little weird. I'm just unsupervised all the time. Seems unsafe."

She laughed and leaned in. "I know I'm supposed to hate you, but I'm just not feeling it."

"Shall we go to lunch?"

She wrinkled her nose. "I can't eat. I'm just a bundle of nerves."

Levi leaned in and laughed. "Having second thoughts?"

Crickets.

His brows popped up. "I was just joking."

She let out a sigh. "I'm good. I think. Just a little nervous."

I pulled her in for a hug. "This will be the best day of your life."

We pulled in front of the house and every time I almost forget how beautiful it was. I knew it would always be the bittersweet memory of the Christmas wedding and Levi. The closure of so many open wounds, yet in the scars they'd be little cuts that would never entirely heal, a new scar within the old. I knew with every fiber of my being he would haunt my thoughts for all of time.

My stomach kurplunked when the front door opened and Royce and Clint walked outside. Their faces told me they'd realized Levi had gone with us and had a few hours to simmer in it.

I hopped out of the van first and gave them a wave.

"Hey guys, how was golf?" I flashed my best smile at Clint to try to give Levi some time to leave. But of course he didn't. I looked back to see that "fuck you" grin he was famous for. *Come on, Levi!*

"Did ya get lots of birdies? Was the *course* with you?" I giggled. "Get it?"

Clint gave me a pissy grin as his gaze slid back to Levi.

Evan walked out with concern written across his forehead. "Hey girls. And Levi." He slapped Royce on the back as he passed and walked to Levi. "Did you get the caterer thing all worked out?"

Kristina pulled her gloves off and threw her arms in the air. "You would never believe it! The Super Saver Serial killer had Emily's wedding food in his freezer in his apartment and then the cops came and said we couldn't have it back! And then Levi and Allie crawled up the fire escape, got in the door, saved the wedding food, and got out just before the cops busted all of us!"

It was that awkward moment when I was trying not to look as Clint stared a hole in me. Just when I thought things couldn't get any more tense, my brother walked out of the house.

My brother walked out of the house!

Will, brown hair, same blue eyes as me, and two years older, was there. Mind you, he didn't know Emily or the groom, but he was there. In Colorado. In the Vrbo. Standing between Clint and Royce, both his friends forever, looking as if he was ready to kill someone.

Someone = Levi, the most hated man in Colorado.

Levi was thoroughly amused as he approached my brother. "Will, it's been a long time."

"Not long enough, Dawson."

Will's eyes narrowed at me. "What the hell happened? You have stitches?"

"I had an ice debacle when I first arrived."

"Debacle?"

"I went over a little cliff and the car rolled."

He stepped closer and took my face in his hands. "Allie, you're okay?"

I stepped away. "I'm fine. Really."

Levi asked. "You here for the wedding, Will?"

My brother took a step toward Levi. "I'm here to make sure you know your place."

Great, the words that would only spur Levi on. "My place?"

My brother looking at me brought fire to my cheeks, and I quickly looked away as Levi walked through them and to the door. "You aren't telling me anything this time, Will."

I walked over and grabbed my brother by the hand. "Let's chat."

Lexi waved her arm in the air. "Emily and Travis are coming over in an hour for a bonfire. I'll get things ready in the kitchen if anyone wants to help." She nudged Rachel. "Of course, wine will be there."

Royce nodded. "I like the sound of that. I'm feeling mentally overworked and a little under intoxicated at the moment."

Kristina pointed at me. "You better join us, Allison. Wine is the only way to deal after this afternoon. Much cheaper than therapy."

I pulled my brother by the hand into the empty living room and to the sofa next to the fire. The room glowed and was cozily perfect if it weren't for me about to rip my only sibling's head off.

"Sit."

He rolled his eyes and plopped down. It was then Clint entered the room and stood next to me.

"Uh, can I talk to Will for a minute?"

"Sure."

He sat in the leather chair next to the coffee table clearly not picking up what I was lying down.

"I'd like to have a word with him *alone*, please."

Clint's expression brimmed with irritation. "Allie, this is ridiculous. Levi has completely crossed the line. Lexi told me he was hiding in the fucking van. Who does that?"

"He saved the wedding reception food."

Will let out a huff. "That's a bunch of crap and you know it. He has motives, and I'm going to make certain this shit stops now."

Clint leaned up in his chair, "Allie—"

"Clint, I think I stated that I want to speak with Will alone."

"Can't you see—"

"I see two people in my life who seem to *not* be aware that I'm a grown ass woman. I don't need or want anyone bossing me around anymore." I pointed to the door. "Clint, out."

"This is bullshit."

He stormed up the stairs as I turned my attention back to Will. "I'm a smart person in every area of my life. Will you stop thinking I can't make a decision without you?"

"When it comes to Levi—"

"It's none of your business."

He stood. "Clint is great and he's crazy about you."

"Again, none of your business." I started pacing. "Since I've been here Royce called Clint who came here, and then Clint called you. I need this to stop. Just because you and Clint are talking doesn't mean I have to be with him. You don't make my decisions. Maybe I don't want to be with anyone."

"Allie, I just worry about you."

"Stop. I'm smart and don't need you jumping on a plane when you think I might screw something up."

"Back then—"

"Back then you made all the decisions for me. I had no say in my life, and I *hated* it."

He stood and pulled me in for a hug. "I'm sorry. I did some things in the wrong way after the accident. I just, we all wanted to protect you."

I pushed away. "Don't do that."

He threw his hands in the air. "Truce. I want a do over." He gave me his stupid googly eyes and a grin. "I'm sorry. Can you stop being mad at me? Mad Allie makes me sad and not glad."

"Shut up." I tried to hide my smile. "You can't stay unless you are civil to everybody I this house. Nobody knew Levi was the cousin of Evan. Can you do that? *Not* be a douchebag?"

"So you want me to be my *normal* self? The awesome one?"

"How's being a full-time asshole working out for you? You need therapy."

He laughed. "I went to a therapist, but I don't think she was supposed to say "wow" so many times in our first session so I quit. Maybe I need a shady therapist who's experienced some shit and could really help me deal with all these dickheads walking the earth."

"Yeah, sometimes there are just too many people and not enough voodoo dolls."

He threw his arm over my shoulder as we headed toward the kitchen. "Voodoo, now there's something I'd like to try."

FIFTY-ONE
LEVI
BROTHERLY HATE

I paced my room as Evan downed a Miller Lite.

"I can't believe Clint called Will. What kind of pussy is he?"

"Maybe the kind seeing you making moves on Allie."

"Whatever. They're not married or anything."

Evan rolled his eyes. "Can't you just wait until we aren't all stuck in the same house to make a move? It's like you have a death wish."

"I'm doing whatever the hell I want. Screw everybody."

"If you have any hope of something with Allie, I think pissing off her brother is not the way to go. Play nice for a few more days. Be cool. Don't let him think you guys are sneaking around."

I nodded and looked down.

"Because you aren't, right? You promised me you weren't doing anything."

"A promise to you? I don't recall." I shrugged.

He stood and walked as his mouth dropped open while he pointed out the window. "Are those your footprints in the snow on the *roof*? Come on, Levi! Are you trying to kill yourself?"

"The opposite. For the first time in seven years, I feel alive."

"Rachel still hates you by the way. She and I had to hatch a "no talking about Levi" pact. And now her brother and Clint? You need to chill out."

"I'm totally chill."

He looked at me. "The bonfire today. I think you should stay in here."

"What? I love a good bonfire."

"Then no liquor for you. You need to keep your head on straight."

"I'm going to the bonfire. It's all cool."

"Worst idea ever, but if you do, you're stay by me so I can keep you on track."

"I'll be good. I'll act like a responsible adult." I nodded. "I just hope Clint doesn't fall in the fire."

"You're driving me to alcoholism. Trying to keep your brain in check is like raking leaves during a hurricane. It's exhausting to worry about who is going to kill you first this weekend."

Once downstairs we pulled on our coats and headed out to the deck as the icy air hit us. The sun was going down and at the bottom of the hill was an impressive fire.

We crunched through the snow.

"Remember, no alcohol."

I nodded and went straight for the cooler to the right of the fire and grabbed a beer while Evan flipped me off. I followed my cousin to the other side of the fire as Emily and Travis headed down the hill.

Travis had black hair and dark eyes and stood with Will and Royce.

I looked at Allie talking to Lexi and everything in me tightened. The glow of the amber fire against her face and hair was breath taking. She lifted the beer bottle to her lips, and I was jealous. Her eyes found mine and the grin I knew well slid across those perfectly plump lips. How could I keep my eyes from her?

That answer came when my gaze shifted left to Will. His clenched jaw and "I want to kill you" resting face were on point as his eyes shot me dead. I raised my beer, took a drink, and realized poking the bear might be a thing after all.

Lexi held a small speaker above her head before hitting a button on her phone and *We Wish you a Merry Christmas* echoed across the frozen forest before the girls started singing.

Rachel pointed. "I put some sleds on top of the hill. The one who goes the farthest while holding a drink above their head wins!"

I stood back while everyone hit it. Watching Allie scream while whipping down the hill was kind of amazing. I couldn't wait to see her later.

"Dude." Evan elbowed me. "Get that look off your face." He head pointed to Clint. "That man is going go ballistic if you don't cut it out."

I finished my beer and tossed it into the trash can. "Nice. Middle fingers up if you don't give a fuck." I shook my head at Clint. *I see your pissed face, and I raise you a fuck off.*

We emptied the cooler, and the girls were all giggly.

Rachel jumped up and down. "My toes are frozen! Let's hit the hot tub! Emily, I have a bathing suit you can borrow. Travis, I'm think Evan has some shorts you can use."

We tromped up the hill, kicked off boots, and everyone scattered. I walked behind everyone to see Clint and Evan enter their rooms. While I had planned to pop in on Allie, it appeared Emily was changing in her room so I hopped in my swim trunks, grabbed a Rockstar from the refrigerator, and was the first in the hot tub with Evan joining me.

"You're holding it together so far, an unexpected point for you."

It was then Allie entered through the door in slow motion. She wore a dark blue bikini that she filled out perfectly. The bottoms were cut high, shining a spotlight on her amazing legs. My only thought was how to get them wrapped around my waist pronto.

Evan splashed water at me. "Stop staring." His eyes narrowed.

Lexi and Rachel climbed into the hot tub. Rachel gave Evan a peck on the cheek and looked at me. Oh, shit ran through my bloodstream, and my eyes ran back to see Allie had not remembered the tattoo. "Damn it. Evan, do you have a t-shirt I can use?"

"What?"

I stood and grabbed a towel from the chair next to the hot tub and threw it over my shoulders to conceal my new tattoo just as Clint and Will entered the pool area.

I sat with my feet in the water as fire shot through me when Clint suddenly picked up Allie and jumped into the pool with her in his arms. I slammed my beer realizing there just wasn't enough liquor to deal with any of this crap.

Everyone around me was jabbering on about something, but I couldn't pull my focus from the pool and the fact that Allie and Clint were talking while only their heads were out of the water. She started to swim away when Clint pulled her to him and appeared to be hugging her under the water.

Quick summary: the most hated man in Colorado had his arms wrapped tightly around the woman I was in love with. Her perfect chest was pressed against his, and I was having trouble breathing as my diaphragm seemed to be shutting down altogether.

I looked away trying to figure out how to deal.

Will sat next to Evan as Allie let out a squeal when dickhead had her in his arms and threw her a few feet away from him. He glanced over with a smug smile that was a kick in the balls.

Everything sucked. Should I leave? Go to my room in order to assure I didn't throw Clint through the window and into the magical Christmas snow outside?

As I contemplated his future, Allie climbed out of the pool with buttmuch on her tail heading toward us.

Lexi slapped the water with her hand. "Allison, get your hiney in here."

She hopped in when Rachel gasped. "Allie, you got a tattoo?"

Her eyes went wide and shot to me and relief washed over her when she saw my perfectly placed towel. "I, well, I did."

Lexi leaned in and examined it. "You know we do these kinds of things as a group. Friendship is doing dumb shit *together*. What were you thinking?"

"I guess I didn't think." Her face grew rosy as the rest of the crew leaned forward to take a look. "Being a grown up is tough, and I deserve to have a cool sticker."

"When?" Rachel scooted closer to her. "When did you get it? It's very pretty."

"When I got here. Yeah, I went to town and decided what the hell." She let out an airy laugh.

Lexi cocked her head. "It's unlike you to just get a tattoo. That's something you totally wouldn't do."

Emily strolled over and plopped in the hot tub while Lexi eyed my visible tattoos, and I quickly looked away.

FIFTY-TWO
ALLIE

OH MOTHER TRUCKER

Shit, shit, and shit!

"I can totally fly by the seat of my pants sometimes." I dramatically threw my fist in the air. "Yup, that's why I got it." My nodding was rapid. "I saw that tattoo parlor and said, Allie, get your ass in there. It's time to live a *hell yeah* life. Am I right, or am I right?"

Lexi shot me a *that's bullshit* stare, and I wanted to disappear down the hot tub drain. "Enough about me. Emily, how are you doing? Big day is almost here." I reached into the water and grabbed her hand. "Tell us every single emotion you're feeling right now."

"Turns out there's nothing like planning a wedding to make you want to punch every person you've ever met in the throat." She gave a nod. "Not you guys, of course."

Travis hopped out and grabbed a towel. "I wanted to sneak off to the Virgin Islands if you remember correctly." He winked. "But your choice was a splashy affair, but I'm sure it'll be great."

She blew him a kiss. "Oh, don't question my choices; you were one of them, buddy."

Kristina laughed. "The wedding will be beautiful."

Emily leaned her head back. "I keep telling myself to put those big girl panties on and shut up. But I've really been debating on hopping into my ass kicker boots and messing some folks up. My mother is driving me nuts, and I'm a little pissed."

"Again, or still?" Evan ran and jumped into the pool and laughter echoed around the room while Will, Royce, and Lexi followed him.

Everybody was getting out when Evan came up behind Levi and put his finger over his lips. In his hand was a big bucket filled with water. A second later he dumped it on Levi as more laughter filled the space.

"Dick!" Levi hopped out and dropped his wet towel to the ground and grabbed another on the table behind him while he chatted with Evan. My mind screamed as my eyes landed on his new tattoo. I held my breath hoping it would be covered soon as he dried himself off.

"Oh my gosh." Lexi spoke quietly.

I follow her stare to the new infinity art on the perfect arm of Levi. Uh-oh.

Rachel stood. "I'm going to get some snacks."

She, Kristine, and Emily didn't notice and walked toward the door while Lexi stood up. Her eyes cut me as she leaned in close and whispered.

"You two got a matching tattoo? *Together*?"

"It's not a big deal. I was a little drunk and—"

Her head dropped back. "You were drunk with Levi? This is so bad."

"It's not. We got a tattoo, no biggie, and I want you to shut your face about this."

I climbed out, grabbed a towel, and headed to my room. No sooner had I closed the door than the hot one sprung inside, closed the door behind him, and yanked me to his chest.

"I have to kiss you right this very second." His lips brushed against mine. "The guys are playing stupid poker and Evan is making me join so I don't think I'll be able to sneak over later."

I kissed his cheek. "I'll see you in the morning then."

His hands on my arms made me tingly and my heart beat in triple time. He brushed aside a whisp of my hair as he green eyes made me want to lock him in the room forever and ever. My breathing stopped for a second as his warm lips were on mine. A restless burning ache spread through my tummy and heated my skin.

I wiggled against him and pulled him closer as my pulse spiked. I didn't want him to leave or even move an inch. He should be in my room all night to provide me every bit of lusty pleasure I could ever hope for.

A little whimper escaped when he broke the kiss and grinned down at me with victory in his eyes, knowing he was still triumphant when it came to heating me up. My cheeks grew hot knowing he could read me like a book.

"Sleep well."

I nodded as he disappeared out the door.

I got ready for bed and headed to the kitchen to get a glass of chocolate milk. I'm a firm believer in the fact that behind every successful woman is a butt load of chocolate. Yes, money can't buy happiness, but it can by chocolate which is kind of the same thing. I was about to enter but stopped around the corner when I heard my name rolling off of Lexi's lips, and I took a peek to find the kitchen table full of poker chips and cards but only Lexi and Will were seated at the table while Levi stood with his back toward me.

"Levi, thanks for today. Well, for yesterday too." She shrugged. "You've kind of kept us out of jail twice."

"You know I'd do anything for her. Then and now."

My pulse ticked up at his words.

"Since we're all here, I just want to clear the air. I know I was out of control with Allie in the past. All I wanted to do was love her, but we all know how that ended."

Will's voice oozed anger. "We're not talking about this, Dawson."

Levi's voice was low and quiet. "Your words at the hospital tore me apart. Saying I would've held her back. We all know she has that amazing intelligence, and you convinced me I'd fuck up her future."

My stomach squished into a ball.

Will's voice was quiet. "You did the right thing when you let her go."

"You never gave her the letter."

Silence.

"You made me a promise. I said the only way I'd leave that hospital was if you gave her the letter, but you never did." Levi's head shook. "I should've never fucking trusted you."

My brain felt like my junk drawer being dumped onto a trampoline. A letter?

"She needed a fresh break."

"Maybe from the eighteen-year-old me, but not when I came back for her every year on our anniversary. The letter told her I'd be at our spot if she wanted us. She was everything, she was my wife."

"Stop saying that," Will hissed.

"I should've just gone after her regardless of you. That letter was the explanation she's never had. She thought I just left her there and *never* contacted her again. How could you let her think that?"

My jaw hit the floor and bounced a few times as my temples began to throb.

"She's moved on."

"Did she? Because her kisses tell me otherwise."

Will's hand hit the table. "Back the fuck off."

"Every day I fought myself to *not* get into my truck and come for her. I thought she read my letter and didn't want me back. The only way I wasn't going to go to her was to move to a different continent. I did that because I believed she wanted to let it all go." I looked into the room to see his head shake. "Do you know how many times I was packed to come back? She was all I thought of."

"Don't kid yourself, it would've never worked."

"I finished college and have a good life and career now. I didn't have your respect back then, and I didn't deserve it. But I've earned that now. I've fucking earned it."

A quick peek showed Lexi looking thoughtfully at Levi. "I think we can agree you have, Levi."

"Thank you."

I took a step away when Will cleared his throat.

"Clint loves her. I'm asking you to stay away, Levi."

"I know what you're asking."

I heard his feet, and I quickly disappeared into the coat closet as my brain tried to wrap around the conversation that included all the missing puzzle pieces. He'd written me and said the words I longed to hear for what felt like an eternity. The explanation that never was.

He'd come back every year on our anniversary?

My heart was skipping beats which I was pretty sure could kill me, while my feet were rooted in the closet as my stomach weaved itself into a French braid. All the blank spaces were suddenly filled. There was a confirmed answer. An explanation for the chunk of my heart that had been missing for so long.

I stayed in the dark closet until I was certain everyone had left the kitchen, and I was a mess. I needed to resuscitate my brain. I dug deep for a pep talk.

Look at you. You're not a total mess. Being awake and stuff like that. You're tucked away in a closet not even stabbing Will right now. You deserve a coffee for being a magnificent little sunbeam.

I finally exited the closet and bolted into the bathroom. Yeah, sometimes in life you just vomit.

Once I'd seen my last meal in reverse, not recommended, I tip toed back to my room. I locked my door and plopped onto the bed. I buried my face in the pillow searching for his scent. Memories zipped through me of being held against the shower wall while he touched me like only he could. Where my name mixed with cursing as he reminded me what it could be like to be owned by him. Because I kind of always had been. My heart was cocooned in warmth.

He'd written me. He'd come back for me every year on our anniversary. He thought I didn't want him.

My family had taken the reins of destiny and sent me in a different direction. Even through the pissiness I felt toward Will, I was floating. Yeah, I'd kill him later. I was literally bursting with joy. Ecstatic was the only word to describe what was bubbling through my veins. I kicked my feet against the bed while I screamed into my pillow.

He had wanted me. He'd always wanted me. So was it safe to assume he still wanted me even though he'd stated clearly as a train derailment that we were only a closure thing? Maybe he was just saying that?

I heard a ping and looked over to see Levi had dropped his phone when he popped into my room. I hopped up, grabbed it, and held it in my hands ready to get it back to him. The case was smooth, shiny, and felt good in my hands. Of course everyone has a screen lock code, but I wondered if he had a screensaver. Although I was alone, I locked the door and pulled the curtains closed.

I ran my finger over the screen and a rustic trail surrounded by trees and water popped up. It was beautiful. I bet it was a Brazilian path where he where he runs. Yes, his bare chest would glisten in the sunlight as his muscly body jogged along causing gasps and horniness from passing tourists. Sigh.

When I hit the button on the side, which I was certain would *not* let me in, I found that smart Levi apparently didn't feel the need for any kind of security on his mobile devise. Clearly, he was a little irresponsible and unaware of shady characters out there.

Allie = shady character.

My eyes darted around my empty room. It would be *completely* wrong to go any further. Every phone owner deserved privacy. I could almost hear the universe scolding me: *Who the hell do you think you are? That is not your phone. Shhh.*

I set it down quickly. The last thing I needed was to be was on the wrong side of karma. We all know that one never escapes karma. Every action is stored and will come back around like a rubber band and snap you right in the ass. Yes, it was a day to have my head on straight.

But do you know what? It suddenly pinged two more times. *Two.* What in God's name was happening in the world of Levi? Why the urgency late at night? Was there an emergency? OMG what if his place was on fire right now?

I should bring Levi the phone immediately. I started toward the door while fighting with myself. But he's the one with zero security on his phone. He clearly had *no* concern for who may see his cell. Right?

As I clicked on a message, even the devil on my shoulder asked what in the hell was I doing.

As I awaited the message to open, I wondered if there was a chance for Allie and Levi after all.

The answer to that question was a swift throat punch.

I stared at the phone while having difficultly comprehending the sight before me.

And I was worried about karma? *Me?*

Yeah, Karma wasn't coming for me. Nope. She was just sharpening her nails and finishing her drink. She would be with Levi shortly I was certain.

My stomach squeezed tight as my eyes landed on a woman in a bikini on the beach and a smile emoji. Her hair was dark and her tan darker while her hot pink bikini barely contained her ginormous set of knockers.

Okay.

Of course he had friends. Like really pretty friends, but so what?

I scrolled over to his contacts. Yes, there were more women than men, but not a big deal. As I went through the A's, I clicked on Ashley and a message popped open and I nearly fell off the bed. There was Ashley alright, sitting on a couch next to a sleeping Levi with no shirt. Yes, apparently Brazilian babes are believers in my "no shirt for Levi" rule.

But I have all sorts of crazy photos in my phone with men. Well, man.

Sure, there's the one where Clint and I went to Texas Roadhouse and he rode the wood horse they bring to your table when it's your birthday. Kinda the same. Okay, not the same.

My door rattled with a knock, and I shoved the phone under the pillow.

"Allie, Do you have any saline solution?"

I bolted to the door, whipped it open, grabbed Kristina, and jerked her inside.

"What's going on?"

"Well, I'm doing something I shouldn't be doing."

Her brow arched. "Should I come back later?"

I shoved her so hard her back hit the wall.

"Shut up. I mean, I've looked at something that I shouldn't be looking at."

She clapped her hands. "Well, let's see?"

"You won't judge me? Believe I have zero self-control?"

"Sweetie, I've cooked for a man I should have poisoned. So yes, I have self-control and know you do too. No judging."

I scooted over, retrieved the phone, and held it out.

"What's this?"

"Levi's phone. And I looked at some stuff. He dropped it here and has no lock code, can you believe that?"

"No code?" She grabbed it from my hand. "Well, that's on him. He's leaving his info out there for the whole world to see. What have we got here?"

I gulped. "Well, I was looking at his contacts and, uh, there are a lot of women in there."

"Let me take a looksee." She plopped on the bed, and I followed. "Actually, me doing this means you're not, so it's really a win/win situation."

She flipped through his contacts. "Let's see what Mr. Levi's messages looks like."

"This is bad." I leaned in closer.

"Shhhh, my little one. It's fine."

She flipped to the B's. "What do you think Bella's last message was?" She clicked on the name, and our collective gasps filled the space. There they were. Levi was sitting on a bed looking at his phone while Bella took a selfie.

She quickly closed the message as a mixture of sadness and irritation shimmied in.

"Maybe we shouldn't look anymore. I mean, if he's not with anyone he didn't do anything wrong."

"You're right. I mean, he said he didn't date or get into relationships, so it is what it is, I guess." Inhale. "Go to the C's."

"Allie."

"C's."

She clicked on Carla and went to the last message to see a blond with big green eyes sitting with Levi in a bar.

Kristina shrugged. "So he likes to, uh, go out a little. He's just a popular guy maybe."

She clicked on the name Chad and after scrolling through some messages a photo appeared of Levi and Chad golfing. Totally normal right?

"Just guy stuff."

She continued to the D's and hit Destiny and a message

popped up with a photo of a sleeping Levi next to two nearly naked women.

The image caused my crying heart to leap from my chest and do a death dive out the fucking window.

"Holy crap." Kristina looked closely. "Wow."

"This is who he is."

She took my hand in hers.

"I'm just one of them now."

"Maybe not."

"He was as clear as a missile strike that he doesn't do relationships. It was us just getting our kicks. I'm so stupid."

"You're not, honey."

"Maybe deep down I thought it might be more somehow. But he was telling me the truth. He isn't the kind to settle down or move in with somebody."

She clicked on Emma and my eyes blinked uncontrollably at the sight of a beautiful woman with thick long black hair wearing white shorts and a blue off the shoulder shirt sitting on a beach with a German Shepard beside her, and a message.

The couch was delivered and looks so good! I did some cooking so now the freezer is stocked with your favorites. See you in a few days!

My stomach clunked to the ground, and I wished my life had background music so I could keep up with whether I was in a comedy or horror show.

Kristina's head shook. "He's living with a woman?"

Her eyes shot to me.

"But he doesn't do relationships." I stared at the words that were burning my corneas.

She exhaled. "Well, is he's buying couches and she's filling up the freezer with his favorites, that sounds like a relationship to me."

My mind was grasping at straws. "Maybe not?"

"Allie, he's purchasing domestic items with a woman, and it sounds like the share a home together."

While my mind was attempting to choke out this new information, prissiness was seeping in. It was one thing if he were honest about being a player and not wanting anything serious, but it was another when he had a woman at home and was with me; he'd made me the other woman.

He planned to be in Colorado and then go home. He didn't know I'd be here. He just wanted to shag and bag me before he left the good old US of A.

Kristina set the phone down. "What can I do?"

"Nothing."

She stood and pulled me to my feet. "Okay, but remember a true friend doesn't ask *what are you going to do* when you tell them you've killed someone. They say *I'll get my shovel*. You text me if you need me."

After a quick hug she exited as my scorched brain processed the new crap that had dropped into my life like a steaming pile of horse shit.

He'd become his father? When I was in high school John Dawson was one of those men who was rough, tough, drank hard, but had an undeniable sexiness that kept him away from his apartment a good chunk of the time. I guess the apple didn't fall far. My life sucks.

He was well aware of the effect he'd always had on me. He just wanted to have another go at it before he went home. To the woman who was probably awaiting his return naked on his new couch.

I allowed myself to cry for five minutes, and the tears fell like rain, and I realized just how far into my heart he was. Again.

I crawled into bed and closed my eyes tightly trying to summon strength.

I tossed and turned bouncing between if it was a toaster-in-the-bathtub or burn the fuckin' house down kind of night. As I attempted to sleep, I realized insomnia is just another word for chit chatting with the demons. Clearly my noggin had decided I would not sleep until I find a cure for my insomnia.

Dear two thirty a.m., we have got to stop meeting like this.

I finally just got up and read my favorite author Mary Lee Painter. Yes, *Wild in Minnesota* took my mind off of the biggest heart breaker on this side of the globe for a while before I took a hot shower.

I applied ointment to my stitches and realized he caused everything. Yup, the second he was in the same state as me my car flew off the road, and I was hurt in multiple ways. Again.

I dabbed on some concealer to hide my cry bags, and blush as if my heart wasn't busted into iddy biddy pieces. It was a *I want to fake my own death, move to Mexico, and live off tacos and margaritas* kinda day.

I just needed perspective. I needed to make it through the wedding and get the hell out of Colorado and deal with my Levi feelings never. While I debated on tossing his phone out the window and into a snowbank, instead I set it on the sofa table in the living room like a normal human before entering the kitchen where laughter assaulted my ears.

I kept my eyes down and made it to the table. I could see Levi at the stove out of the corner of my eye so I sat with my back to him. I could not see his beautiful face.

Clint, Will, and Lexi were seated at the table. Rachel walked in behind me and gave my shoulder a squeeze.

"Good morning. After all that activity yesterday, did everybody sleep well?"

Behind me I heard silverware falling onto the tiled floor. The whole table turned to see Levi's red face. "Oops."

"No. It was a *terrible* night, from top to bottom."

More dropping utensils.

Clint pushed me over a mug. "I guess coffee is in order."

"Or vodka. Is it too early for vodka?"

I grabbed my phone pretending to read something when Levi appeared and placed overflowing plates in front of us. I refused to lift my eyes.

"Bon appetite."

His deep voice rattled me, and I was glad when he returned to the center island and stove. My heart gave me a disgusted huff. How was I going to survive being trapped in this place with the man who turned my legs to spaghetti with a glance?

And what about my new tattoo? Shit, a daily reminder of what a dumbass I was. How could I be soooo stupid? Word of the day! Dipshitidiot; when dipshit just doesn't cover it.

I took a bite of breakfast and irritation pumped beneath my skin; damn the hot man who can create a delightful breakfast of fluffy French toast and bacon with the perfect amount of crispness.

I focused on eating slowly because I wanted to inhale this masterpiece when his voice filtered through the room. "How's everything?"

I was shocked when Lexi nodded. "This is good grub, Levi."

I could imagine the smile he wore at her words. It made me

want to slap him around a little. Edit, a lot. I had a moment of joy hit me at the thought of beating him senseless with spatula and hog tying him with the Christmas tree lights around the window.

I held my fork in the air. "Not my favorite. Good try, I guess."

All eyes shot to me as my tone was a little more grizzly than I'd expected.

FIFTY-THREE
LEVI

WHAT IS HAPPENING?

I couldn't figure out what in the hell was happening in the kitchen.

Was this her pretending to hate me again to keep everyone from planning my disappearance? If so, she was succeeding with flying colors.

I turned off the burner. "Anyone want the last slices of bacon?"

Allie's voice was as sharp as a switchblade. "Nobody wants fuckin' bacon, Levi."

The wind was knocked out of me as Clint and Will exchanged a look while Kristina gave me pity eyes. I scratched my head fairly certain this was an act? Yeah, it had to be.

Evan raised his hand. "I'll take the bacon. And thanks for cooking."

"Sure." I cleared my throat. "Evan, I wanted to see if you and Rachel would like to run into town. I saw a coffee shop I thought looked interesting. Anyone else like a mountain coffee shop?"

That was when Allie stood and brought her plate to the

sink, but her eyes stayed down. "I'm sure Colorado coffee blows ass. Most things in this freaking state seem to."

With that she turned and walked out of the room.

I rinsed the pan, put it in the dishwasher, and knew I needed to locate Allie and find the answer to whatever the hell happened this morning.

Once everyone adjourned to the living room, I sprung up the stairs and to her room and turned the knob, to find it locked.

"Langley." I whispered through the door but was met by silence. I tapped. "Allie."

"Go away."

While I had hopes of the door flying open and being pulled inside, it appeared things had taken a turn.

"Are you okay?"

"Yes, I'm fucking okay."

"You just seem a little, uh, annoyed."

"No, I'm not annoyed, ya jackass. I'm just rolling my eyes and speaking in a condescending tone because you're so fucking wonderful."

There had to be an explanation. Amnesia? "Well, I'm a little confused."

I jumped as the door whipped open. "You're confused?" A sarcastic laugh which scared me a little flew out of her. "Let me clear it up for you. Closure is over. And it's such a shame for you, I'm sure." She whispered, "Your sneaky intention of messing around with me is done. You think you can just come in here and have sex with me all night?"

I shrugged. "Last night?"

Her nose wrinkled. "Shut up. Closure is done. You go back to your life and stay the hell away from me."

Yes, it was definitely amnesia. I decided instantly to do the only thing that could bring her back to reality. In one swift move I had one arm around her waist and lifted her into her room while shutting the door with the other.

"You let me go—"

It was then I pulled her close and kissed her. She pushed me away but then her arms went around my shoulders, and we were back.

For three seconds.

She squirmed out of my grasp. "You get out of here right now. This whole thing is done." She straightened her shirt. "Go get back to your life in *Brazil*."

"I need to know what in the hell is going on with you."

She pushed me towards the door. "What's going on with me? My brain has begun to function again, that's what's going on. You are bad news through and through, and I want you gone."

With another push I was in the hall and took her arms and pulled her to me. I stared into her eyes searching for the answer to whatever the fuck this was. She was squirming so I lifted her up so her feet were off the floor, and we were eye to eye.

"Tell me what's happening."

Her head shook. "Let me go. Leave me alone."

"What—"

Her head shook as she whispered, "Please go."

I put her down. "But Allie—"

"Go."

FIFTY-FOUR
ALLIE
SHITTASTER

I closed the door on Levi and us. Clearly, he had Brazilian bombshells around every corner awaiting his return and that's where he belonged.

I just needed to pull my shit together and for him to stop popping up around every corner just wanting sex.

My heart whispered that he needed to be gone. While she was leaning towards a permanent solution to the problem certain we could get away with it, I just wanted *anything* that would just keep him away from me until I was wheels up on a plane. A temporary solution was what I needed to conger up. All Levi pings and pangs I'd file into my "fuck this" and "fuck that" drawer when I got home.

I needed to find a cluster fuck fixer. A superhero who's an expert and can unfuck any situation in a single bound. A calm genius who is levelheaded and would help me give zero fucks about the womanizing man in the house.

I suddenly regretted holding in one fart for the mother trucker.

I realized this whole thing was making my arm pits sticky, gross, so I swapped out my tee for another and pulled my burgundy cardigan over it.

Then Taylor's *Cardigan* lyrics ran through me and a few tears escaped.

The man I knew long ago was gone.

I reapplied my mascara and curled my eye lashes swearing this was it. I was a tough chick and had gotten over Levi once before, and I could do it again.

A knock at the door brought on a prickling sensation to the back of my neck. I inhaled deeply knowing I had to keep the dumbfuckery to a minimum today and use the mediocre brain God gave me, although I was fairly certain at this point, he would consider letting me exchange mine for a new one.

"It's Kristina, can I come in?"

I opened the door. "Hey."

She examined my face. "How are you?"

"Well, I spun the wheel of attitude this morning. It landed on bitch."

She walked in and sat on the bed. "Yeah, I noticed that a little at breakfast. I wanted to check on you."

I stood in front of her running out of places to look.

"I'm here if you need to talk. You know I'm loyal and anything said stays in this room."

I nodded and sat next to her. "I kind of just don't want to talk about it. I want to forget about it. Everything."

"I see. That could be what you do. But if you need to talk, I'm here, okay?"

I took a breath. "I told you we were close while here, and then we would move forward and never look back."

"I think I heard Dr. Phil talk about closure once."

Gasp. "You heard that too? It's bullshit, closure does nothing but add some confusion into the recipe of a shit-taster." I forced out a breath I didn't know I was holding.

She nodded. "I don't wish death on anyone, just diarrhea while stuck in traffic for Levi. With many sneezes."

"I hate him."

"I want to make this better for you, Allie."

I dropped my head back. "I just want to go home. Be in my bitch cave, where I can take off my stupid damn bra, wear jammies, consume all the alcohol, and have no shitty fucking assholes around."

Her shoulder nudged mine. "Oooh, a bitch cave. I want one." She took my hand in hers. "I'm sorry you're going through this. Twice. Someone treating you like this is all the closure you need. What can I do to help?"

"Well, he keeps showing up everywhere and wants to kiss and say words that melt me. I just need something that will keep him away."

"Oooh, you could act like you're into Clint. I know you've been avoiding him, but just pretend, while in Colorado, and you can deal with all that once you're out of here."

"Yeah. I can do that. I've been in here praying for a super-hero, and it looks like that might be you."

Her hand went over her heart. "Yes, I want to be the super-hero! I'll help you and my power could be, uh, the filler. I'll fill you with ideas to get rid of evil Levi and other stuff. Yeah, if you have an empty wallet, boom, it's filled with cash. Cup empty, boom, it's full."

"I love that."

Her gasp nearly sucked the curtains from the window. "Do you know what I just realized? *Levi* and *evil* are made of the same damn letters."

My eyes locked with hers. "I am *stunned* I haven't put this together before. There it is, the universe was trying to warn me from day one, and I missed it."

FIFTY-FIVE
LEVI
WTF?

I stood next to the Christmas tree as *We Wish You a Merry Christmas* played quietly in the distance while fat snowflakes fell outside the window making it a picture perfect day.

But my morning was quickly swirling down the toilet. What in the bloody hell happened to change perfect Allie to a fire breathing hate machine?

I paced the living room when Evan entered. "We have a few hours before the wedding; you want to play cards?"

"Cards on are my list of things I don't give a shit about."

"Wow."

"Sorry, but everything's taken a turn this morning, and I don't know why. It's hard now."

He shrugged. "Life is a dick, sometimes it gets hard for no reason."

"You're clearly the fountain of knowledge I'm *not* looking for today."

"Calm down Karen."

He sat in the chair next to the roaring fire I suddenly wanted to toss him into.

"Everything was good with Allie." I looked around to make sure we were alone. "And now she suddenly hates me. Like *hates* me."

"She's probably overwhelmed. All her friends are here, Clint, and now her brother. If you didn't do anything wrong, maybe just back off and give her some time."

"Maybe. Nothing happened or changed, she's just dealing with a lot. Yeah, that makes sense."

Allie and Kristina walked down the stairs, and I whispered to Evan. "Get Kristina out of here."

Evan sprung to his feet. "Kristina, Rachel's been looking for you."

"What?"

He walked past her. "Follow me."

With that we were alone.

"Can I have a word with you?"

Her hands popped on her hips. "I thought I smelled something burning, are you trying to think again?"

"Allie, I don't like this attitude."

"That's a shame. I'll need one minute to recover from that tragedy."

"Why are you saying these things?"

"If the things I say shock you, can you even imagine the things I've left unsaid? It'd blow your effing mind."

Lexi came in from the kitchen as her eyes darted between us. "Allie, I made a little coffee bar in the kitchen with mocha and all the yummy stuff. Can I get you some?"

"I'll have a vodka valium latte, please."

I sat on the couch as Will came down the stairs and

pointed to Lexi. "Hey, can you get everyone in here for a minute."

Lexi yelled and everyone filtered in and found seats. Allie was looking everywhere but in my direction, and other than kidnapping her, I couldn't think of another way to get a conversation to figure out what the hell had transpired today.

I stood next to the fireplace as Royce and Clint came down the stairs. Some days the supply of available curse words isn't sufficient to meet my needs.

Evan walked over and spoke quietly. "Hey, are you feeling calmer?"

"No, as a matter of fact I think I'm going maybe kidnap Allie for a while just so I can figure out what's going on. Not really kidnapping, just an ordered discussion?"

"In my opinion that's a bad idea."

"A good place for your opinion is up your ass."

He punched my arm. "I see we're playing stupid again. Looks like your winning."

Clint walked to the center of the room, grabbed Allie by the hands, and pulled her to him.

"First of all, I wanted to thank everyone for welcoming me here."

Nods around the room, and I would've been blind to not notice the fucking overjoyed look on Will's face. I couldn't recall seeing him happy. Ever. But there he stood, arms across his chest, wearing a smile.

I hate being hated by him.

Clint turned. "Allie, I know I surprised you by coming here, but sometimes absence clears things up."

He reached into his pocket, and every ounce of oxygen was squeezed from my body when he pulled out a little red velvet box and dropped to his knee. I'd reached the point in my life where I need a stronger word than fuck.

"Allie, I don't want to imagine another day without you."

Everything was in slow motion, and my vision was hyper focused. Her eyes went wide as he opened the box while douchbag wore a fucking smile that could curdle milk.

"Allie, will you marry me?"

Everything froze. I couldn't breathe and felt Evan's hand on my arm. And then it happened. Allie's hands went to her cheeks as she stared at the ring. I don't know shit about diamonds, but as he pulled it out of the box all I knew was that it was big. A large, shiny diamond that made me want to hurdle the coffee table, grab dickhead, and drown him in the lake out back.

Time stood still as I awaited her refusal. There was no fucking way she wanted to marry this dude after our time together. We were back—Allie and Levi.

"Yes."

My ears melted off my head. What in the hell was happening?

Clint slid the ring onto her finger before standing and hugging her as the room burst into applause, and I couldn't seem to suck in any air. I wanted to leave, to disappear, but my feet were stuck. While Clint hugged her, Kristina's eyes were on me.

I stood there while all the ladies went and looked at the ring as Allie held out her hand. She had a few tears under her eyes she wiped away.

FIFTY-SIX
ALLIE
LEVI = EVIL

I stared at the ring as the voices in my head were requesting booze pronto. Sobriety and whatever in fuck this was were not mixing well.

This could be the worst idea in the history of time, but it was my steppingstone to get where I wanted to go. A way to get out of Colorado, and I'd deal with it once I was home. Or maybe I'd move away and start a new life with a new less fucked up identity.

This morning was a time for fake smiles and head nods all in the spirit of getting away from Levi. He'd hatched up the closure plan knowing he made me weak. One look and he made my bra want to pop open.

My mind was racing with visions of the last few days hurling through my brain like an asteroid. Currently it seemed my brain had ten tabs open, a GIF of a guy falling down, and an alarm going off; I was in the danger zone. My life is like when you're holding your laundry basket and a sock falls and you pick it up and two more fall, and eventually everything is everywhere.

He had beautiful women in Brazil and he just wanted to be shagged and bagged in Colorado because he'd grown into an awful human. I wondered if the one in his home knew of the other ladies. He needed to burn in hell.

He wasn't my Levi anymore.

Levi = evil.

I turned to find Will beside me and pulled me in for a hug. "Congrats, Sis."

I stepped back and just looked up at him. He'd dropped everything and flew across the country when he learned Levi was in the same house as me. Because he knew Levi was bad, and I was stupid. This engagement was the answer for him.

I stood silent as mime while happiness buzzed around the room. Lexi and Rachel were beaming while laughter and chipper voices were crushing my eardrums. I kept my gaze from Levi, but could see him out of the corner of my eye by Evan.

Lexi clapped her hands. "Okay, as much as I'd like to bring out the bubbly to celebrate, we all have to be at the church in less than two hours."

I grabbed Kristina's hand and bolted up the stairs and into my room. I locked the door and turned to her.

"Allie, he proposed."

"It'll keep Levi away. I'll deal with it all once I'm out of here."

Her head tilted. "I saw Levi downstairs. The look on his face said he wasn't staying away."

My heart was beating against my ribs, and my thoughts were as clear as mud soup. "I need to get out of this room. He might come here."

"The door's locked, you're good."

I pointed. "He comes to my window."

Her hand went to her heart. "He scaled a two-story snowy roof to come here?"

"It's how he's always come to me." It came out in a broken whisper, and I cursed the fact that he knew with one look he had me any way he wanted me. "You get ready in here and I'll change in your room. I can't risk him showing up."

"You're engaged now."

"It doesn't matter. He knows he can have me whenever he wants. I'm like the wounded deer. He circles until I'm too weak to do anything."

I grabbed my dress and makeup before heading down the hall.

FIFTY-SEVEN
LEVI

PICKLED HERRING

I did the only thing I could to prevent bodily harm to dickhead, Royce or Will; I changed and sat in Evan's car until people came out and got into the van.

We drove through the magical Christmas town that now had a black cloud over it. The street where we kissed, got a tattoo, and her panties caught on fire in the private dining room at the Bistro; it was a punch to the gut.

"I can't believe this."

"They had a pretty good thing when they were together. I know it sucks, but shit happens."

"This is all jacked up. She doesn't want to be with him, I know it."

"She's a smart girl. You have to respect this."

I stared out the window. "There are approximately 1,010,000 words in the English language, but I can't string enough together to express how much I want to hurt you right now."

"Levi."

My mind was a mega maniac solution seeking vessel at the

moment. It was out lassoing up anything that would help me find a way to get her alone.

The big van stopped and as if reading my mind Allie flew out of it and into the church. A few moments later the others exited, and I followed them inside.

My stomach clenched as my eyes spotted the two perfectly decorated Christmas trees on the altar causing memories of the storage room to take flight. How I missed the good old days.

The girls entered a room down the hall from the sanctuary. As pussy of a move it was, I jumped behind a large fake plant at the end of the hall and watched Will, Evan, and Clint enter the sanctuary.

As my focus returned to the hall, Allie exited one door and entered another. I power walked down to see she was in the ladies room. I opened a door next to the bathroom to see a Sunday school classroom filled with little tables and a window. Bingo.

I closed the door behind me and entered. Once the screen was out, I hopped through the window and into the snow before examining the other window in front of me; it was a good window that slid up. Old and workable.

I pushed with all my might and got it opened about ten inches.

"Allie." I whispered. "Langley?"

I jumped when she appeared in front of the window.

"Go away, Levi."

"I need to tell you something."

"Well, I need to tell you that *Levi* and *evil* are spelled with the same letters. Yeah, how did I miss that shit? While I may have had dumbass stamped across my forehead in glitter recently, I'm well aware of the reality, and it's time for you to go straight to hell."

"Well, that's just plain mean."

She flashed a toothy smile. "I know. Bye."

She started to turn when I reached in and caught her wrist. "No."

"No? You're not the boss of me, Levi Dawson." Her eyes went wide. "I hate you."

"Langley, tell me what's changed here? I mean last night—"

"Last night sucked." She pulled her wrist, but I didn't let go.

"You're not marrying Clint."

"I don't give a tiny little rat's ass what you think. Clint is a good man. Good for me."

"So is pickled Herring."

Her nose wrinkled. "What?"

"Yeah." Where was I going with this? "It's rich in omega-3 fatty acids and Vitamin D."

"Huh?"

"Some things *seem* good for you but are fucking garbage."

She pulled her wrist again, but I held on.

"You just shut your face. Maybe I want to be with him."

"You're lying."

She gasped. "Me? Me *lying*? You are the biggest liar in the history of the world. You have dark motives and think you can use your stupid smile to get under my skin."

"You're adorable when you're pissed."

"Just leave me alone."

I pulled her closer. "You can't close your eyes without seeing me."

"That's it! I'm telling Will and he will kill you today."

I chuckled. "We both know that won't happen."

"Let go of me before I scream. I hate you."

"Why? Why do you hate me?"

"Just shut up."

"Langley, this makes no sense."

"I saw your phone, okay?"

"Okay?"

She leaned in close, and my heart jumped when I smelled her perfume which sent images of her mouth on mine. That body moving against me.

"I saw your stupid Brazilian women."

"Brazilian women?"

"Yes. And who doesn't have a screen lock anyway. You're dumber than I ever imagined. Everyone has the right to be stupid, but you're abusing the privilege."

"Allie—"

A sadness washed over her. "Just let me go."

"Yes, I've been with women. Too many women, and it's been wrong. Every time someone might be getting too close to me, I bolt. Nobody could ever be what you are."

"That's bullshit." She spoke in a harsh whisper. "I know about the couch!"

"Couch?"

Her voice dripped with distain. "Like you don't know what I'm talking about."

"I don't know what you're talking about."

Her whisper was razor sharp. "You're in a relationship buying domestic items with that woman. You were all *I don't do relationships* but you're in one. You lied to me and made me the other woman! Does she know about your posse of women? You are the worst kind of man ever!"

"She's works for me—"

Gasp. "You're the scum of the earth. Hurting people and breaking, probably, like every HR rule in existence." Her eyes were fire. "I hope the worker people who deal with these issues track you down, and, well, do whatever they do to people who break HR rules. Yeah, they'll put you away!"

Was it a shitty time to have laughter escape me? The answer was a strong yes.

"I hate you."

"Her name is Margo and she's dog sitting while I'm here. That's it."

She tugged her arm again. "More lies. Do you even know what the truth is? I saw she *cooked*. Yes, only a woman who thinks she's in a relationship cooks up a storm. There you go, you're caught and the worst kind of two timing liar ever."

"She cooks because she's in culinary school. She cooks for our whole office almost every day."

"Bull shit."

"She let the furniture store in to deliver a couch because I accidently caught the old one on fire."

Her eyes narrowed.

"Yeah, don't even ask. The bottom line is there's no *relationship* with anybody. Not once since it was you and me. You're the only one."

"I—"

"On our anniversary, every year, I come home and wait for you on the Sugar Creek Bridge. I'd left a letter with Will at the hospital telling you that's where I'd be on that day every year if you wanted me. Our spot. I was there 64 days ago, and already have my ticket bought for next October. There can never be anyone else when all I think about is the possibility of you and me."

Her head tilted.

"I wait from sunup to sundown, every time, hoping to see come around the corner." I leaned my forehead against the glass. "I thought you didn't want me. That you'd moved on and couldn't forgive me. For the accident or leaving."

The little wrinkle between her brows made an appearance.

"I've been trying to play it cool in Colorado. Letting you think I only wanted closure, but it was bull shit. I just wanted to be close with you." My chest tightened. "Forgive me for the lie, but I knew you'd be here. I figured it out and I was done hoping. I came here for you. To make you mine again. You're all I've ever wanted. Needed. It's always been you."

Her face softened.

"I let people tell me what I needed to do that day, and I've regretted it every minute of every day since. And as time passed, I knew you'd moved on, and I was afraid of never being what you needed in your life."

She took a step toward the window. "So those women—"

"I'm a stupid guy. I've had women in my life over the years, but I couldn't let anyone get close. That space in me is owned by you. If I couldn't have you, nobody would ever have me. You're the only one who's ever had me."

She took another step toward me. "I had you?"

"You've always had me."

We stared at each other through the glass.

"Open the damn window, Langley."

Her little grin grabbed me by the throat. She lifted the window, and I leaned in.

Her minty breath hit my face. "Hi."

"Hi." I wrapped my arms around her. "We were supposed to be, Allie. You and me. All along it was supposed to be us." She rested her forehead against mine. "I'm not leaving this state without you."

Her hands went around my neck. "So, you're saying you really dig me, huh?"

I laughed. "I dig you so fucking hard it hurts."

She giggled as she kissed my cheek. "So, you don't want to live without me?"

"Nope, I can't do it. Won't do it."

"It's you and me?"

"You and me."

Kristina suddenly appeared in the bathroom with freak out all over her face.

"You guys!" She closed the door and leaned back against it. "The girls are coming." Her finger pointed at Allie. "Aren't you engaged?"

"Not for long."

Kristina clapped before throwing her arms in the air. "Yes!" She walked over and pushed my chest. "But you get out of here now. It's almost wedding time and anyone dying would turn Emily into a monster. In the last twenty minutes she's already laughed, cried, and had a tantrum."

Allie's smile lit up the bathroom in the First United Methodist Church. "I know. She's a little fragile today."

Kristina adjusted her boobs. "Not fragile like a flower, fragile like a fricking bomb. Levi, you need to disappear like now."

Allie stepped away but I grabbed her arm and pulled her to me for another kiss before Kristina walked over and pushed me. "Out!"

FIFTY-EIGHT
ALLIE

LEVI & ALLIE

Once back in the bride's room I jumped into the beautiful deep red bridesmaid dress that was strapless and sucked me in in all the right places. The hair stylist did my hair in a half up-do, and I applied my lip gloss while I swear to God I floated through the air. For the first time in years, I was light as a feather.

What circumstances took away all those years ago, Levi had corrected. It would be us again. But better because we knew what it was to be without our other half and that's what we were together. Whole.

As I made my way to my spot in the front of the church my eyes landed on Levi in the fourth row, and my heart grew three sizes at the grin he wore. My vision blurred for a moment as my heart digested that this was our new beginning.

As the three-string orchestra filled the air with Pachelbel's Cannon in D, I knew it was now our new song. The one that would always remind me of the handsome man declaring his love for me outside of the church bathroom while standing in a snowbank. Be still my beating heart.

Emily made her way down the aisle, and she was beautiful beyond words in her wedding gown that was chic and classic with a sprinkling of bling. But my gaze kept sneaking back to Levi whose eyes never left me, and my heart sang opera for the first time ever.

It was an absolutely stunning luncheon reception in the beautiful ballroom with spectacular views of the snowy mountains in the distance. The hearty Italian cuisine was the bomb and consisted of yummy lasagna (yes, please), tortellini with bread sticks, and a beautiful chocolate fountain she'd decided on because of little old me. Sigh.

Guests enjoyed the most delectable holiday treats including red and green cake balls, Christmas Trifle, cupcakes with crushed candy canes topping the thick white frosting, and cookies. Thank God the Super Saver Serial Killer didn't ruin this amazing affair. (Our group did steer clear of the desserts.)

Clint stuck to me like a cheap shower curtain, but my eyes didn't want to leave Levi. I decided I'd get out of my recent engagement once we got back to the house. Sure, Levi and I might have to disappear into the forest once Will found out, but I didn't give a rip. They may hate us together, but there was no stopping us this time. Yup, from now on I do a thing called *what I want*.

The D.J. played some tunes and before I knew it Clint had me on the dance floor. We swayed standing near Royce and Lexi.

"Are you okay?"

I nodded. "Yes, it's just been a busy few days."

I looked at Levi with Evan standing at the bar. The second his eyes connected with mine there was electricity. One look. How could one look liquefy me at a glance?

Once Emily and Travis exited in a horse drawn carriage and disappeared down the beautiful Christmas street, our crew said goodbyes and walked down the stairs outside of the reception.

My heart was floating, and I swear to God glitter was pumping through my veins; Levi was free. I was free. So we could be tied up together forever. Sigh.

Our group stopped when we hit the sidewalk.

Will rubbed his hands together. "Well, since we have the afternoon free, should we hit the brewery in town? Online I saw they have a variety of Christmas beers. Spiced ales and winter warmers if anyone's interested."

Levi's dirty grin hit me as his eyes locked with mine. His wink reminded me that I was his.

Clint reached over and grabbed my hand as Rachel pulled on her gloves. "I have ninety-nine problems but I'm going to have some alcohol and ignore every single one."

Will pointed. "It's right down the street so we can walk."

We all strolled down the sidewalk.

"Wait." It was Levi's deep voice.

We all stopped, turned, and his grin tickled my tummy.

He nodded as he took a step in my direction. "Allie, marry me."

A collective gasp came as Kristina started jumping and clapping.

"I love you, Langley. Marry me today."

Clint released my hand and took a step toward Levi. "What the fuck are you doing?"

I screamed. "I'll marry you right now!"

One hand went over his heart and the other punched the air. "Yes!"

Rachel grabbed my hand. "Allie, what are you doing?"

My heart did a triple back handspring with a twist. "I'm marrying the only man I've ever loved."

Will shook his head. "This is not happening."

I threw my arms in the air. "I don't care what you or anyone thinks."

Levi took a step and grabbed my hand. A second later Clint had Levi by his coat and pushed him hard. "Get the fuck out of here! You're not marrying anyone."

Levi leaned in. "Watch me."

With that Clint punched Levi in the jaw and he stumbled back.

Levi let out a sarcastic laugh. "That all you got? She's always been mine, we all know that."

Levi nailed Clint in the face as Rachel screamed. Clint stood, lunged forward, grabbed Levi by the jacket, and pushed him so hard he went off of the sidewalk and into the street.

My heart stopped when a passing car hit Levi and sent him onto the hood of the car and over the top. I heard screams and tore into the street behind the car to find Levi lying on his side. My heart beat violently, with a frantic pounding in my ears. What?

I dropped to my knees, everything being hyper-slow, as fragmented thoughts tried to comprehend what was happening. His eyes closed, how still he was, the blood coming from his head.

A numbness wrapped around me; this wasn't happening. Was this real? It couldn't be.

There was commotion all around me but in the space between Levi and me, there was silence. I leaned down and cradled his head in my arms as my white coat was turning red. I took my scarf and held it against his head and my vision blurred.

I couldn't lose him.

❄

They'd just rolled him into the hospital room after surgery and my soul ached looking at him. Evan sat in the corner of the room and Will was smart enough to be in the waiting area outside after the girls sent Clint away.

Kristina knocked and walked in. "Hey. Can I get you some coffee or water?"

I shook my head as a nurse entered and checked the machines next to Levi's bed. "The doctor will be in soon to discuss the surgery."

Kristina leaned down. "What can we do? Anything you want, I'll do."

"Bring a Christmas tree here. And lights, lots of lights."

"What?"

I wiped my eyes. "He loves Christmas, it's his favorite. And tomorrow is Christmas."

Kristina squeezed my arm. "Honey, I don't think they allow that in ICU."

The nurse looked over. "Normally not." Her eyes told me the chances weren't good. "But I think a small tree would be just fine."

"The girls and I will go get one right now, okay?"

I nodded as I looked at Levi. His face was calm while all hell was breaking loose inside him.

I stood when a man in blue scrubs and a white doctor's coat entered and extended his hand. "I'm Dr. Ferguson."

"I'm Allie."

"Please have a seat." He sat in the empty chair beside me. "I apologize I wasn't able to speak with you prior to the surgery. We wanted to get in there as soon as possible."

He motioned to Levi. "He has a condition known as a cerebral edema. It's something that turns our most precious organ into a battleground."

My agonizing heart twisted so hard I saw quick spots in front of my eyes. "What is a cerebral edema?"

He spoke with his hands. "Imagine your brain as a delicate sponge, normally content within the bony skull we all have. Because of the accident, the sponge has slowly expanded, pressing against the unyielding skull. Basically, it's a buildup of fluid that causes the brain to swell, and, unfortunately, can lead to a cascade of neurological concerns."

The back of my eyes burned as I attempted to blink back tears. He grabbed a box of tissues from the counter behind him and handed it to me.

"Thank you."

"The acute phase of brain swelling is like a high-stake drama on TV. His brain is in full crisis mode right now. It was kicked off when the accident occurred, making the next twenty-four hours very crucial. His accident, colliding with the car, was the equivalent to a motorcycle accident where the rider had no helmet on with the trauma he's experienced. We acted fast with the surgery to try to relieve some of the pressure, which is good, but, uh, things are up in the air right now. We're monitoring and trying to control the intracranial pressure. It's like a fire and we're coming at it from all angles, but we'll have to wait and see what happens in the next day."

His eyes were telling me things I didn't want to know.

He was going to die.

An hour later Kristina, Lexi, and Rachel had a Christmas tree in the corner filled with white lights which put a soft glow in the room. The red and green balls reflected, and it was beautiful.

Levi would love it.

Lexi set a little speaker on the table next to Levi's bed, hit a button, and *I'm Dreaming of a White Christmas* softly filled the space. She pulled me to my feet, wrapped her arms around me, and we cried together. After a long moment she pulled back and dabbed my eyes with a tissue.

"I'm sorry, Allie. For then and now. I didn't give him the chance I should've." She pushed hair over my shoulder. "Please forgive me."

I kissed her cheek. "I love you."

"I'm going to go get you some food."

"I'm not hungry."

"Too bad. You will eat. Don't flip my bitch switch." She squeezed me. "I stole your line."

She left, and I took his hand in mine and prayed. I prayed for strength and healing and for a Christmas miracle. I hated the doubt I had that anything could save him as his head bleeding in the street was running through me.

There was a knock at the door and Will entered.

"Not now, Will. I don't want you here."

"Allie, nobody meant for this to happen."

"I don't believe you! You didn't mean for this accident to

happen, but you came here to make sure he was pushed out like you always had. Screw what I wanted or anything else."

He took a controlled breath. "He's not good for you—"

"I'm so sick of that sentence! You *never* knew him. You never gave him a chance. Yes, he was wild and lacked direction back then, but he would've walked to the ends of the earth for me."

"He was—"

"Don't you dare tell me what he *was*. You didn't know him then or now. You *never* gave him a chance to show you who he was. You, mom, and dad decided everything. Levi didn't cause the truck to run into us, he didn't do one thing wrong, but you didn't care. You wanted him gone. You sat in my hospital room tearing him apart, making him responsible for an accident he didn't cause. You used it to get rid of him. My husband."

"Don't say that."

"It's true. You and our parents changed the whole course of my life. I never had a say. You all decided everything. And what about the letter?"

His jaw clenched.

"Yeah, I heard you talking last night. He left something for me that would've changed everything, and you never gave it to me. You *never* gave me the chance to decide my life. You tore it away from me. There were years you could've told me about it, but no. You just kept lying to me. And he thought I wanted him gone forever."

"I was wrong, Allie. I'm sorry. We were all trying to do the right thing and, well, we were wrong."

I took the breath and turned back to Levi. "Not this time."

I heard him walking toward me.

"Stop right there. If you aren't supporting my prayers right now, you go."

"Allie—"

"He is the only man I've ever loved. The only man I will ever love. If you're not for us, you're against us, and I want you gone right now."

"You can't be—"

I turned to my brother. "I can be whatever the fuck I want to be. You either support me or get the hell out." I wiped my face. "I have a minister from the church in town coming here and if he opens his eyes for even a minute, there will be a wedding. If he doesn't, there will be a commitment ceremony. Do you understand me?" The back of my eyes burned. "I will be his wife when he dies."

The girls wanted to stay with me but when it got late, I insisted they go back to the house. I wanted to be alone. As soon as they were gone, I pulled the little loveseat over next to the bed, as close as possible.

I held his hand and stared into his face. I loved him so much it put an ache deep in my soul. As I prayed, it seemed every sound including my own blinking eyes was magnified.

The beeps of the machines were like a ticking time bomb, and the monotonous drip of the IV bag and even the quiet swish of the nurses' scrubs as they pass by his room were almost painful to my ears.

The dim fluorescent bulb across the room was too harsh, with the light bouncing off the polished sterile metal equipment causing my eyes to be jumpy and unable to settle in one place.

I gulped air still trying to process all the fucking things that had gone wrong as worry seemed to have clawed through my ribs and was now attacking me from the inside out. Everything was on a tilt and my senses were overwhelmed. The place I sat was cold, yet my skin clamy, and my clothes scratchy.

My heart was bathing in sorrow realizing how close we were. So fucking close. We almost had it all; almost.

I don't know how long I was sleeping, but it was still dark when I opened my eyes. My chest tightened at the sight of my mother sitting next to me on the sofa. Her auburn hair was pushed behind her ear as she sat with her hands folded, and eyes closed.

"Mom."

My vision blurred as she hugged me and peppered my face with kisses.

"If you're here to do anything—"

Her voice was almost a whisper. "I'm here because I heard there's going to be a Christmas wedding."

She held me in her arms.

"Dad and I took the red eye. We wouldn't miss it. And I knew you'd need this." She reached into her purse and pulled out a black velvet box she handed to me.

I lifted the lid and my heart sputtered at the sight of the gold ring. The wedding band Levi had picked out for me at the pawn shop just outside of Vegas.

"I've known you hid it in the back of the dresser in your old room for years." She sniffed.

Hot tears streamed down my face. "It's not fair."

She pulled me to her. "I know it's not."

"He's all I've ever wanted, and there were years of wasted time. Years I should've been with him. I should've gone and found him. I should've done it all differently."

She pulled back and cupped my face in her hands. "I'm so sorry for everything. We were afraid, trying to protect you. Please forgive me, Allie."

We sat silently for several minutes.

"He's going to die, Mom."

We sat holding hands watching him.

I took Levi's wallet from the table beside the bed. I opened it, went into the secret pocket, and pulled out his ring then whispered. "Look, Mom he had it with him every day."

She held me tightly while I cried my heart out.

The door opened and light streamed in from the hall as my father entered. I jumped up and he hugged me.

"Allie, I'm so sorry, honey."

I buried my face in his chest and although I swore I had to be out of tears, I was wrong.

A few hours later Kristina, Lexi, and Rachel walked in carrying flowers and bags. My mom hopped up and hugged everyone.

"Girls, I'm so glad you're here." She looked over at me. "You all have been Allie's rock forever."

Lexi walked over and pulled me to my feet. "Well, it's time to get Allie into her wedding dress."

"Dress?"

She laughed. "You told me the story of your Goodwill dress. And sure as shit, we found one at the Goodwill right here in Colorado, and I believe it's perfect."

"Thank you."

A knock at the door and my heart stopped as John Dawson

entered. Tall, like his son, same green eyes, but the hair that used to be salt and pepper, was just salt now.

My father stood and shook his hand, and my mother gave him a hug. "We'll give you some time alone."

My parents led the girls out of the room. "We'll be outside when you're ready." She reached out and took John's hands. "We're praying for Levi."

His eyes welled as he nodded, and she gave him another hug.

Once the room cleared, he spoke softly. "I talked to the doctor last night and got on the first flight I could." He scooted a chair close to Levi and sat down. "I can't believe this."

"I know."

"I let my son down so many times over the years. I was nothing but a mean alcoholic when he was growing up. But then he shows up and makes me go to Brazil with him a few years ago." He looked at me. "It was his willpower that got me sober."

He ran the back of his hand over his eyes. "A man like that deserved a lot better than me."

I leaned down and put my arm around his shoulder. "But he wouldn't be the man he is without you. The things you and he went through made him strong and brave."

He patted my arm. "But when it was you in the hospital bed, I broke a part of him by making him go. You both were young, but for me and your family to pull the shit we did, it was wrong."

"But we found each other again." I wiped my eyes. "He asked me to marry him yesterday."

His head whipped in my direction.

I nodded. "I'm marrying your son today."

"You are?"

I nodded. "Even if he doesn't wake up, the minister is coming and will marry us." I looked over at the most perfect man in the world. "So when I go to heaven someday my husband will be waiting for me." I forced a smile. "We'll have our forever then."

He stood and pulled me into his chest and we both cried. Tears for past mistakes, wasted time, and lost futures.

There was a knock at the door, and my dad walked in.

"The minister just got here. The nurse set up a little room for you to get dressed in if you're ready."

Thirty minutes later the girls had helped me into the white dress that was understated and classic with zero puff or bling. Straight white satin with spaghetti straps over the shoulders giving a little Grace Kelly flair. They did my makeup but didn't even bother with the mascara as I seemed to be tearing up every two minutes.

Rachel stood back. "You look beautiful."

Lexi put the simple white veil on my head before holding up her blue Air Jordan's. "Something borrowed."

I pulled them on and smiled as she gave me the little bouquet of pink and purple flowers.

FIFTY-NINE
EVAN
THE END

I sat in the chair next to John. I'd visited them in Brazil last summer and knew he regretted how Levi was raised. That it took him so long to get into a good place with Levi. But they'd grown close.

John stood. "I'm going to grab some coffee. You need anything, Evan?"

"No, I'm good."

He exited, and I grabbed my phone and walked down the hall. As I leaned against the wall and texted Rachel, beeping at the nurse's station across from me filled the air. A nurse tore around the counter and ran into Levi's room.

I followed and when I went through the door, my cousin was sitting up in bed pulling tubes from his arm. "Allie!"

"Sir, you need to stop!" The nurse tried to hold his hands when I sprinted to the other side of the bed.

"Levi, stop it, calm down!"

"Allie!" His voice was filled with pain and anguish.

"Calm down!"

He groaned and held his head with his hands for a second as he threw his feet over the side of the bed as the nurse yelled.

"Sir!"

"Allie!" He grabbed my shirt and pulled me to him before putting his arm around my neck as he groaned. He stood, leaning against me, at the same time John ran into the room.

"Levi, she's not here—"

He looked over at me. "She's here. I can feel her."

He leaned on me and led me to the door as a second nurse appeared in the hall. "Sir, you need to stop this. You had surgery."

We stood just outside the door in hall when Levi yelled with such a primal urgency it shook the walls. "Allie!"

She stepped out of a door down the hall and froze as if she'd seen a ghost.

Instantly Levi let out a breath. "Allie."

She took off running toward us and threw her arms around him. "Levi."

She pulled back and kissed both cheeks and then his lips. "You're here."

A relief washed over me as he grinned. "I'm here."

The nurse waved her arms in the air. "We need to get the groom back into bed, please."

A CHRISTMAS MIRACLE

The thank you prayers were overwhelming my brain as Levi leaned on Evan to get back to the bed, but he didn't release my hand.

Everyone left us alone as the nurse got him reattached to the machines while he laid his head back against the pillow.

I kissed his cheek. "Rest Levi. You just had surgery."

"I'm not resting until you're my wife." He wore a tiny grin. "You're so beautiful. Like thirteen out of ten."

I fluffed my hair and rolled my eyes. "Well, I don't know about that."

He kissed my knuckles. "A fucking thirteen, Langley."

Will entered the room and approached as he shoved his hands in his pockets.

Levi winked at me. "Will, you look like shit."

He took a deep breath. "I want to apologize to you. For everything. Back then I let fear cloud decisions, and what I did was unforgiveable."

Levi nodded. "I know you did what you did because you were scared. I get it." He looked up at me. "Now I hope you'll understand that me marrying your sister today is because I'm scared. I know life without her, and I don't want it. I'm going to marry her today and never stop protecting her. All I want is to be with her until my last day." He looked at the nurse. "That isn't today, is it?"

She giggled. "It appears you might just be too stubborn to die."

"That does sound like me." His emerald green eyes returned to me. "I want to do nothing but make you happy, keep you safe, and make babies with you."

Will groaned. "Oh jeez."

Levi chuckled. "But Will, I think I could use a best man today, if you're up for it."

Shock was Will's. "Are you serious?"

He nodded. "All the shit from the past is done. We leave it there and go forward."

Ten minutes later my father walked me down the hall to my Mr. Perfect. I sat on the edge of the bed and Lexi took my flowers as his ginormous smile was all because of me. Well, he was on some pretty good meds too, but whatever.

"Hi."

He took my hand in his. "Hi."

The minister spoke and everyone melted away. He was going to make it. He was strong.

"You have your own vows you'd like to share?" I glanced up at Pastor Williams as Levi nodded.

"I Levi, take you Allison Langley to be my everything. To protect you, take care of you, and share every day with you until it's my last. To be the person you need, and to be your home," His eyes pierced mine. "It's our time. It's you and me."

Lexi sniffled and when I glanced over she gave me a nod before I looked back to him.

"I Allison, take you Levi Dawson to be my everything. To be your person for life. To hold your hand through all the things, and be the one you turn to for strength and support. It's you and me now."

ONE YEAR LATER

While this was technically our second marriage to one another, Allie was insistent that we meet on the Sugar Creek Bridge on the day of our anniversary.

It'd been a crazy year. She'd talked her employer into letting her work remotely and flying in when necessary and we got her all packed up. My business partner took over the daily operations in Brazil, and I'm working on commercial projects stateside as well as a residential project, which allowed us to figure out where we wanted to settle.

After many discussions we chose to go back to where it all began. Where we could be close to her family and my father. The town that gave me a second chance.

We've been renting a tiny house for the time being across from the water tower in town. From our deck, if you look closely, you can still see a faint "Allie Langley" coming through the white paint. Seeing it seems to make her want to kiss me a lot which is totally cool.

Some other things have changed, too. Would you believe

that Will is not only my ice fishing partner, but agreed to come on to be the financial guy for my company?

Who says hell can't freeze over?

While he wants to deer hunt with me, that spot's reserved for Allie.

The Sugar Creek Bridge is a few miles outside of town and remote enough so nobody ever drives by and was our fishing spot this fall. Nothing was better than football on the radio, beer in the cooler, and Allie by my side all afternoon.

Today I brought two chairs, a little table, and grilled cheese sandwiches I wrapped in foil and put in my cooler. Of course, I have a bucket of Dove chocolates and chocolate milk because she deserves all the things she loves at all times.

I brought wood for a little bon fire and pulled the Christmas tree off the back of my truck and plopped it in a tree stand and set it next to the table. When I left the hospital Allie had taken all of the decorations from my hospital tree and put them in her "special box" which I'd snuck out of the storage closet this morning.

I now stand on the bridge waiting. Unlike the other seven times I stood in this spot, I knew she was coming to me. I watched her car come around the corner as the sound of crunching gravel grew louder.

While I'd just woken up with her by my side this morning, I couldn't wait and started walking toward her when she jumped out.

"Freeze!"

I stopped in the center of the bridge.

"Since the moment I heard that you'd waited for me here every year, I've imagined it." She walked to the edge of the bridge, and her hands went to her cheeks when she saw my makeshift dining area by the fire. "Are you kidding me right now?"

"Anything for you, Allie."

Her head shook. "I can't believe how beautiful this is."

"I can't believe how beautiful you are."

Her head tilted. "Did you really just say that?"

"I know, a little pukey."

"No, it's perfect."

"Can I move yet?"

She walked to me and threw her arms around my neck. "Just give me a second to soak this in."

"Well, don't take too long, our lunch awaits."

"Oooh, lunch?"

I took her hand and led her to our table by the fire.

"Have I told you you're the most thoughtful man I've ever known?"

"And handsome?"

She took her seat. "And handsome."

I opened my cooler, pulled off the foil, and placed her grilled cheese in front of her.

"Well, it's not totally cold."

She looked up at me. "It's totally perfect."

"It's a rare couple who has their anniversary on Christmas."

She gave me a knowing nod. "The rarest. Only super cool couples are Christmas couples."

I set bottles of chocolate milk in front of us and took my seat. "Do you want your present?"

Her hand clapped as she kicked her feet under the table. "Yes! Yes, to the present!"

I reached into my coat pocket and pulled out the red envelope and slid it across the table. "Happy Anniversary, Allison."

She giggled as she opened it and pulled out a piece of paper before her baby blues returned to me. "What is this?"

I sat back in my chair. "I bought an acre of land for the house I'm going to build you."

Her mouth dropped open.

"Right here."

"What?"

"Our house will sit right over there. The same field they used to chase us out of, is now ours."

She jumped up so fast her chair fell over and sat on my lap as she peppered my face with kisses. "Are you serious?"

I let out a laugh as I pushed a curl from her face. "Yes. It's ours now."

"I can't believe this." She leaned back and took my face in her hands. "You are the sweetest man."

Eye roll. "I kinda am. You got real lucky with me, huh?"

"I did." She giggled. "Okay, my turn. Close your eyes."

I closed my eyes as she continued to giggle so much I was giggling.

"Open them."

I opened my eyes as she held something up. "Happy Anniversary."

My eyes went from her to her gift.

"What's—"

She pointed to the two lines on the pregnancy test.

I don't know what expression I wore, but she burst out laughing as she cupped my face in her hands. "You okay?"

I stood and held her in my arms. "We're having a baby?"

"We are."

"I can't believe this!"

"I know it's a little unexpected—"

"I've never been happier in my life."It's going to be great."

"I still can't believe it." Her nose wrinkled. "I bet my belly will be ginormous."

I laughed. "I can't wait. I hope our little one has your wild hair and those baby blues."

She looked so deeply into my eyes something twisted. "I love you so much, Levi."

I leaned my forehead against hers. "There's no beginning and no end. It'll always be us."

We spent the crisp Christmas afternoon kissing a lot by the fire on the spot where our past and future would be connected for all of time.

ACKNOWLEDGMENTS

Thank you, God.

To you, the wonderful person who chose my book out of millions, thank you from the bottom of my heart for giving my words a chance. You've made my wildest dream come true.

NK Winter, the incredibly talented artist, thank you for a cover I'm in love with. You are amazing to work with and somehow took my ideas and made them cool. Nkwinter.carrd.co/

Kayla Bramante for being so supportive, happy we're a team.

A huge shout out to the Bookstagram and Book Tok communities. The love and support have been tremendous, and I'm left awe struck by your creativity and love of books. Yes, to a book cruise.

Satin Romance for being a joy to work with and for taking a chance on me.

While he will never know, I have to give a huge thank you to Bailey Zimmerman. When I was thinking of a holiday story I happen to hear his song *Holy Smokes*. By the time the song was over, I knew what this entire book was going to be about.

To my amazing mother. I love you and am grateful beyond words for you. You were always the cool mom who sacrificed and gave everything you had for us while filling the house with laughter. Sure, you were laughing at us a chunk of the time, but still, thanks.

Dad, I miss you every day. Our adventures and your story telling are something I'll always hold close to my heart.

Love to all the Millers, Kirkles, Kirchners, Hardinas, and Lingenfelters. Lucky to call you my people.

Angie and Bob Cope for always being there. Whenever I'm sad I think of your fainting goats and smile.

Josh, Taylor, Jameson, Penny, Jake, Tori, Eden, Samuel, Everhett, Rachel, Tyler, Anna, Dontavius, and Zakari-love you all more than chilled Reese's Peanut Butter Cups. That says a lot right there. Looking forward to all the future holds.

Lynn for always being my built in bestie. From the Barbie house where it was always Christmas, our road trips to Inver Grove, and the way you can read my mind, I lucked out with you. #whitecastlerules

Candy and Lori for being there since we were fifteen. Abby, Amy, Katie, Pam, Little Katie, and the Millard Heights three-mile club for always making me smile.

I also want to thank Coke for being fizzy enough to wake me up at 4:45 a.m. to write, chocolate for lifting me up when I'm feeling low, and 132nd street from Millard to Springfield – you've been responsible for many story ideas.

And Brian. Thank you for all you do and for putting up with me. Your ability to be supportive even when I don't entirely know what I'm doing is impressive. In case I don't say it enough, you're the coolest.

THANK YOU FOR READING

Did you enjoy this book?

We invite you to leave a review at your favorite book site, such as Goodreads, Amazon, Barnes & Noble, etc.

DID YOU KNOW THAT LEAVING A REVIEW...

- Helps other readers find books they may enjoy.
- Gives you a chance to let your voice be heard.
- Gives authors recognition for their hard work.
- Doesn't have to be long. A sentence or two about why you liked the book will do.

ABOUT THE AUTHOR

Mary Lee Painter and her family reside in Omaha, Nebraska. She enjoys spending time with family, watching Minnesota Wild hockey, chasing kids, writing, and day dreaming. Mary Lee has a deep appreciation for chocolate along with road trips that involve discovering local treasures and fun basement bars.

maryleepainterbooks@gmail.com
maryleebooks.net/maryleebooks

instagram.com/maryleepainterauthor

ALSO BY MARY LEE PAINTER

The Other Fork in the Road

Wild in Minnesota

Holiday on the Rocks